PRAISE

Under Her Care

"The action never wavers, and the surprises are unending. Berry is writing at the top of her game."
                                    —*Publishers Weekly* (starred review)

"[It's] a humdinger . . . Perfect for suspense fans."
                                    —*Kirkus Reviews*

"Lucinda delivers every time. Unputdownable."
                        —Tarryn Fisher, *New York Times* bestselling author

"Lucinda Berry's latest, *Under Her Care*, is her best thriller yet! A dark, riveting read that will keep you up late, racing to the chilling end."
            —Kaira Rouda, *USA Today* bestselling author of *The Next Wife* and
                                                    Somebody's Home

"Lucinda Berry's *Under Her Care* is stunning, diabolical, and gripping, with one of the best and most gasp-worthy twists I have read in a very long time. Fast paced, fabulous, and enthralling, the pages practically turn themselves. Absolutely captivating."
            —Lisa Regan, *USA Today* and *Wall Street Journal* bestselling author

"Creepy and chilling, *Under Her Care* is a tense page-turner that leaves you questioning everything you ever knew about motherhood and the family bond."
            —Tara Laskowski, award-winning author of *The Mother Next Door*

The Secrets of Us

"Those looking for an emotional roller-coaster ride will be rewarded."
                                    —*Publishers Weekly*

"Combine Lucinda Berry's deep understanding of the complexities of the human mind with her immense talent for storytelling and you have *The Secrets of Us*, an intense psychological thriller that kept my heart racing until the shocking, jaw-dropping conclusion. Bravo!"
—T. R. Ragan, *New York Times* bestselling author

"*The Secrets of Us* is an unputdownable page-turner with two compelling female protagonists that will keep readers on their toes. Fantastic!"
—Cate Holahan, *USA Today* bestselling author of *One Little Secret*

"Lucinda Berry's *The Secrets of Us* is a tense psychological thriller that explores the dark corners of the mind and turns a mind can take when it harbors secret guilt. The interplay between sisters Krystal and Noelle and their hidden past is gradually revealed, and in the end, the plot twists keep coming. Right and wrong can be ambivalent, and this story explores all shades of gray, from their dysfunctional family to an old childhood friend to a husband who may or may not be too good to be true. Berry's background as a clinical psychologist shines in this novel with a character so disturbed they spend time in seclusion lockdown at a psychiatric ward. Don't miss this one!"
—Debbie Herbert, *USA Today* and Amazon Charts bestselling author

"*The Secrets of Us* is an utterly gripping, raw, and heartbreaking story of two sisters. Berry's flawlessly placed clues and psychological expertise grab you from the first word, not letting go until the last. Compelling, intricate, and shocking, this inventive thriller cleverly weaves from past to present with stunning precision. I was absolutely enthralled."
—Samantha M. Bailey, *USA Today* and #1 national bestselling author of *Woman on the Edge*

"The past and present collide with explosive consequences in this addictive, twisty thriller from an author at the top of her game. *The Secrets of Us* grips from the first page and doesn't let go until the final shocking twist."

—Lisa Gray, bestselling author of *Dark Highway*

The Best of Friends

"A mother's worst nightmare on the page. For those who dare."

—*Kirkus Reviews*

"*The Best of Friends* gripped me from the stunning opening to the emotional, explosive ending. In this moving novel, Berry creates a beautifully crafted study of secrets and grief among a tight-knit group of friends and of how far a mother will go to discover the truth and protect her children."

—Heather Gudenkauf, *New York Times* bestselling author of *The Weight of Silence* and *This Is How I Lied*

"In *The Best of Friends*, Berry starts with a heart-stopping bang—the dreaded middle-of-the-night phone call—and then delivers a dark and gritty tale that unfolds twist by devastating twist. Intense, terrifying, and at times utterly heartbreaking. Absolutely unputdownable."

—Kimberly Belle, international bestselling author of *Dear Wife* and *Stranger in the Lake*

The Perfect Child

"I am a compulsive reader of literary novels . . . but there was one book that kept me reading, the sort of novel I can't put down . . . *The Perfect Child*, by Lucinda Berry. It speaks to the fear of every parent: What if your child was a psychopath? This novel takes it a step further. A couple, desperate for a child, has the chance to adopt a beautiful little girl who, they are told, has been abused. They're told it might take a while for her to learn to behave and trust people. She can be sweet and loving, and in public she is adorable. But in private—well, I won't give away what happens. But needless to say, it's chilling."

—Gina Kolata, *New York Times*

"A mesmerizing, unbearably tense thriller that will have you looking over your shoulder and sleeping with one eye open. This creepy, serpentine tale explores the darkest corners of parenthood and the profoundly unsettling lengths one will go to, to keep a family together—no matter the consequences. Electrifying and atmospheric, this dark gem of a novel is one I couldn't put down."

—Heather Gudenkauf, *New York Times* bestselling author

"A deep, dark, and dangerously addictive read. All-absorbing to the very end!"

—Minka Kent, *Washington Post* bestselling author

ONE
IN
FOUR

OTHER TITLES BY LUCINDA BERRY

ONE IN FOUR

LUCINDA BERRY

THOMAS & MERCER

Published by Thomas & Mercer, Seattle

www.apub.com

Amazon, the Amazon logo, and Thomas & Mercer are trademarks of Amazon.com, Inc., or its affiliates.

EU product safety contact:
Amazon Media EU S. à r.l.
38, avenue John F. Kennedy, L-1855 Luxembourg
amazonpublishing-gpsr@amazon.com

ISBN-13: 9781662526046 (paperback)
ISBN-13: 9781662526039 (digital)

Cover design by Kimberly Glyder
Cover image: © Junebug Studio's / Shutterstock; © DanielBendjy / Getty

Printed in the United States of America

To Scott

CHAPTER ONE

I gave my wife a wicked grin and pulled my hand out of her pants before grabbing my phone off the nightstand. "Gia, it's almost two in the morning. You cannot call me like this. How many times have I told you that?" I rolled my eyes at Noelle. We'd barely gotten started when Gia started blowing up my phone.

"Ohmigod, Laurel, you have to get down here! You have to get down here now. Right now! We need you. Maddie bled out in the hallway. There's blood everywhere. Literally everywhere. It looks like a massacre. I've never seen so much blood. Spencer and Preston are covered in it. They were the first ones to find her, and they won't even let them wash it off. It's so disgusting. The clients are totally freaking out. Completely losing their shit. I don't know what to do. What are we going to do? Ohmigod. I can't believe this is happening. Spencer just bolted. Two officers took off after him, but they still can't find him. Hurry up, Laurel, seriously—hurry. You have to get here!"

I leaped off Noelle. All thoughts of sex gone. "What are you talking about?" Everything was calm when I left the house three hours ago.

"Maddie!" she shrieked. "I told you—Maddie had an accident. Why aren't you listening to me? You're just as bad as the police. They're everywhere, by the way. Crawling all over the damn place. They won't let anyone leave the house or anybody else inside. We're on total lockdown. Nobody can use their phone. Not even staff. They barely even let me call you—I know, I know," she interrupted herself, snapping at someone who must be in the room with her. "They gave me permission to call her."

A male voice. Low and deep. Muffled. Said something, but I couldn't make it out.

"That guy!" Gia snapped at whoever she was talking to again. The same way she snapped at the production crew. "He said I could call her. He gave me my phone. And I'm pretty sure he's the one in charge and not your incompetent self, so maybe you should talk to him instead of me!"

"Gia, settle down and just tell me what's happening," I ordered while I scrambled to find the jeans I'd tossed on the floor seconds ago. But she wasn't listening to me. She was screaming at people. Whoever was there with her. It sounded like multiple voices now.

"She's their therapist, and they need her! I already told you that! Look at them," she shrieked, and was probably waving her hands wildly around just like she did on set. "Have you seen that one over there, picking her skin in the corner? Or how about her? See how she's crying so hard she can't breathe? You want to be responsible for not getting them proper mental health treatment when all this is going down? At a time when they so obviously need it?"

"Ma'am, give me that phone. You're not allowed to be on your phone right now." This time there was no mistaking the sound of a man's voice. He came in crystal clear and meant business.

"I want my attorney. You can't just take away our phones like this and keep us here all night without any contact with the outside world. We haven't done anything wrong. We have rights. We're not criminals. I—"

Sounds of a scuffle like they were fighting over the phone.

"Gia?" I yelled into my phone just as the call dropped.

I quickly called her back, but it went straight to her voicemail.

"Shit." I shoved my phone in the back pocket of my jeans.

"What's going on?" Noelle asked as she tossed me my shirt. Her eyes as wide as mine probably looked.

I shook my head, bewildered. "I'm not sure, but it sounds like Maddie had some kind of terrible accident and the police are at the house. Apparently no one can leave? Which makes no sense and probably means it's bad, so I'm going over there."

"Hon, really? It's so late, and are you sure it's safe?" Concern immediately etched her face. "Why not wait until the morning or see if Gia calls you back? Talk to her first before you do anything."

"I have to go, especially if Maddie's hurt." Maddie was the baby of the house—barely nineteen—and my favorite, even though you weren't supposed to have favorites. I quickly kissed Noelle's forehead and brushed the hair out of her eyes. "Don't wait up for me, okay? I have no idea how long this will take." I kissed her again. This time on the lips. "I love you."

"Love you too," she responded, but I'd already turned around and headed out of our bedroom. I hurried to my car and wasted no time driving to Crystal Meadows. Thankfully, we were only fifteen minutes away, and without traffic, I got there even faster.

I spotted the police cars and emergency vehicles before I rounded the corner on Edgecliff Lane. Their flashing red lights danced through the trees. My stomach sank at the sight of the yellow tape—the telltale sign of a crime scene—partitioning off the entire property. A couple of the neighbors had gathered to watch on the sidewalk in front of the house. Their bathrobes wrapped tightly around them like blankets. Other people's tragedies always drew crowds. Tonight was no different. A few eyes peeked out from huge bay windows with the shades drawn back. None of them had wanted us in their uberwealthy suburban neighborhood to begin with, but we'd promised the city there'd be no drama. Up until tonight, there hadn't been. At least not outside the house. All our dysfunction was kept behind closed doors.

I pulled up along the sidewalk and scanned X as I walked up to the police-tape barricade to see if there'd been anything posted. I stopped in my tracks at the comments:

@comeback kids OMG!!!! Did you see that sh$t!!!! wtf just happened?

@comeback kids Is Maddie dead? She looked dead.
| She's not dead.
| Looked dead to me.

@comeback kids it had to be faked. It was staged.
| Bro that was real
| Facts.

Oh my God. No.

Maddie wasn't dead. She couldn't be dead. Gia would've told me if she was dead. She said she had an accident. I shook my head, refusing to believe Maddie was gone. You couldn't believe what just anyone said on social media.

Were the cameras still running? They couldn't be. Even if that's what we'd promised people—an uncut, uncensored, twenty-four-seven look at the lives of seven former celebrity kid stars as they struggled to get sober. I switched to YouTube because it hosted all the live feeds. Constant streaming, just like *Big Brother*. We hadn't turned off cameras since the show started. But there was nothing except empty black screens:

Video Unavailable: This video has been removed by the uploader

This wasn't good. Gia never shut down the live feeds, no matter what was happening on set.

"That's part of the deal!" she'd screamed into her headphones when Tripp was going off on his racist rant, calling Kendall all kinds of slurs, and half the crew wanted to shut off the cameras. But she refused to let them. So we, along with all of America, watched one of the most

4

disgusting and blatant displays of racism I'd ever witnessed play out on live TV. I was sure they'd shut down the show after that. At least kick him out. But none of that was the case. Our ratings skyrocketed. People wanted more of Tripp, not less, so that's what Gia gave them, even though she'd been the target of some of his worst insults. It was all so sensational and dramatic, but that was the point.

There'd been plenty of other drama too. It was why people loved the show. It sparked life into a dying cable network. Tripp's rant wasn't even the worst thing the cameras caught, though. Viewers witnessed a drug overdose after Javon's boyfriend smuggled in gummies during their visit and she ate the entire bag in one sitting. There'd been so many memes created afterward, and the video of her peeing in the middle of the kitchen had over two million views on TikTok. It was still one of our most-watched episodes. Lyriq's seizure in the middle of our first group session also had high ratings.

But if Gia cut the cameras, we were in serious trouble.

Surprisingly, the front yard was mostly empty, except for the lone police officer standing guard at the end of the long driveway. He was busy talking to one of the reporters that arrived right before me. I'd spotted the KTLA news vans behind the ambulances when I parked. I didn't want to ask permission to go inside and risk him saying no, so I quickly ducked underneath the yellow tape and walked up to the front door like I was supposed to be there. Like it was any other day in the last twenty-seven days of me going to work. Just as I was about to grab the handle, the officer from the end of the driveway rushed up behind me and yanked my arm, pulling me away from it.

"What do you think you're doing? You can't go in there, ma'am. That's an active crime scene. I'm going to have to ask you to step away from the door." He said it like he was being polite, but his voice was firm and he hadn't released his grip on my arm.

"Officer Malone," I said, reading the name on his breast pocket. Swole underneath his navy shirt. "I'm Dr. Harlow, and I'm the therapist that's been treating all the patients here for the last twenty-seven days.

I'm not sure if you know this, but Crystal Meadows is an inpatient treatment center. Every person inside this house is suffering from a chronic addiction. Many of them with severe mental illnesses on top of that, and I understand there's been some kind of crisis, so I'm here to help stabilize the situation, and check on the status of my patients. I—"

He interrupted me, shaking his head as he spoke. "I don't care what you do for a living or how you help those people. Nobody goes in there. It's an active crime scene and can't be contaminated."

"Please, the director, Gia, called me a few minutes ago, and whoever is in charge of this investigation is right there with her. He gave me permission to come down. He was the one that let her use her phone to call me in the first place. He's obviously okay with me being here," I lied, but did my best to look sincere.

He wrinkled his face at me for a second while he thought about it, but ultimately, he wasn't convinced. "Again, ma'am, I'm going to have to ask you to step aside from that door and to get behind that yellow line over there." He pointed to the tape with his other hand. The one that wasn't holding on to me.

"Sir, Officer Malone, I know you're only following protocol and I respect that, but I'm worried there are people inside that house in significant distress. My patients need me right now."

He repeated himself and pointed at the tape. "Like I said, I don't care who needs you right now or what's happening in that house. I only care about what I need from you, and that's for you to get off this porch and behind that yellow line over there." Any hint of politeness gone.

I raised my hands in the air like I didn't want him to arrest me and backed away from the door. "Fine, but will you please call whoever is in charge of this investigation and let them know I'm here? Dr. Laurel Harlow. They're expecting me."

Just then his police scanner crackled. "Priority one. Code two. 816 Edgecliff Lane. 419. Coroner is—" He flipped the switch, silencing the dispatcher's voice, but not before I'd heard the last part.

"Did she just say *coroner*? Why is there a coroner headed here?" I asked, knowing full well there was only one reason a coroner would arrive on any accident scene.

CHAPTER TWO

I stood just outside the yellow tape with my phone in my hand, replaying the video of Maddie stumbling out of her bathroom over and over again, like I'd been doing for the last twenty minutes, ever since the police officer brought me over here and told me to stay put. They'd taken the video down. Halted all production on the show, but not before people had saved it. They were putting it up on all the social media platforms faster than it could get taken down.

Besides the bathroom, every single room in the house had multiple cameras, including their bedrooms. At 12:42 a.m., Maddie's bathroom door opens, and she falls to her knees as soon as it does, spilling her into the hallway of her bedroom. She tumbles onto the carpeted floor, both hands gripping her head. One on each side. Blood pouring through her fingers. She tries to get up from her knees, but falls every time, until finally she just gives up and crumples on the ground like a wounded animal. Seventeen long seconds pass while she lies there motionless. Blood draining out of her head. You can't help thinking she's dead. I hold my breath just like I do every time I watch it. Even though I know exactly how the video ends, I keep hoping there's a different outcome.

But there's not.

At eighteen seconds, Maddie's body convulses like she's suddenly shocked with electricity. Violent, bloody seizures, one right after the other, pummel her tiny frame. Or maybe just one long continuous one. It's so hard to tell from the video. And then there comes the sound. The terrible crack her skull makes as it bashes against the wall behind her. Unlike anything I've ever heard before. A loud, deafening crack where there's no mistaking a bone breaks. It woke Preston first. He's there almost immediately. Rushing into the room and finding her flopping on the ground like a fish that's been tossed on shore and desperately trying to get back into the water. She writhes and flails about. It's so hard to watch, but as with any bad accident, I want to cover my eyes, and yet, I can't look away.

Spencer arrives next. He lets out a bloodcurdling scream at the sight of her. That's when chaos ensues. Staff flies into the room. Everyone's up. Someone else screams. It sounds like Javon. Then Tripp darts into the hallway. He's the last thing you see before the screen goes dark. Before someone finally cuts off all the live video feeds.

I looked up, eyeing the front door of Crystal Meadows for any change in activity, hoping whoever was in charge would come out and let me in, or at least give me some answers. But there wasn't anything going on. From the outside, Crystal Meadows looked like every other sprawling ranch on the block. Unless you lived in the neighborhood, you'd have no idea it's home to the most-watched reality TV show in America right now. It was the one thing about the show we'd managed to keep a secret. It helped that it was a gated community too. We'd chosen that on purpose. Taken every step possible to protect the confidentiality and privacy of our clients, which seemed a bit absurd given they were going to be living their entire lives in front of the camera.

But it was for their safety. Not really their privacy. Every celebrity—no matter how small—had at least one stalker or someone obsessed with them, and no fan was creepier or scarier than the ones obsessed with child stars. Even though our clients were grown, in the eyes of their fans, they'd always be kids. It's why the neighbors were just as invested in keeping their location quiet. They weren't any more interested in that kind of scary pedo fan stumbling into their space than we were.

The coroner had been parked in the driveway for an hour, and nothing had been wheeled out. A couple of guys dressed in hazmat gear went in, but besides that, it'd been quiet. Police officers put up a barricade at the end of the block once other news vans started showing up. Nobody was in their houses anymore. Everyone filled the streets. A few minutes ago, a woman across the street started bringing people coffee like it was some kind of sunrise block party.

Did it usually take this long to bring out a body? Was it really Maddie?

The front door opened, interrupting my thoughts. Two officers flanked Gia as she finally stepped outside the house. She looked like she'd aged overnight. Her face was pale and gaunt. Eyes wide. Pupils dilated with shock. Half her dark hair in a ponytail and the other part haphazardly sticking out everywhere. Wearing only a tank top, like she'd gotten too hot and taken off all her other clothes. Her jeans slung low on her hips. Her always-present combat boots. Totally appropriate for the situation, because she looked like she'd been to war inside that house. I've never seen her so wrecked. She was always so put together.

"Gia!" I yelled out to her, waving my hand wildly like I was behind a security line at a rock concert and she was the talent whose attention I was desperately trying to get.

She spotted me immediately and broke free of the officers, running straight to me. She threw herself into my arms like she'd been waiting to fall apart. Silent sobs shook her small frame while she hid her head in my chest. I held her tight as she cried, but it was only a few moments before she pulled herself back and wiped her face with her hands. Thick mascara coated the skin underneath her eyes.

"It's Maddie," she said, struggling to control her emotions. "She's gone, Laurel. Maddie's gone."

A wave of disbelief throttled me. Denial is that powerful. I'd held on to hope until the last possible moment. Not sweet Maddie. We'd just lain on the floor of my office earlier today. A cup balanced on her belly while I taught her how to breathe. The same way I taught the kids at my workshops, because she was practically a baby. Just like them.

She couldn't be gone. She was too young.

My knees went weak, and I clung to Gia as much as she clung to me. Both of us shaking now. Waves of shock coursing through my body.

"You have to come inside and help," Gia said. The officers stood behind her, unmoving. The yellow tape between us. "They're not going to let anyone go until they've been interviewed by the detectives, and the clients are really struggling. How are we supposed to keep them sober through this? I'm afraid of what's going to happen. I think they are too. That's probably the only reason they allowed me to come out here and get you. They've called in a crisis response team, so I told them if they're calling in anything like that, then you had to be a part of it. They couldn't keep you out, especially since you're the one that knows them the best." She glared over her shoulder at the two of them.

"I can go inside?" I asked, directing my questions to the officers.

They nodded their heads at the same time, and I quickly ducked under the yellow tape before they could change their minds. Lights flashed all around us as the news crews shifted their attention to the police hurrying us into the house. They snapped our picture while we walked up the sidewalk, like we were the celebrities and they were the paparazzi. The crowd had grown larger by the minute. Ever since the coroner had shown up. I couldn't imagine what it would look like in a few hours or how all this would play out in the media.

Mostly, I couldn't stop thinking about Maddie's mom. This wasn't the first time I'd had a client die on me. When you work with people battling addiction and alcoholism, it's part of the job. But this one hit hard because she was so young, and I knew her mom intimately. Almost as well as I knew Maddie. It wasn't because she was an overbearing mom manager, though. Not like some of the other parents. She wasn't on the show to give her daughter a chance to be in the spotlight again. All she cared about was Maddie getting better. She'd been so desperate during family week.

"Please don't let my baby die. I'm so afraid she's going to die," she'd cried when I met with her for her private session. Three months ago, they'd found Maddie in her bedroom, overdosed on pills with a belt around her neck and barely breathing. She swore she wasn't trying to kill herself, but nobody believed her. Especially not her mom, Hilda. "You have to understand that this isn't her. All this stuff she's doing? These drugs? Hurting herself?" She shook her head while she wiped the tears away from her eyes. "It's not who she is." She shook her head again. "My baby's not the same, and you have to find out why. She won't tell me. Make her tell you. Because something happened to make her this way. I know it did. Please."

I shook off the memory and braced myself for what I'd find in the house. Did the hazmat team clean up all the blood, or was it still there? I hated blood. I used to pass out at the sight of it when I was a kid.

"I'm so glad you're here," Gia said, still holding tight to my arm. Her fingernails digging into my biceps. "I didn't even know what to do, and they still haven't given me back my phone. They won't let us talk to anyone. They're treating all of us like we've done something wrong."

Before I had a chance to respond, another officer opened the door and motioned for us to come inside. All the words left my head as we stepped into the foyer.

The house was thick with death and smelled like blood. Metallic. I never knew blood had a smell, but there it was—dense and heavy—clinging to my clothes like sweat. So many people were crying. Their sobs bounced off the walls. Half the crew paced in and out of the common areas, treading circles through the house. The other half waited in lines to be interviewed. Groups of officers circled around them, ferociously scribbling notes. More officers scurried in and out of Maddie's bedroom, collecting evidence and bringing it into the kitchen, where they'd set up a makeshift command center.

We stepped around people and slowly moved into the living room, unsure of where we should go now that we'd actually made it inside. My eyes immediately moved toward Maddie's bedroom. A puddle of blood seeped into the hallway, but it wasn't bright red like I expected it to be: it was dark brown, almost black. Like all the life had been sucked out of the blood the same way the life energy had been sucked out of Maddie.

I'd never seen so much. I felt woozy and grabbed the back of the couch to steady myself. I quickly looked the other direction and away from the blood. But that wasn't any better.

A sob caught in my throat at the sight of the body bag by the back door. I could smell the rubber of the bag. Like new tires. That's how strong it was. Did everyone get a brand new one, or was it just for Maddie? Did they have different sizes? She was so tiny. How would she fit in an adult bag?

I took a deep breath and turned to Gia. Her head was down and her hair falling forward in her face, her eyes purposefully avoiding looking at the body bag or the blood. I wished I hadn't seen them either. I'd never been this close to death. Not close enough to feel it. Or touch it. Taste it in the way it coated the back of my throat, making it hard to breathe.

I quickly scanned the room again and noticed none of the clients were in the common spaces. Mostly it was the production crew standing in long lines like they did when they were starving and the food was late. Their arms crossed. Nervously moving back and forth. The desire to move coursing through their bodies while they waited to be interviewed.

Gia noticed me searching for the clients. "They put everyone in their rooms after Spencer took off—which, by the way, we still haven't found him. The police almost lost control of everyone. They were worried that the others would run too. So was I." She pointed down the long hallway to the patient rooms. Three on the right side—Preston, Maddie, and Spencer. Four on the left—Lyriq, Kendall, Tripp, and Javon. A camera on each end of the hallway. A police officer underneath each camera. Strategically placed so if anyone else decided to run, they'd be there to stop them.

I looked at the officers, then back at Gia. "So, what do you want me to do? Where should I start?" I didn't see any of the crisis response team members anywhere yet. Their bright-red polos always set them apart from everyone else at a crime scene, but they were nowhere in sight.

Just then, a woman stepped out from the back. Tall and lean, with shiny black hair pulled back into a tight ponytail. She wore a badge and a gun slung low on her hip. She was staring at her phone, but within seconds, she lifted her head and spotted me, immediately noticing someone different was in the room. She strutted up to me like she was on a mission.

"You're the mental health therapist we've been waiting on?" She eyed me up and down, clearly not impressed with my jeans and the old Wellesley hoodie I'd quickly slipped on over my T-shirt.

I stuck out my hand to shake hers. "Yes, I'm Dr. Laurel Harlow. These are all my patients. I've been working with them—"

She cut me off before I could finish my sentence. "These are your patients?"

I nodded, feeling like a protective parent. I was desperate to check in with them and see how they were doing. I couldn't imagine going through something like this at such a fragile time.

The woman shook her head. "Um, no," she snapped. A huge scowl taking over her entire face.

"What do you mean?" I asked. "I'm here to help."

"You're not helping in a crime you might've been involved in," she barked at me. She whipped around and yelled into the room at no one in particular, the same way Gia always did when we were filming. "Who let this woman into this house, and where is the real crisis response team?"

Instant silence. Shifty eyes. Nervous movement. Everyone looked everywhere but back at her.

"I mean it! Who let this woman in?" She pointed to me like anyone was confused about who she was referring to. Her eyes angrily scanned the room. Gia wasn't kidding when she said they were treating everyone like suspects. Another few moments of awkward silence followed, before the officers who'd come out with Gia stepped forward. They hung their heads like two children being scolded.

Finally, the short, stocky one spoke. "We thought she was the lead therapist on the crisis response team."

"Who told you that?" she demanded with her hands on her hips. The other one pointed at Gia. "Don't listen to her. She's no longer in charge here. Understand?" She scanned the entire room again, making pointed eye contact with everyone before snapping her fingers and turning on her heels in the other direction. "Someone find me the real crisis response team therapist, and separate these two."

HER

(THEN)

She used to live in the world of smiley, happy, beautiful people. You know the kind. The bright ones. The ones that sparkle. That shine because their insides are full of light. So much goodness. Pure. That used to be her. She was one of those people, and even though she lived in those same spaces, her light had gone out. She'd felt it that awful night. As real as if someone had just blown it out like a candle.

Poof.

It'd been so easy. Who knew it was that easy to kill another person while still keeping them alive? It's the worst death.

How many people are walking around in the world with their lights turned off? The switch inside them faded to black? People just like her. Still wearing huge smiles on their faces. Filling rooms with their infectious laughs and bubbly personalities. Still pretty. Still sparkling. Still saying all the same lines. But gone.

She recognized them everywhere now. This club. That she didn't know existed until she became a member. But she didn't want any part of it. She never asked to join.

She didn't spend time thinking about what turned her light off. She didn't want to relive those moments ever again or talk about them with anyone either. She tried that once. It didn't work. But she did spend a lot of time on wondering if her light would ever get turned back on. Like, once it went out, did it stay that way forever?

In the beginning. The early days following the dark night. That's what she wondered. It used to freak her out to consider that it might never come back. That she might exist as a zombie. Being alive, but not really. She'd never understood more the meaning of *undead*.

That was the sad part now. More and more, she didn't care. It didn't matter so much to her if she ever got it back, because the more days that passed without it, the more she forgot what it even felt like to truly be alive. Present. In your skin. Breathing. Feeling. Experiencing.

She just wanted to feel something again. That's what happens when you disassociate from your body. You're cut off—not just from the bad and the pain. All the emotions, and she missed them like they were actual people. Really missed feeling. She wanted to feel again. To come back inside the body. Her empty-balloon body. Filled with no air. She wanted to be back inside. Alive.

Hurting yourself starts off like any other drug—the first time is always amazing, and you spend the rest of your time chasing that first high. Lots of girls at her school cut. Carrying around their razor blades in soft velvet pouches like they were heroin kits. But she didn't like the blades. She preferred the belt.

That's how it started. By complete accident.

Almost like she was possessed. No thought beforehand. No plan. She didn't wake up that morning and think *I'm going to hurt myself today so I feel better*. It just happened.

She watched herself do it. Saw herself pull her belt out of her jeans when she was changing into pajamas that night. The $14.99 belt she'd gotten on sale from Tillys the week before. Black woven fabric. Dark clasp. She pulled her arms wide and snapped it. One hand on each end like a taut rope. It made a beautiful slapping sound. And she liked the noise. The crispness. Especially the slap. There was something about that zing.

She was still wearing jeans when she just slapped it again. But this time on her leg. As hard as she could on her left thigh. She screamed and dropped the belt. Jumped back immediately. It stung like she'd just been attacked by a thousand fire ants.

She quickly pulled down her jeans and couldn't believe the mark she'd made on her leg. It was inflamed—angry, red, and raised. She took off her jeans and put on her favorite sweatpants, feeling a strange exhilaration and flooded with the adrenaline of doing something wrong and not wanting to get caught. She spent the rest of the night rubbing the swollen welt on her thigh over and over again. Keenly aware it was there. And every time she touched it, a weird satisfaction and strange pride filled her, unlike anything she'd felt before. It made her smile, and it'd been so long since she smiled. Really, truly smiled from the inside. That's where that one came from. The deepest part of her soul. It felt good. That was all she knew, and nothing had felt good in a long time.

She had to have more.

CHAPTER THREE

My eyes burned as I stumbled into the front door of my house shortly after sunrise. I must've drunk six cups of nasty coffee while the police interviewed me. My stomach was in knots. Twisted with anxiety and too much caffeine. But they'd kept bringing it to me in those small Styrofoam cups, so I just kept taking it. One right after the other.

Noelle raced forward and threw her arms around me. "How are you, babe? What happened? Do you want something to eat? Drink? What can I do for you?" I felt bombarded by her questions, and now that I was home, the exhaustion pummeled me alongside her concerns.

"I'm *so* tired and really just want to go to sleep, but I have to shower first." I set my bag on the entryway bench and took my shoes off, placing them next to hers. "I can't go to bed like this, though. I've never felt so disgusting in my entire life." I felt covered in death. Like she'd be able to smell it on me the same way I'd smelled it when I walked into Crystal Meadows.

She wrapped her arm around my waist and led me over to the couch in the living room. There was a cup of tea in my favorite mug waiting for me on the coffee table. No doubt filled with chamomile and my special honey from New Zealand. She fluffed the pillows behind my back and set me down gingerly like I was a young child or an elderly person. "You just relax, and I'll get you a bath ready. How's that sound, babe?"

I just nodded back at her. It felt like if I opened my mouth, I'd start crying all over again and I didn't want to cry anymore. I was spent. I'd sobbed the entire drive home. I couldn't believe Maddie was gone. Beautiful. Sweet. Innocent. Maddie.

She'd brought her baby blanket with her to our first meeting. The same blanket she'd been sleeping with since she was two years old, totally tattered and torn, stitched together by her mom, Hilda, numerous times over the years. She wrapped herself up in it like she was being hugged, for the entire ninety minutes of our session. The only time she cried during that first session was when she talked about Hilda, and how much she'd hurt and scared her mom when she'd overdosed. She never cried when she talked about herself. She obviously loved her mom as much as her mom loved her.

God, she was so young. She had an actual chance. A real one. Not like the ones we promised the others. Again, you weren't supposed to say that as a therapist. You weren't really supposed to even think it. But I knew the facts. Every single one of the statistics. After all, I had a doctorate in addictive disorders and recovery studies. The younger you were when you received intervention, the greater the likelihood of a positive outcome. It was easier to treat five years of trauma and addiction than it was twenty. But you didn't need a PhD to tell you that.

The mean detective—the one with the black hair—had drilled me with questions about Maddie for over an hour. Right after she finished with Gia. They worked their way through the entire house, and we were the last ones to go. Probably as a punishment for Gia sneaking me into the house when she wasn't supposed to.

"How did she seem to you tonight?" the detective asked. Two other men sat next to her, wearing plain clothes. They'd introduced themselves as detectives too. I couldn't remember either of their names, and they weren't wearing badges.

"We have therapy groups during the afternoon, and she was in really good spirits for all of them. Also, today happened to be our individual therapy session, too, and she did lots of positive work there as well. We focused on learning new breathing techniques. Ways to calm and center herself when she felt upset." The image of her lying on my office floor with a cup balanced on her belly flashed through my mind again, along with her huge smile when she moved the cup with only her breath for the first time. She was always so proud of her achievements. My heart squeezed, making my chest hurt. Tears filled my eyes.

"Did she get upset often?" the detective asked next, moving on quickly and not wasting any time on my feelings.

"She was an emotional wreck, but that's pretty much expected when anyone gets sober. Early sobriety is brutal. Every day is a roller coaster, going from these incredible highs where you think life has the possibility of being amazing again and you're finally going to get it together, to the next minute thinking life is absolutely terrible and never going to get any better so why even bother living or trying. Maddie was on that roller coaster. So are all our patients. That's why I wanted to meet with them so badly." I wasn't going to let the detective off the hook for that one. It still wasn't right that she hadn't let me check in with any of them. But she ignored me and stared at her notes.

"How did she usually handle her tough emotions?" The man on her right spoke for the first time since he'd introduced himself.

"She spent a lot of her time crying, and in her room. But that's not unusual, either, when people get sober, especially for someone that young, whose brain is still developing. It's all very overwhelming. Maddie cried a lot, but that was just her body's way of letting go of all the big emotions she'd repressed for so long."

"Was she on medication for any emotional or mental health disorders?"

It'd gone on and on. I felt like a parent giving an intake on their child. And by the end of it, I wasn't any closer to knowing what actually happened to Maddie or how any of my other clients were doing. I pulled out my phone to see if Gia had texted with any updates about Maddie or Spencer, but there was nothing. He was still missing when I left tonight. Everyone was worried about him. Relapse was contagious, just like the flu, especially when you were so newly sober. Nothing was more precarious than a newly sober person. I knew that from experience. It took me three years before I had any confidence in my sobriety.

"Your bath is ready," Noelle called sweetly from upstairs, and just the sound of her voice made me feel a little better.

I took another sip of my tea and set it back on the coffee table before climbing the stairs to the bathroom. Noelle sat on the wooden stool next to the huge white porcelain soaking tub. She'd insisted on the tub when we remodeled the bathroom, and it'd been worth every penny.

She hadn't turned on any of the lights. Just lit a few of the candles scattered around the room. Oriental Noir from Urban Apothecary filled the small space. I peeled off my clothes and tossed them into the laundry basket in the linen closet. The water steamed: so hot all my skin would be red when I got out—just the way I liked it. I gave her a grateful smile before slowly climbing into the tub. I sank underneath the sudsy water, submerging myself completely. I held my breath for as long as I could before bobbing above the surface and sitting up, hugging my knees in front of me.

Noelle poured water on my shoulders and rubbed my back for a few minutes while we sat in silence. Each with our own thoughts. "Do you want to talk about it?" she asked after a few more minutes had passed. Her cheeks were flushed.

This had been our ritual for years. Me lying in the bath while she washed the horrible day off me. She was a kindergarten teacher, so her days were filled with crayons and ABCs. Even on her worst days, it was kids crying and runny noses. Nothing like mine. Life with addicts and alcoholics is heartbreaking. It never gets easier to watch people destroy themselves. Or the way they take down everyone close to them in the process. My highs were just as high as theirs, and my lows equally bad. I needed her light to cancel out all the darkness that was in me. It was one of the things I loved the most about her. She was the safest of spaces. She always asked if I wanted to talk about my difficult clients or tough days, but never forced me, which was probably why it was always so easy to talk to her about things.

"I just keep thinking about her mom," I said, running my hands through the bubbles. No matter what. That's where I returned all night—Hilda. To her pleading face. Her desperate voice. I wasn't a mother, but I didn't need to be in order to feel the depth of her love for Maddie. And her equal concern. "Maddie was her only child. Her everything."

Noelle's faced crumpled, and she looked like she wanted to cry too. "Poor thing."

"I promised to take good care of her—that's what I'd said to her mom on the last day of family week, when I walked her to her car. Can you believe that? I told her that her daughter was in the best hands she could possibly be in." My voice hitched.

I'd live with that guilt forever. I was grateful someone else was breaking the news to Hilda. I was capable of a lot of things, but looking Hilda in the eye after I'd told her all that wasn't one of them. How would I face her the next time I saw her?

Noelle shook her head at me, practically reading my thoughts. "This isn't your fault, Laurel. Whatever happened isn't your fault."

The logical part of my brain knew that. My heart, on the other hand, did not, and felt the weight of the responsibility on my shoulders. "I just can't believe it. She seemed fine the last time I saw her. Excited to get out. Committed to working together. I even had a check-in with her right before I left tonight, and besides having a headache, there was nothing wrong with her. She seemed happy."

"Do they know what happened to her yet? I was following all the stuff on socials for a while, but people were saying so many ridiculous things that I finally stopped looking. Some of the stuff was so dumb. Like someone broke into the house and hurt her. I was like, *Um . . . do you even watch the show?* If someone broke in, everyone would've seen it and someone would've called the cops immediately." She rolled her eyes.

"They don't really know anything other than she was alone in the bathroom when it happened, and you see that clearly because it's all on camera." The reason I'd hesitated to do the show was the very thing I was most grateful for now. "The last person to see her was the night staff member when they did bed checks at ten thirty, and she was already asleep by then. She fell asleep before lights-out on the unit. I watched all of her video feeds while I was waiting to be interviewed by the police. She curled up in bed early to read a book around ten, but barely made it through a few pages. She had such a peaceful angel face while she slept. Until she rearranged herself on the bed. That's when it got strange."

It was the way she'd lain in bed that was slightly troubling. Once the crisis team finally arrived, they weren't any more interested in my help than the detective had been. It didn't matter to them that I'd been working with everyone in the house since before they got into treatment and knew all their histories intimately. Instead of talking to my clients, I'd watched everything leading up to the incident and what happened afterward, studying it like it was my final exam.

I'd never seen anyone sleep the way she did. Flat on her stomach. It wasn't just that she was sleeping on her stomach. It was how she was sleeping too. With her arms crossed against her chest underneath her, and her legs crossed tight at the ankles. A form of self-regulation or protection—I wasn't sure which one yet.

"That's the weirdest way to sleep," Gia commented on our third pass through. She'd snuck over to join me. I couldn't agree more. Had she always slept that way, or was it a coping mechanism she'd developed while she was here?

Either way, she was dead asleep until she stirred right around twelve thirty. That's when she got up and shuffled to the bathroom. We rewound and watched that part over and over again, looking for the slightest hint of something wrong. But there wasn't anything off about her walk. She just looked like someone sleepily making their way to the bathroom. Her flannel pajama bottoms with tiny pink hearts dragging on the floor. She was in there for eighteen minutes—eighteen point six minutes, to be exact—before she tumbled out the door and fell into the hallway. I shifted my attention back to Noelle.

"The only thing we knew for sure about what happened, besides being alone while she was in there, is that she hit her head on something. There's no way to know yet if she slipped and fell, or if she fainted. Maybe she had a seizure. Of course, she obviously could've been high, which would've made her disoriented, and also could've caused a myriad of other health issues. But you can't tell any of that from the video." I didn't know how I was going to sleep, with all the images from tonight replaying in my head sure to come as soon as I closed my eyes.

"What happened after all the cameras stopped?" Noelle asked like she wasn't totally convinced she wanted to know.

"Once she got in the hallway, she just stopped breathing. Her entire brain hemorrhaged, and she basically bled out right there in the hallway. Javon did CPR until the paramedics arrived, but they couldn't find a heartbeat. She'd already lost too much blood. They pronounced her dead on arrival."

Noelle paused a beat before asking her next question. "How's Javon holding up? I know it's awful for all of them, but how hard would it be to be the one trying to save her and then she dies?" She shuddered.

"I know. It's so horrific." I let out a deep breath. "She pretty much hasn't stopped crying since it happened. You could hear her sobbing even though her bedroom door was shut. It's one of the reasons I wanted to talk to her so badly, but the police weren't having any of that. I'm so worried they're all going to get high again as soon as they're discharged, and all of this will have been for nothing . . . just a huge tragedy."

"I'm sorry. I know this is so hard." She ran the washcloth up and down my back. Softly humming underneath her breath to soothe both of us: *Midnight Train to Georgia*. How many years had it been our song?

"Do you know they have actual companies that come in and clean up your house after someone dies in it?" I asked after a few minutes had passed and a few of my tight muscles had finally relaxed.

"What do you mean?"

25

"Real companies where that's their only job," I explained. "A place called Aftermath Services came to the house after the detectives finished interviewing everyone and the forensic team tore the place up. Which, by the way—I've never seen anything like what they did to the house. The entire downstairs is wrecked."

Tonight was the first time I'd been inside an actual crime scene. I'd never seen pictures of a real one. I didn't even like watching that stuff on TV. Lots of psychologists and people were into that kind of stuff. All the true crime and based-on-real-life cases that dug into the deepest and darkest parts of humanity. Solving brutal homicides and other terrible crimes. But not me. I wasn't into that version of psychology. All that stuff scared me.

"There was blood all over the house. So many people had walked in and out of Maddie's room, so tracks were everywhere. And the forensic team is required to remove every single piece of physical property that's been touched by blood as part of their investigation," I explained.

"I suppose it makes sense." She shrugged, not seeming all that impressed.

I shook my head at her. She didn't get it. I wouldn't have, either, if I hadn't witnessed it firsthand. "No, you don't understand what I mean when I say everything is removed—I mean *everything*. They took big chunks of plaster right out of the wall. Even the drywall. Her entire hallway outside the bathroom? That little area? Totally gutted and demolished. There's nothing left but the studs. They ripped up all the carpet from the floor. And not just the floor in her bedroom. Everywhere around the house where there'd been any blood. So, now the entire place has all these missing patches of carpet and linoleum all over. The walls look like someone punched holes in them. I've never seen anything like it."

"Where are you going to put all the clients?" Noelle asked. "They can't stay there with the place all torn up like that, can they?"

"For now, they're at the Langham. They all wanted to stay together, so they're in rooms on the fifth floor. We didn't know what else to do, so we just put them up there until we figure it out. None of them wanted to go home even though there's only two days left of treatment."

Day twenty-eight.

This was the day they would've written their goodbye letters to drugs and alcohol. They would read the letters out loud to each other in their final group together. But there'd be no letter writing today or final group. Not like that, anyway.

"Are they just going to keep them there? How are you going to end the show?"

I shrugged. There were so many parts of this that were unknown. Everything still felt heightened and distorted even though I'd left Crystal Meadows. It'd been so disorienting being there. The walls in the house had warped and warbled while I walked through. For a moment, I thought maybe I'd been drugged. Perhaps that's what happened. Someone pumped gas into her room. Then I realized—oh, this is what they mean. I'm in some weird state of shock, right along with the rest of them. And even now that I was home, surrounded by bubbles and candles with my wife's tender hands massaging me, I felt the aftereffects. Coupled with a throbbing headache.

"Do you think she overdosed?" Noelle asked, softly rubbing my head, as aware of my impending migraine as I was and doing her best to stave off the effects.

I shrugged. "It has to be. Either that or she had a seizure or stroke while she was in there. That happens sometimes when people are detoxing."

"Is there any way she could still be detoxing after all this time? Treatment's almost over."

"It's not likely. The acute and dangerous effects of withdrawal are usually gone within the first couple weeks, but there are definitely times when the withdrawal hits later. It tends to be with people that are longtime chronic users, though. And that's the thing with Maddie. She really wasn't. She'd barely gotten started."

Noelle held out her hand, and I nodded, signaling that I was ready to get out of the tub. Ready for this night to officially be over. Even though the sun was already up, peeking its way through the blinds. She helped me out as her other hand offered me a towel. I dried my hair while she grabbed my bathrobe from the hook behind the door. The fatigue seeped into my bones. She wrapped me in my robe and gently guided me into our bedroom like she'd guided me onto the couch downstairs. She'd already pulled back the covers. Arranged the pillows just like I liked them. I didn't realize I was crying until she wiped my cheeks.

"I'm sorry," I said.

"Stop that," she scolded. Sliding in next to me and wrapping herself around me, hugging me with her entire body. "You know we don't apologize for having emotions in this house."

That's all it took for me to release the feelings I'd been holding inside ever since I got the phone call. Maddie was dead. The tears silently shook my body while Noelle rubbed my back.

"It's going to be okay," she whispered into my ear, over and over again, until I cried myself to sleep.

CHAPTER FOUR

Being interviewed by the police was an entirely different experience down at the station than it was at Crystal Meadows. So were the detectives. Gone were the ones from last night, and they'd been replaced with Detective Wallace and Detective Boone. One man. One woman. Both serious, and so obviously playing good cop versus bad cop from the moment we walked into the interrogation room together.

Detective Boone didn't even sit down. She stood, just leaning against the concrete wall with her arms folded on her chest. Her legs crossed at the ankles in her heels. I admired a woman who could rock a good suit, and she was definitely slaying in her black Armani. Detective Wallace was as frumpy and disheveled as Boone was put together. His wrinkled collared shirt was barely tucked into his pants and hung over his belt.

We'd done introductions in the hallway, and they wasted no time diving into their interrogation. He pointed to the table with the aluminum chairs next to it. Two on each side. "Take a seat."

"Thank you," I said, sliding into the chair like we were about to have dinner rather than an intense conversation about a young woman who had just died. He handed me a cup of coffee. "Oh no," I quickly declined, pushing it back across the table. I'd already decided on my drive over that I wasn't touching their sludge today. I'd paid for last night's even more this morning.

"I know you just went through all of this before with the detectives, but we have some additional questions, and we apologize in advance if some of this is redundant," Detective Wallace opened, giving Detective Boone a brief nod. She responded with an approving look, and he continued, "Why don't we start with you telling us what the show was like?"

"Okay, um, let's see . . . there were only seven clients living in the house even though there was room for more people. They didn't want a huge group, so we purposefully kept it small. Gia and the other producers wanted it to be intimate and personal, and you lost that, the more people you added to the group. They wanted viewers to feel like they really knew the clients. As if they were sitting down in the living room with them and having a cup of coffee. Like they were their very best friends." Cameras followed them as they went through twenty-eight days of inpatient treatment, and it was filled with all the demon battling, soul searching, and occasional breakthroughs that you'd expect from such an intense treatment structure. "They were there to get better. For another chance at things. We pitched them as desperate drug addicts at rock bottom who'd traded in their Disney childhood stardom for dirty sheets and empty streets, crack pipes, and folded tinfoil." The last line was copy straight from our marketing materials. It was dramatic, but a good description of the show nonetheless.

"Can you take me through the process?" Detective Wallace stared at me from across the table, his face still a blank slate.

"It was chaos those first few days. Everyone arrived totally wasted. Gia and the others were so surprised, but I hadn't been shocked in the least. That's what you did—when you knew your drugs were being taken away, you got as much of them inside you as you could. Like, the more messed up you are, the longer it'll stay in your system. And people with addictions have to say goodbye to their drugs like they're committed lovers, so that's a big part of it too. Getting as messed up as possible beforehand. It was a lot to manage in the beginning. They were under strict medical monitoring for the first seventy-two hours because detoxing can be so dangerous. Everyone felt terrible no matter what drug they'd been on." I shuddered, remembering my last detox thirteen years ago. I wasn't a fan of AA, but one of the things I agreed with them about was the necessity to hit rock bottom before you became willing to get sober, and mine was seared into my consciousness in a way that no amount of time would erase—cold concrete floor, *Family Guy* T-shirt, and no pants. Vomit crusted in my hair. Scratches all over my legs. Lost pieces of the night.

I cleared my throat and continued. "We live streamed all of the detox parts, from the throwing up to the diarrhea to the sobbing. Viewers loved it, and it wasn't long before they were committing to getting sober with the clients on the show. They suffered through the first seventy-two hours right along with them. Some of the big content creators filmed their own detox journeys the same way we did. Obviously, the network immediately came out and issued a statement releasing them from any responsibility or liability in what might happen to those that were doing it, but they loved the publicity it brought the show. Some of their videos had nearly as many fans and views as our show. The most popular feeds were the YouTubers that narrated the live streams. *Comeback Kids* became a viral experience." It was already up for an Emmy and the season wasn't even over.

Detective Boone interjected from her spot, leaned up against the wall. "You didn't feel like you were exploiting them when they were at their weakest?"

"Us exploiting them?" I pointed to my chest like there was no way she could be referring to me. "They were the ones monetizing the situation. They had the most to gain from the experience. Not me. They were probably paid more than all of us."

"They were paid?" She asked like it was the first time she was hearing about it. Detective Wallace had the same look. I couldn't tell if it was real or if they were faking it.

I nodded. "Yes, and very nicely. None of them would've done it without it." It was the main reason I'd doubted their commitment and authenticity from the very beginning. No one would've been there if they weren't being compensated. Truth was, they weren't all that interested in participating when we first pitched them the show idea, and it wasn't until after we mentioned the stipend that they seemed excited. We had their full attention then. "I never forgot that none of them would've been in treatment if they weren't getting paid. Well, except for Maddie. She . . ." My words stopped in my throat. The enormity of her loss hitting me all over again, reminding me why we were even in this room to begin with. "She was the only one who might've come to Crystal Meadows even if she wasn't getting paid. Did you know her mom actually offered to pay us to treat her? At first, Gia thought she was just being one of those moms. You know the ones. So desperate for their kid to be a star and vicariously living through them that they would do anything to catapult them into the spotlight. But all you had to do was meet with her for one second and you could tell her feelings about Maddie being on the show were rooted in genuine concern for her daughter's welfare. She wasn't trying to fool anyone."

"You don't think you can be fooled?" Detective Boone raised her eyebrows at me.

"That's not what I said at all." She was twisting my words. "I said her mom seemed like one of the most genuine and real people I've ever met. You'll see when you meet her." She'd know then. Exactly what I was talking about.

"What else can you tell me about Maddie?" Detective Wallace asked next.

"Here's what you need to know about Maddie, besides her being the only one here for the right reasons." I folded my hands and leaned across the table. "She was different than the rest of them, who'd already destroyed their careers. They're all in their late twenties and early thirties. They've been out of the industry for years. Some of them have already staged their comebacks and failed. Multiple times. But Maddie? She's still in the Hollywood scene. She's just beginning to slide, at the start of a very slippery slope. And unlike all of them—she wanted to stop herself before she spiraled."

"She wasn't doing it to boost her career?"

I shook my head. "She just needed to get her shit together and she would've been fine. People still thought of her as a kid. They're much more forgiving of children. Plus, they're super invested in her story."

Maddie was what kept the dream of being discovered alive. Getting discovered rarely happened, but it did to her. Maddie was plucked out of obscurity. She just happened to be walking down the mall in Baton Rouge at the same time the EVP of FilmNation was grabbing a pair of running shorts from Lululemon. They had just signed a huge movie deal and were looking for the female teenage runaway for the lead. She spotted Maddie outside Dairy Queen and knew she was the perfect person for the role.

Maddie catapulted into stardom almost overnight. The screen loved her. So did everybody else. She'd been working full time as an actress ever since. Landed multiple roles on the Disney Channel. Her face was synonymous with the new Tide commercial. She was the closest thing we had to a real celebrity in the house.

She'd barely crept into the tabloids in a negative light. Only had a few of those kinds of headlines. Most of hers were still positive. The media had just started asking the question: Would Maddie Hernandez succumb to the Hollywood-kids curse, or would she be able to keep her spot in the limelight as she lost her cute-kid look and transitioned into adulthood? Hollywood was the worst narcissistic relationship you could be in. So glamorous while it loved you, but it could discard you as quickly as it'd love bombed you. The ultimate discard. How could you expect them to survive that?

"Still. You didn't feel like you were taking advantage of people when they were at their most vulnerable?" Detective Wallace switched the words up but asked the same question Detective Boone just had a few minutes ago. Seemed like a very cop thing to do.

"No." I shook my head. "Take away the cameras, and then you'd really see them at their most vulnerable."

He didn't try to hide his surprise at my response. "Really? You don't think you could capture their vulnerability on camera?"

I burst out laughing. "I'm not Gia." I smiled at them both. "Don't get me wrong. I love Gia. Absolutely adore her." I treated her for her own nasty Percocet addiction after shoulder surgery four years ago, I wanted to say to them. But I couldn't. Unlike everyone at Crystal Meadows, all her information was still strictly confidential and bound by HIPAA guidelines. I'd never work again in this city if I broke her anonymity. "But she's in the industry. Me?" I shook my head. "I couldn't be further from it. I don't come from TV land. Prior to the show, I'd never even been on any kind of set, even though I've lived in LA for over a decade and most of my clients are connected to the industry in some way. I don't actually know anything about it."

"So, why'd you do the show then?" he asked.

"Because I believe in helping other people get clean, and honestly"—I leaned forward and cupped my hand around my mouth like there was an actual chance someone might hear us—"I needed the job."

Detective Boone let out a laugh. Her first one. Some of the tension in her forehead softened. "I hear that." She smiled at me, then cocked her head to the side. "The gig must've paid pretty well."

"Indeed it did," I said. "Big reason why I took it."

When Gia emailed me about the job last year while she was thinking about putting together the show, I'd shot her down immediately. Spending twelve-hour workdays in a house full of seven spoiled former celebrity kids sounded absolutely torturous at the time. But three months later, when we met for drinks at Soho House in LA during the Grammys and Noelle had just lost her teaching job—her job that paid half the mortgage and bills—and she asked me about it a second time, it seemed incredibly more attractive. By our second drink date, I was sold. I'd brought Noelle along with me on that one, and she'd been mesmerized by Gia from the moment they met. But everyone was like that when they first met Gia. She had that extra-special charisma. The kind that made you excited about life just by being around her. Something as mundane as going to Target felt like a big deal, and she was always surrounded by all the important people. She knew all the talent. Had access to all the private parties. The VIP spaces. It's why so many people applied for the show. They loved her too.

"Why you?" Detective Wallace asked, interrupting my thoughts.

"Why me?" I repeated his question back to him. The classic stall to give yourself more time to think, since I hadn't expected his question.

He nodded. "Yes, why you? Out of all the chemical dependency counselors in the world—in this state—why'd the producers pick you for the show?"

"They wanted someone with experience in providing an alternative treatment approach to getting sober than the traditional twelve-step one," I explained.

"What's wrong with the traditional way?" Detective Boone's interest was immediately piqued, as if I were controversial in some way, but it wasn't anything like that.

"Nothing, but everybody here has already been through multiple twelve-step treatment programs. All of them have gone at least twice. Most of them three or four times. They've all attended the meetings once they got out too. Sometimes the twelve-step approach works for people, but there are lots of times when it doesn't. That's where I come in."

"The alternative to the twelve-step approach? You mean like AA and all that? What is it that you don't like?"

I shook my head at Wallace. "It's not that I don't like it, and there are certain parts of the philosophy that I agree with, even. But I practice a much different approach." I leaned across the table. "The traditional twelve-step approach teaches you there's a sober self and an addict self at war within you constantly. Or if you like, a good self versus a bad self. Either way, it's based on a philosophy deeply rooted in Christian-fundamentalist beliefs, and I just can't get down with that. I can't teach people to live in a constant war with themselves. That's just not healthy." Not to mention empirical research from the last ten years showed that most people—regardless of treatment approach—cycle in and out of sobriety and those associated behaviors for most of their lives. Those hardcore-fundamentalist approaches weren't any more successful in keeping people sober than their counterparts, but I didn't want to step into that whole debate with them.

"What sort of an alternative approach do you provide?" he asked in a certain tone, as if my approach might have something to do with what happened here.

"Like I said before, they'd all been to treatment numerous times. Expensive treatment centers. Those luxury rehabilitation places that are like spas. Ones that cost fifty thousand dollars to attend. But none of those fancy centers kept them sober after they'd been discharged or made a lasting difference in their lives. Most of them were high within three days. And do you know why?" I paused, giving them a moment to let my words sink in and get them ready to digest this next part. "Because those places are the most unrealistic environments on the planet and nothing like real life. It's super easy to work through your problems on the beach with the ocean breeze gliding through your hair and the sun shining down on your face, sipping on a green detox smoothie packed with vitamins. All the while being massaged by professional masseuses. Not to mention being served the healthiest food cooked by certified nutritionists. Exercising with personal trainers. Taking scheduled naps and daily meditation. But here's the thing." I shook my head. "None of that works long term. It's like being on a fancy vacation. It keeps them in the endless cycle of sober and using. Getting high until you bottom out, then getting sent to luxury rehab. I mean, if you don't feel amazing after one of your stays there, something is seriously wrong with you." They both gave obligatory-looking smiles.

"So, what do you do differently for them?" Detective Wallace asked.

"The same thing I do for my individual clients, but in a group setting. Teach them how to function in the real world and in real life. To have jobs. Be responsible in their lives. Become productive members of society. Build relationships. I swear I end up being more of a relationship coach than anything else. But addiction breeds in isolation, so I spend a lot of time encouraging social relationships. That's why we were so different, and why we function the way we do—did—at Crystal Meadows," I quickly corrected myself. We weren't doing anything at Crystal Meadows anymore. Probably ever again. I continued explaining our unique approach. "They all lived like a real family under one roof, and it's all relational based. Most treatment centers have staff doing everything for them the entire time they're there—housekeepers, cooks, gardeners—but not us. Our clients are responsible for maintaining and running the household, so if they wanted a clean house while they were there, they had to do it. Maintaining a house teaches them responsibility. It makes them work and also teaches them how to work together. Everyone's assigned housekeeping duties, and they rotate through them on a weekly schedule. So, our staff is very light in comparison to what you would see at most treatment centers where there's staff waiting on the clients twenty-four seven. Most of it was the production crew, and besides their intrusive cameras and microphones, they stayed out of the way."

"We understand you were the only mental health therapist on the unit for the clients?" Detective Boone asked, shifting gears. I nodded. "And you felt qualified to handle all seven clients on your own?"

"I did," I said definitively, unsure where she was going with all this. These weren't the types of questions I'd suspected. I'd been ready for more of last night. Could Maddie have gotten drugs inside the building? What was our policy for screening visitors? Did I have any idea if Maddie had relapsed in the last few days? Did she have any preexisting health conditions that could be complicated by drug use?

They kept asking the same versions of those questions over and over again, trying to trip you up. Asking them in slightly different ways. But these questions? I hadn't expected anything like these kinds of questions.

He looked over his notes. "Every single person in Crystal Meadows has a fairly significant rap sheet."

He was right. Everyone had been arrested at least once. Most of them numerous times. "We wouldn't have much of a comeback story if they didn't have anything to come back from," I said pointedly, and it wasn't lost on him.

He scanned his notes. "I'm okay with that. I'm just particularly concerned about the ones that are violent." He scrolled through. "Like Spencer. Three different domestic violence charges. He beat up a 7-Eleven clerk after he refused to sell him alcohol because he—meaning Spencer, of course—was clearly intoxicated. Oh, and assault on a police officer after he was pulled over for his second DUI." He finally looked up. This time he was the one to give me a pointed look. "Correct me if I'm wrong, but isn't Spencer the one that took off last night as soon as the police got there? The one they still can't find?"

"Yes, but that doesn't mean anything. He's a drug addict whose first impulse is to avoid and run away. He quite literally ran away from a very emotional situation."

"Or he had something to do with it."

I balked, sliding back in my chair. "Something to do with it? What do you mean? Maddie was in the bathroom alone."

He shrugged. "We still don't know what caused her death, and until we do, we're keeping all possibilities open."

"Including the possibility that someone else hurt her?" My brain scrambled to consider how something like that would work. How anyone else could've been involved with what happened to her when she'd been alone in her bedroom since ten o'clock last night? There was no disputing it given the cameras. What were they thinking?

"Maybe." He shrugged again. Gave a quick glance at Boone, then back to me. "We take it seriously when someone dies, especially when someone dies on camera and the rest of the world is continuing to watch how we do our investigation. You better believe we're making sure we've got every single one of our bases covered. How's that saying go? We're dotting all our i's and crossing all our t's?"

I nodded. I definitely understood that pressure. Doing your job while the rest of the world watched was incredibly nerve racking.

"Did they have secrets?" Detective Boone asked.

"Are you kidding me?" I burst out laughing. "Of course they did. They were full of them. That's all addiction is based on—secrets. The life force motivating so much of it. So, yes, there was probably no bigger group of people living with so many secrets under one roof."

"What about Maddie? What kinds of secrets did she have?" Detective Boone's eyes dug into mine.

That was the thing. Something terrible had happened to Maddie. It'd shifted everything for her. Transformed her from bright and bubbly to dark and withdrawn. Hilda needed to know why. That's what her mother had begged me to find out when she called the show.

And there was trauma there.

No doubt.

Deep, dark, bury-yourself-in-your-unconsciousness kind of trauma. It was just beginning to peek out. The truth was I hadn't gotten to Maddie's worst secrets yet, and I knew it. She had plenty of painful secrets. That much I was sure of. She just never told them to me.

And I hadn't pushed because I thought we had more time. I was going to work with her after she got out of Crystal Meadows. We'd already set up her first appointment. But those secrets couldn't possibly have anything to do with this—could they?

HER
(THEN)

He was out there still. Every day. She felt him. Watching her . . . that was the last thing he whispered in her ear. After he thought she'd fallen asleep. She faked it well.

"I'll be watching you, my little love bug," he whispered into her ear in that deep throaty voice that two hours ago had been the sexiest voice in the world. But now it sent quivers of fear throughout her body. Zaps of electricity. Her body desperate to move.

But she forced herself to be still.

Acquiesce.

She didn't want to find out what he'd do if she fought. She tried that in the beginning. Let out a wild scream when he first grabbed her panties and pulled them to the side. He clamped his hand over her mouth and nose. His hand was so huge. Just completely enveloped her face, and she couldn't breathe. But he didn't care. He was the first one to attack and the last one to finish.

We lived with predators, and then they told us to not be afraid. And once you've seen a predator? Well, you can pretty much spot them almost everywhere. That's what she wanted to yell from the rooftops— *Mamas, grab your daughters and lock them up. It's not safe to exist in these parts. On these streets.*

But she didn't. She shoved all the silent screams deep inside.

Just like she did that night.

Acquiesce.

They say that means you didn't fight. That you somehow gave in or, even sicker, that you wanted it. But that couldn't be further from the truth. Any good fighter will use whatever tactic they need to stay alive, and sometimes the best tactic in the world is to play dead. She'd known that from the moment he brought his fraternity brothers into the room.

It's not just fight or flight. Sometimes it's freeze.

So, she froze while he whispered all those other horrible things in her ears. Pretended to be dead while he moved his hands across her body. Buried herself deep in the most beautiful mahogany casket lined in silky white as he handed her off to the other monsters. That didn't matter. She was already on her way to meet the angels.

She stayed in that coffin until it was over. Nestled against the softest pillow. Like the ones from the Westin. Those ones she liked. Right there. When it was finished—finally over—he whispered more vile things into her ear, spewing his hate like venom.

Why did he hate her so much? What had she ever done except walk into the party? She'd barely smiled at him from across the beer pong table. He took her nervous smile and used it as an invitation.

She watched him, too, though. That's what he didn't know.

All the time. It was so easy. All his social media profiles were public, and he posted constantly. Tagging his location. Tagging who he was with. All the pretty girls draped all over him. He was having so much fun. Shining his light so bright. It wasn't fair. He just got to go on with his life like nothing happened. Hers was over.

She woke with his voice in her ear at night, or any other time she tried to sleep. Whispering those horrible things. And she woke screaming. Dripping in sweat. Sometimes urine, depending on how scared she got. Because she was one of those now too.

A bed wetter.

CHAPTER FIVE

I glanced at the clock on the wall. It'd been three minutes since Boone and Wallace stepped out of the room, but it felt like hours. Felt even longer that I'd been answering their questions, but it'd barely been an hour.

This was exhausting, and I hated that I still hadn't been able to check on anyone else. They spent the last ten minutes drilling me on how I taught people to make friends with their brains rather than be at war with their thoughts. But as much as I loved talking about what I do, I didn't see how it had anything to do with figuring out what happened to Maddie. They still said they didn't know. Was that possible? Or were they just not telling me? Why would they keep it a secret?

The door opened, and they walked back inside. A noticeable shift in the energy. This time they both pulled up a chair at the table. Detective Wallace nodded at Detective Boone, signaling her to go first, like they were politely taking turns.

"Was there anyone in the house who might have wanted to hurt Maddie?" Detective Boone asked, and I was immediately taken aback.

"Hurt Maddie? What do you mean, hurt Maddie?"

She looked at me like I was purposefully playing dumb, but I wasn't. Her question had taken me by complete surprise. "Was she fighting with anyone in the house? Anyone in particular that didn't like her? Or maybe she didn't like them?"

I shook my head. "Absolutely not. Nothing like that. I told you—everybody loved Maddie."

Detective Wallace raised his eyebrows at me and leaned across the table. "You're trying to tell me that group of former celebrity kids getting sober and vying for the media's attention didn't fight?" he scoffed.

"Of course there were fights, but nothing like she's suggesting. When you spend every day living together and doing intense therapy, there's an immediate closeness that develops. You become like family really quick—a dysfunctional one—but a family, nonetheless. It's part of the process. Getting sober is a huge traumatic event, so you're basically trauma bonding with everyone in the group." I laughed, but I was only half joking. "And yes, they fought. All the time, but over stupid things. Same as you would in any family—not emptying the dishwasher, leaving clothes in the washing machine. Misplacing one of their things. Eating someone's food without asking. Or frustration. There was plenty of that too. Emotional outbursts over nothing because being in early sobriety puts your nerves on edge, obviously. But none of it was serious. Even when they argued, everyone made up afterwards, and they were back to being friends in no time."

"Was Maddie fighting with anyone in the group?" Detective Boone asked, stepping back into the conversation.

"Maddie was the baby of the house in every sense of the word, and not just because she was the youngest. Everybody loved her. Everybody wanted to protect her. And she could do no wrong in anyone's eyes. She really was the sweetest thing." I swallowed hard. I wanted to ask about Hilda, but I couldn't bring myself to do it. Not yet. It'd crumble me to pieces, and I didn't want to fall apart in front of them.

"So, everyone loved her. You said they all wanted to protect her?" Detective Boone asked, with the look that, I was quickly beginning to recognize, meant there was something underneath it. Some kind of reason for her asking.

"I mean, just like in a general way," I said, unsettled again.

"It's so interesting you say that, because Maddie was really worried about her safety. In fact, it sounds like she didn't feel protected at all."

I wrinkled my face at her. "What do you mean? Maddie never said anything like that."

"Are you sure?" Wallace asked.

"Yes, I met with her multiple times a day. She would've said something to me if something was happening to make her feel unsafe." I crossed my arms on my chest. She might not have told me all her secrets, but we were close. She trusted me.

"What sort of procedures did Crystal Meadows have in place in case a client felt threatened or uncomfortable with another client?"

"We had all sorts of scenarios and procedures if anything like that should happen, starting with warnings, all the way down to removal from the house. We were prepared. But I can assure you that Maddie never expressed any concerns for her safety. At least not to me." I racked my brain for any memory of anyone ever saying otherwise, but came up empty handed there as well.

"What happened with Tripp?"

"Tripp?"

"Yes. What happened with Tripp when he got so angry that the police had to be called?"

The memories from that day came flooding back immediately, and I shook my head at Wallace. "It sounds way worse than it was. It was during their first week, and Tripp was coming off some pretty tough stuff. For a second, he had a brief psychotic break." Their eyes widened in surprise, but his behavior wasn't that unusual, especially not for someone who'd used so many hard drugs and for as many years as he had. "You don't understand. That sort of thing happens all the time when people are withdrawing from drugs. Psychosis is a part of it, and he had a moment. But it was only a moment."

Detective Boone raised her eyebrows at me. "One where the production crew was concerned enough for their safety that they called 911 to talk him down."

"Off a picnic table," I said softly, because I didn't want to sound combative, but I also didn't want them painting a violent picture of Tripp. He was so mellow and calm except for that instance, and it wasn't really even his fault. His withdrawal medication had worn off, and the nurse missed his second dose. He got really agitated and crawled up on the picnic table in the backyard, perching on top of it like a bird. He cracked his knuckles over and over. The moment anyone came near him, including one of the camerapeople, he spit at them. "He jumped up on the picnic table because he was upset, and yes, he seemed very aggressive. But if they would've just left him alone for a few minutes, he would've been fine as soon as he got his medication. It was just having the cameras in his face at such a delicate time, when he was so paranoid. He thought people were trying to attack him."

I wished for the thousandth time that staff or Gia had called me while it was happening. I'd left early that day for a doctor's appointment or I would've been there, and I would've been able to talk him down. Or at least get everyone to leave him alone long enough for him to calm down. Which he would've. I could've de-escalated the situation.

Wallace glanced down at his notes. The same notebook he scribbled away on while we talked. I wanted a notebook, too, and a pen in my hands. I didn't do therapy sessions without them. It was more than jotting down client notes, though. Sure, I wrote down important information to remember and questions I wanted to ask, but I also liked the feel of the pen in my hand. Sometimes I just doodled. It was a way for my constantly moving brain to focus and pay attention.

"Are you aware of . . ." Wallace paused, reaching into the folder sitting next to him on the table. He'd left it sitting there untouched up until this moment. He pulled out a blue notebook and placed it on the table in front of him. "The tenth-step journal?"

"Yes, it's really common in treatment centers, and we created a modified version for all our clients to use." It'd been my idea. I did the same thing with my clients outside Crystal Meadows too. It was a great tool.

"Can you tell me more about it?" he asked, sounding like any well-trained psychologist.

"It's a journal that we ask the clients to write in first thing every morning and the last thing they complete at night. It helps them keep track of their progress. In the morning, they pick some key goals to work on. Usually things they've identified as important in their treatment groups or one of their sessions with me. They list ways they're going to meet the goals, and then at the end of the day, they reflect on how they did. We try to keep it positive. Gratitude in the morning. Successes at night."

"Along with some additional questions, too, right?" He didn't wait for me to answer. He looked down. Opening the journal he'd just taken out of his bag and reading from it. "Like, *Is there anything you've kept to yourself today that should be discussed with another person at once?*"

"Yes, that's one of the questions. A way we keep them accountable. People struggling with addiction keep lots of secrets, and secrets eat away at their insides, giving them a reason to use. So, we give them an opportunity at the end of every day to dispel the poison and save their lives."

"It sounds intense," Detective Boone said.

"It is, but it has to be," I assured her. Sobriety was a life-and-death matter. Clearly.

"Looks like Maddie had some pretty alarming answers. There were lots of things she was keeping to herself." Detective Wallace stopped and gave me a dramatic look. I was officially over the police interrogation. I couldn't stand that they had all the information and I had none. Asking questions they already knew the answers to, and I just had to play along like I didn't know what they were doing.

"I'm sorry, but I don't know what you're talking about." They were both staring at me expectantly now, like I'd caught myself in their trap. I just stared back until, finally, Boone reached into her bag and pulled out another notebook.

She slid the journal over to Wallace. I recognized the mandala on the front. The same one that was on everybody's notebook at Crystal Meadows. Purple and yellow with tiny white flowers. Noelle had helped me and Gia pick them out. She loved that kind of stuff. Wallace opened it and flipped a few pages before stopping and reading out loud.

"*I'm scared to say anything. What if nobody believes me?*" He paused, staring at the pages without looking up at me, like he was really taking it in for the first time too. "June fourteenth." He cleared his throat. "*Nobody is going to believe me. But it's happening. Again. No matter what I do. It's never going to stop.*' She writes another one a few days later— June nineteenth. '*Somebody make it stop.*" His voice was pressured and hurried as he continued reading. "June twentieth. '*Don't you see it? Please. Look. Open your eyes. Look at the camera.*' June twenty-first. '*Somebody please help.*'"

Wallace closed the notebook. He folded his hands on top, and his eyes drilled holes into mine. "What do you think about these entries?"

I shook my head in disbelief, stunned. Still trying to make sense of what he'd just read. "I don't understand. Who is she talking about? She never said anything like that to me or anyone else, as far as I know. They would've told me. Something like that would've been reported at once." I just kept shaking my head. "We would've helped her if we thought she was in any kind of danger. This makes no sense."

"Well, it makes a little sense. Victims often don't disclose their abuse for fear they won't be believed, or usually, because they're being threatened." Detective Boone leaned back in her seat and crossed her arms.

"Yes, I understand that part. Of course," I said. But maybe I didn't. Maybe I'd fallen victim to the same stereotypes I'd spent most of my life fighting against. "I don't know what's going on, but she couldn't have written those things. She never said anything like that. Not once. And we were close."

Wallace held up the journal. "This isn't her notebook?"

Maddie's name was scrawled all over the cover. Her *i*'s dotted with hearts, just like she always did them. The tea stain in the right corner. She'd squealed and leaped up from her chair when it happened the first week of treatment, but she hadn't moved in enough time to save the corner from getting wet. It'd been permanently stained ever since. Didn't matter that Preston had grabbed paper towels and tried to dry it up right away.

"It's hers," I said, trying to understand how those things were written in her notebook and we somehow missed them. It wasn't possible. There had to be some kind of mistake. A misunderstanding somewhere. But where? How?

"And correct me if I'm wrong, but Gia indicated that you're the one responsible for reviewing these journals?" Wallace asked, leafing through the pages, pretending there were things in there he hadn't seen. But I was sure he'd diligently combed his way through it multiple times before this meeting.

"That's why I'm so confused. I've gone through her notebooks, and there's never been any mention of distress or being afraid. Not in her words and not in any of her sessions. There's been nothing like that. I've never seen those messages." I pointed at her notebook. "I get notified if there's anything that remotely raises any concerns, and these would've definitely been brought to my attention immediately." I clenched my hands underneath the table. If night staff had missed something like this . . . but there was no way. One time maybe. That was possible, but they'd have to miss it multiple times. There were numerous entries. I tried to slow my thoughts so I could sort them, but they were coming too fast. There were so many questions.

"It's her last entry that's the most disturbing." Boone cut in to my panic. "Would you like to read it?"

Wallace didn't wait for me to answer Boone. He slid the journal across the table. I quickly skimmed the pages—pages I'd already reviewed, just like I'd told them. I always went back to the beginning whenever I got a chance to go over them, and today was no different.

All the staff had ever flagged in hers was how she complained about all the weight she was gaining and calling herself fat. I flipped through the pages, reading as fast as I could, including my own comments I'd scribbled into the margins.

Good job, kiddo.

Proud of you.

Just try again tomorrow.

All my words. Written right there along with hers.

They put the notebooks outside their door every evening, and the overnight staff reviewed them. There were only two—Ethan and Natalie. They split the week. We purposefully kept the number of staff in the house small, just like we did the number of clients. Ethan and Natalie provided comments in the margins of every entry, no matter what. Little words of encouragement. All positive stuff. They noted anything concerning for me to review in the morning and then slid them back underneath the clients' doors so clients could see them first thing when they woke up. We wanted them to start their day off with positive feedback. We tried to fill them with as much hope as possible during the few short weeks we had them under our care.

I looked up and made eye contact with each detective. "I don't know what's going on, but none of these comments about being afraid were there when I looked at the notebooks or when staff read them either. I don't know how they got there."

"Maybe someone else put them there." Boone shrugged nonchalantly, but there was nothing casual about what she was implying. Did she think it was me? That I'd somehow gone back and written in Maddie's journal? Why would I do that?

"The overnight staff took pictures of anything clients wrote that was alarming and recorded it in their charts. Have you been through their charts? Maybe there's something there that can help you," I offered. If they could look at those pictures and the date stamps, maybe they'd be able to tell things didn't match up. Because there was no way we missed something this important that many times. But I didn't know if the client charts were available to detectives in an investigation like this or if they were still protected information. Did the same laws of confidentiality apply?

"We've issued a request to review all the records, but it'll be a few days at least before the judge approves the subpoena." Detective Wallace nodded.

Detective Boone jumped back in. "What do you think about her last entry? The one she made the night before she died? You still haven't said."

"Oh, right," I said, returning my attention back down to the pages.

All Maddie's entries scribbled in her looping scrawl. Blue ink. Scary, ominous words written in bubbly letters. I quickly flipped through the last few pages, scanning each one as fast as I could until I got to the last page. This one was written different. All her other notes had been at the bottom of the page. This one was in the side margin. The spot where the night staff would enter their comments.

My stomach curled with each word:

If something bad happens to me tonight, it wasn't an accident. Please tell my mom. I never wanted to die.

CHAPTER SIX

I buzzed Gia's Ring camera over and over again, anxiously looking behind me. I didn't even know why I was so paranoid. Like somehow the detectives had followed me to her house. But even if they'd followed me, who cared? It's not like I was doing anything wrong. I'd been with Gia every day for the past three months. I spent more time with her than I did my wife. Noelle teased me about it all the time, calling her my second wife. Except this was the first time I'd ever been to her house. I only knew the address because I'd sent a car for her once and it was still saved in my phone. Normally, I wouldn't dream of showing up at someone's house unannounced, and definitely not someone so big and decorated in Hollywood as Gia. But these circumstances weren't anywhere near normal. My meeting had me shook.

And scared.

Why would Maddie write all that in her journal? What did any of it mean? Why wouldn't she tell us if she was in danger? Did she even write it? I pressed the button on the gate for the third time. It was the way they asked about Maddie's safety again. They'd opened up so many possibilities I'd never even considered, and now that they'd opened that portal, I couldn't just close it. My thoughts had spun to all these horrible dark places.

"Go through the house. I'm in the back," Gia's voice finally called out through the intercom right as I was about to give up and go home.

She hadn't answered any of my calls or texts either. This was my last resort. Showing up like this.

When the door finally opened, I rushed inside. Gia's place was as impressive as I'd imagined it'd be. Lush desert landscaping in the front with expensive terra-cotta pots lining the walkway leading into her house. The massive wooden door was surrounded with glass on both sides. An impressive entryway, and if I weren't in such a hurry, I would've taken so much more time to marvel at her gorgeous house, but I didn't. The design was a completely open concept with everything leading to the outside, and with all the sliding glass doors open, she was easy to spot in the back. A seamless transition from indoor to outdoor space.

She was tucked away in the corner, back by the sparkling L-shaped pool. The water glimmered in the sunlight. Diamonds twinkling around it. Just like the huge rock on her hand. The one she'd given herself for her fortieth birthday. She sat in one of the chairs, manically scrolling through her phone with one hand and holding a cigarette in the other, though I'd never seen her smoke before. By the looks of the ashtray, she'd been out here awhile.

"Do you know cigarettes are almost twelve dollars a pack right now?" She didn't even lift her head to look at me. Fully immersed in whatever she was reading. Probably something awful they'd said about the accident and the show. They said all press was good press, but I wasn't sure about this. They were saying some pretty awful things. I didn't care about it. My career would be fine. I wasn't in show business. I worked in the addiction field. I would disappear into the same obscurity I'd come from. But Gia? What would this do to her career? Did something like this ban her from television? Make people stop wanting to work with her or give her shows?

"I got a vape at first, you know? So much safer and better for you and all that, but it just wasn't the same. Sucking on a piece of plastic. You ever tried it?" She motioned to the other end table. "It's right there if you want some of it. Something to do with Skittles. At least you know how they get the kids." She let out her sarcastic laugh. There were empty bottles of wine next to cigarettes. No glasses. Straight from the bottle was never a good sign. She still hadn't showered or changed her clothes. Dressed in the exact same thing she'd been wearing last time I saw her.

"Gia, honey. Doll. Love." I smiled at her, using all the pet names I used on set, too, when I was trying to get her to calm down from one of her almost daily rage fits. This instantly brought a smile to her face, like it did then. It always worked. It's why I used it. "In the time since we left the house, I've had two showers, and by the looks of it, you've still had none. I'm not sure what you had planned for the day, but whatever it is, it's got to include a shower, especially if you're going anywhere near my car."

"I just can't believe someone died on the show, you know? And Maddie of all people. I feel so responsible. Like I should've seen it or I could've done something about it. All they keep asking me is how she could've gotten drugs in. Who might've brought them to her. All our policies. And I just don't know . . . we were so careful." A sob caught in her throat, but she didn't let herself cry. "It was a weeknight too. Nobody from the outside had even been there in three days."

"We were careful. I told the detectives the exact same thing. We were as diligent as any treatment center can be. Probably even more restrictive than most, given our clientele." I raised a finger as I listed the things we'd done, reminding her of how intentional we'd been about keeping our clients safe from using drugs. "They only got visitors during family week, and we screened all their stuff when they came inside. Did all of the urine analyses. Every other day. At different times so you couldn't predict when the drug tests were coming. They didn't even get to leave. If anyone brought it to her, it was the staff." I didn't even think of the implications of what I was saying until the words had rolled out of my mouth.

Gia grabbed on to it as soon as I said it. Like it was the juiciest piece of meat on the plate. "Oh my God, I never even thought about that. Do you think one of them could've given her something?"

I shrugged. "It's possible."

We did our best. We even tested staff—granted it was only once a week, not every day like we did with the clients. The thing about us, like so many other treatment centers, was that we hired former drug addicts as staff. The only people that truly understand and can reach other addicts are the ones that have been there themselves. Myself included. I'd been in LA almost thirteen years and been sober just as long. We called the ones working during the day *junior clinicians*. They spent as much time with the clients as we did. But the night staff? They barely spent any time with them. They arrived as all of us were leaving and were gone in the morning when we headed back in.

"What about the production crew? Do you think someone could've given her anything?" Gia's eyes were huge. No doubt the police were already thinking these things and asking these questions. It'd just taken us a bit longer because we were so deeply connected to it. You couldn't see things when you were right in the center of them. It's why you were never supposed to work with family members, counsel anyone close, or operate on a loved one. You just couldn't be objective.

"Here's the thing," I said, leaning forward and at the same time eyeing the bottle of wine that still had some red left in it. That desire never went away. As seductive as any other forbidden lover. I focused on Gia. "Have you talked to the police today?"

She shook her head. "No, but I spent all night with them, and they want to meet with me this afternoon after they've had a chance to interview everyone again. Apparently, they're doing a second round."

"Well, I've just been with them for mine, and that's why I'm here." We'd gotten lost in our emotions and trailed away from the fact that I'd showed up at her door unannounced and refused to leave until she answered the door. I dropped my voice low, like you automatically did whenever you were telling a secret, even though I was sure they'd share it with her when they met this afternoon. "Supposedly, Maddie wrote some disturbing stuff in her nightly journal. That's what they're really focusing on right now. Those are the kinds of questions they asked me about today. Like, was she fighting with anyone in the house? Was she scared of anyone? Did we have protocols in place if a client felt threatened? Things like that."

"What?" She grabbed me and practically pulled me off my lounge chair. "Why were they asking questions like that? They don't think Maddie overdosed? I just figured that's what everyone thought. She smuggled drugs in somehow and . . ." She motioned shooting dope into her arm and then dramatically closed her eyes, cocking her head to the side like she was dead. "They think someone hurt her?" She shook her head looking as bewildered as I'd felt when they told me earlier. "There's no way anyone hurt Maddie. We would've seen it on camera."

"Exactly. That's what I told them. That's why it doesn't make any sense. But they have her journal, and she writes that she's scared more than once. The very last entry of her journal says if something happens to her, it wasn't an accident."

"Are you serious right now? What in the actual fuck?"

"I know. I felt the exact same way when they were telling me." I still felt sick to my stomach with the news.

"Wait, but don't you go over those? Why didn't you say something?" she asked, sounding just like the police, except her questioning was innocent.

"Yes, I've gone over every single one that night staff pointed out. Hers only got flagged a couple times and never for anything like that." Not like some of the others, who said something concerning at least once a week. We'd created all the protocols together. Spent endless hours hashing out how it'd all work. Everything we did was intentional.

"What did it say?"

"Weird references to being afraid. That someone was trying to hurt her, and she couldn't tell anyone because no one would believe her. That she needed help. She—"

Gia slapped the table, sending the ashtray flying onto the ground and scattering ashes everywhere. "Are you kidding me? That's the most ridiculous thing I've ever heard. And even if it were true—which it's not, but let's just for one second pretend that it is—there's no way the night staff wouldn't bring that to your attention immediately."

"I know, that's exactly what I said. It's super weird that they didn't. I just don't understand why they wouldn't. And her entry from last night is especially troubling." I tried to recite it verbatim as best as I could. "*If something happens to me tonight, it wasn't me. I want to live.*" I shook my head. Still as baffled as Gia was.

She couldn't sit in her seat a second longer. She sprang to her feet, running her hands through her hair, which was completely out of the ponytail now. Just long and scraggly, going everywhere.

"Were they trying to create their own little movie and something went wrong? Is that what this is about? I don't get it. But maybe that's what it was."

That had been our biggest concern from the very beginning when we selected our participants or even discussed the show after she brought it to me that first time. The fact that every single one of them had been a celebrity kid who'd fallen from Hollywood's graces and was desperate to regain the spotlight. That was the carrot dangling in front of them, motivating their sobriety, which meant they were looking for their moment and would likely do anything to create it. That's why we never knew half the time if the crises or traumas they dramatically described were true or if they were just performing for the cameras. Trying to have the saddest story so they could tug at the world's heartstrings the hardest. Get people really invested in their characters because everyone knows you have to be emotionally invested in a character in order to care about what happened to them.

We never forgot that they were all actors. Not once.

"Here's the deal." I stood because it felt odd to stay seated while Gia frantically paced around. "If it was one of the others, I would absolutely say that it was possible they'd tried to create an elaborate plot to gain attention and viewers, a plot that went horribly wrong. One hundred percent, without a doubt. But Maddie was the only one who didn't need to do any of that."

That was the thing about Maddie. It was exactly like I'd told the detectives. She was still in her fame. Hollywood hadn't tossed her away yet. She'd only just begun to get in trouble. She was the celebrity talent that brought people to the show. She was the number one reason they watched, because she was still hot. Still trending. Everyone was rooting for her. They wanted her to get sober.

Which explained why someone else might try something super dramatic to shift the attention on to themselves. But Maddie wouldn't have to do that. All the attention was already on her, and would stay there even after the show ended.

"Who was on duty last night?" Gia asked.

"Ethan," I responded. I'd checked the schedule on my drive over.

Gia turned around and motioned for me to follow her. "Come on, then. We have to go find Ethan and talk to him. Plus, he can tell us why he didn't mention any of Maddie's other journal entries." She hurried through the house, scanning for the keys she was always misplacing, just like she did at work. I grabbed her elbow to slow her down and make sure she was paying attention to what I was going to say next.

"You're missing the biggest point, though. Whenever anyone's journal entries got flagged, I always skimmed everything that was there. Gave it all a quick review. Maddie was no different, and there was nothing there. None of the stuff those detectives showed me today."

"What are you saying?" she asked, whipping around to face me. "That someone else put it there? Why would someone else put it there?"

"I have no clue, but it makes about as much sense as Maddie writing them. Because here's the deal—I just know it wasn't there when I looked at her journals before, and now it is. Which changes everything about what happened to her if that's the case. Also makes sense why the detectives were asking such different questions about her safety."

She shook her head in disbelief. "Come on, let's go. We have to talk to Ethan." She hurried inside, and I quickly followed, grabbing her arm to stop her after she scooped her car keys from the counter.

"First, you have to take a shower," I said. "You can't go out in public looking like a hot mess. No one will take you seriously. They'll all think you're being hysterical."

She eyed me, instantly wanting to do what she wanted to do, but I held on to her arm and gave her another knowing glance. Women had to be put together if they wanted to be taken seriously. It wasn't fair. It wasn't right. But it was the patriarchy we lived in. She set her keys back on the counter and started walking to the other side of the house. She stopped halfway through the living room and turned around.

"What about Spencer?" she asked.

"I haven't heard from him. Have you?"

She shook her head, forehead creased in deep thought. "Could he have anything to do with what happened? He completely freaked out and left the house. His reaction was way over the top. Don't get me wrong. Maddie's death was awful. I'm not saying this entire thing isn't terrible and tragic. But to be such a mess over it and leave the house like that? Not come back?" She raised her eyebrows at me. "The one thing we know about Spencer is that he was quite violent and terrible when he was drinking."

I slowly nodded my agreement. "The detectives brought him up too. If they're thinking this was something more than a freak accident, it definitely makes me a bit more skeptical of Spencer taking off last night. It does change things."

"Maybe one of us should go talk to Ethan about the notebook, and one of us should find Spencer? See if he's acting funny or suspicious?" She paused like she was second-guessing herself. It was so hard to know what to do in this situation. We'd planned for lots of possible events on the show. Never this.

"You're right," I agreed. "One of us should talk to Spencer." I motioned to the stairs in front of her. "You go take a shower and talk to Ethan. I'm going to head out and find Spencer. I might have better luck, and I have a feeling he's going to be a bit more difficult to find than Ethan."

People running from the law always were, especially ones that might be high. But thankfully, that was my specialty.

CHAPTER SEVEN

You never forgot the under-the-bridge smell of a six-person homeless encampment—a mixture of urine, feces, and rotten food. I looked over my shoulder before I walked down to it, glancing at the five-million-dollar homes just steps behind me. Most of these kids probably came from those homes. The first newly sober person I worked with, Conrad, lived right behind me on this block. He was where I learned that lots of the people living under the bridges and overpasses in this city—especially this one tucked underneath this particular bridge—came from these homes. They were the sons and daughters of some of Hollywood's wealthiest and most elite.

Spencer was no exception. He didn't live directly behind us, but his parents lived only a few blocks away in Colfax Meadows, a similar affluent neighborhood. He taught me wealth didn't get you sober, even if it might get you out of consequences. And he'd definitely been saved by his parents from his share of consequences.

It was probably why I hit my bottom so fast—I didn't have rich parents or anyone with money in my lineage. There was nobody to bail me out of trouble once I started getting into it. I was the youngest of four kids, and my parents were so busy working that I was mostly raised by my older siblings. My dad worked so hard that he worked himself to death, dying of a heart attack when I was only sixteen. He just dropped dead in the driveway. His lunch box splayed open beside him. A turkey sandwich next to his head. That's when my world fell apart, and I really started drinking. It's why I understood the clients I worked with so well. I used to be one of them, and nobody knows how hard it is to get sober than someone who's had to do it themselves. Or the trauma that's there to meet you when you do. Becoming conscious is so painful.

The mud stuck to my shoes as I made my way down the bank toward the LA River. Thick sludge, and I tried not to think about what else might be in it. I hadn't told Detectives Wallace and Boone about my history. I left that part out because no matter how far we've come in decreasing the stigma around addiction, we've still got a long way to go. And anyone who's never personally struggled with the beast usually doesn't understand what it's like, and they form all sorts of judgments. I didn't want them judging me any more than they already had.

I kicked the trash away from my feet. Paying careful attention to any sign of Spencer at the same time I was pretending like I wasn't staring or looking for anyone. I didn't want to draw any attention to myself and wanted to get out of here as quick as I could. There were dirty clothes in an Alo bag leaned up against a beat-up shopping cart stuffed full of other junk. I almost laughed out loud. That was what I meant. Their children living out here, but not discarded. The most well-cared-for group of unhoused. There were plants in pots. A broom standing next to where they'd swept. Neatly piled trash. Groceries set outside their tents. Fresh blankets. Their parents took care of them still, even while they were out here.

Spencer's parents included. They'd been bailing him out of trouble since he started getting into it when he was fourteen. Their tale was as old as time.

"He turned into a different kid overnight." That's what they both said. But that's the thing parents never understand—by the time you recognize those signs, it's already too late, and you can't save anyone from a downward spiral if they're intent on going down. Doesn't matter if they're a teenager.

While Maddie was our youngest celebrity in the house, Spencer started in the spotlight the youngest. He was a professional skateboard kid. Sponsored by the skateboarding circuit by the time he was eight. I knew absolutely nothing about the sport. But apparently, he was a big deal. He had all kinds of sponsors. Cameras following him everywhere. And then he got hurt training for the Olympic trials. It ended his short career. Blew out his knee in a way he'd never recover from. Also when he started popping pills. Pills he chopped up and snorted until, eventually, he was shooting them into his arm in the same way the two people behind the mounds of trash were doing now. I looked away from their blue tent and kept walking. Head down while still scanning.

Spencer gave a whole new meaning to peaking in high school. Cycling in and out of the best and most expensive treatment centers in the country. His parents threw all the money at the problem, trying to save him. They gave him the best therapists. Coaches. Alternative treatments. All of it. But never successful. And never a true consequence, because they bailed him out of jail each time he landed there.

As spoiled as these kids were, I still felt sorry for them.

"I don't enjoy the experience of living." That's what Spencer told me the first time we met. And really, how could you blame him? Famous at fourteen? To go from twenty-four-seven attention. All the love, adoration, and praise. Constantly getting your picture taken. The parties. The events. The sponsors. Guest spots on TV. Regular life is just too dull and boring after you've been raised in Hollywood's glitz and flashing lights.

I caught the movement of two people leaning against a mattress on top of a beaten-up couch. They were intense and focused as the young man pressed the needle into someone else's arm. It felt so intimate, like I'd peeked into the window of a house and caught someone having sex. I quickly looked away, but not fast enough.

"What the fuck you looking at, lady?" the guy sitting on top of an abandoned toy carton snapped at me. I hadn't even noticed him there. He was tucked behind a framed Monet poster someone had abandoned, which they'd dragged over next to their pile of broken bike pieces. A dirty gray sweater hung from a clothes hanger on the chain-link fence behind him.

"Sorry." I quickly apologized and looked away. "I'm just trying to find my friend Spencer. Have you seen him?"

"Who she looking for?" the girl next to him piped up. She rubbed his back. It was impossible not to notice her pregnant belly, swollen in such sharp contrast to her rail-thin body. She was so skinny. How could she keep herself alive? Let alone someone else? But I quickly realized it could easily be the advanced stages of cirrhosis or any other kind of organ failure brought on by chronic drug use making her stomach so distended.

"I'm looking for my friend Spencer. Something bad happened to a friend of ours, and I want to check on how he's doing. Make sure he's okay. That's all. I'm just worried about him." I shifted my eyes away while I talked so I wouldn't make them more paranoid than they already were. I didn't want them to think I was the police. "You know him? Seen him?"

The girl cocked her head to the side. "Short stocky kid?"

I nodded.

"Red hair? Talks with this weird clipped accent, like he's from Jersey or something, but he's a total LA boy?" she asked next.

This time I laughed. "Yes, that's him." Lyriq said the exact same thing about him. How she'd assumed he was from the East Coast because of the way he talked. It was her favorite thing to tease him about.

"Pretty sure he went with Ray over to Moorpark." The girl motioned to her left.

"Okay, thank you! Thank you so much!" I gushed. I fought the urge to give them money. Not because I didn't want them to use it for drugs, but because it was like putting a Band-Aid on a knife wound. People had been giving them money to help them their entire lives. That was part of the problem.

I hurried through the last three blocks and back over the embankment to my car, resisting the impulse to run. Moorpark was close enough to walk, but I didn't want to miss him. Who knew if the girl had seen him this morning or last night.

Luckily, I found a great parking spot on the street, and it wasn't long before I was scouring the park for any trace of Spencer. I searched alongside the fence down by the river on the other side, glancing up at the Laurel Canyon traffic bridge as the cars roared past. Javon used to talk about it in our sessions. How the bridge she ran by in the morning, swearing she was never drinking again and going to get sober, was the same bridge she had to talk herself out of jumping off every night when she was drunk. I'd never heard a more perfect description of addiction.

I hurried along the pathway, staying away from the park equipment, where all the parents and nannies were playing with their small children. If Spencer was here, he would be on the other side of the park, as it was an unwritten rule that the unhoused persons and anyone using drugs were allowed to stay in the park if they left everyone else alone. For the most part, they did. That's how we existed. The desolate on one side, searching in trash cans for the items rich folks threw away. I didn't see anyone resembling Spencer, though, on either side. I was just about to abandon my search and head back to the car when I spotted him coming out of the bathroom. He was in the same clothes he'd been in the last time I saw him, and I could tell just by the way he walked that he was high. Short. Jerky. Hunched over like he was hiding. And talking to himself. Always a telltale sign.

He lifted his head and saw me coming toward him. For a second, he froze like a deer in headlights. He wanted to run. His eyes skirted everywhere.

"Spencer, I just want to talk to you. It's okay." I put my hands up as if to say *I come in peace.*

He took a few steps backward. Looking behind me like he was weighing whether or not someone was following me. Why was he so paranoid? He hadn't done anything to be this paranoid about. All he'd done was get high and leave the center. Pretty much the most common thing to happen in any treatment program.

Or was there more?

Was Gia right to be worried about him? Were the police?

Could there actually be a chance that he'd hurt Maddie in some way? But how?

I finally got close enough to him to tell he wasn't just high. He reeked of alcohol too. He hung his head in shame, raking his hands up and down his arms.

"Hey, Spence," I said. Even though I was close enough to touch him, I made no move to do it. It'd scare him away for sure. As it was, I felt like, at any second, he might bolt. He refused to look at me. Just kept hanging his head low. Too ashamed to make eye contact.

"I know what you saw must've been so frightening. I just wanted to—"

He cut me off and jerked his head up. His eyes lit with anger that quickly. "Don't talk to me like I'm a little kid."

"I wasn't talking to you like that. I—"

"*I know what you saw must've been so frightening,*" he mocked, jeering. "Please. Don't treat me like I'm an idiot."

"I understand wanting to lash out at me right now. Believe me. I do. You've got a lot of powerful and big emotions happening, and you're not used to—"

"Pff, there you go again." He waved me off. "All that treatment bullshit. I'm not trying to hear all that." He turned around and started walking away. I held back the urge to grab him and instead fell in line next to him. I hadn't expected this to be easy. It never was. Thankfully, I'd talked to plenty of people in this exact spot.

"Look, Spencer, I didn't come find you so that I could drag you back to Crystal Meadows. I'm not demanding or forcing you to talk to the police either. Truth is, I don't care if you stay out here and get high." I swept my arms around us and the wide-open space of the park. "Sure, would I like you to not be doing what you're doing right now? Absolutely. I would prefer you don't go down this road again, but I'm not trying to stop you." His walk slowed. Some of the tension left his body. He settled into position next to me rather than trying to pull ahead. I kept talking while we walked, staying on the west side of the park. "I know you might think this is all treatment stuff, and you don't have to believe anything I say, but I actually care about my patients. Truly care about all of you and genuinely want you to live as your best selves. That's it. And I know that you're not usually at your best self when you're high. But I won't stop you. You can feel free to get as high as you want."

I had never been one to stop them. Addicts stop when they're ready and not a moment sooner. It doesn't matter how much you love them. Or equally hate them. Punish them. Reward them. Yell at them. Coddle them. There's nothing you can do to keep an addicted person from using. It's why I didn't try.

And sometimes they don't stop. Ever.

Sometimes they die.

But sometimes they don't.

The ones that don't are condemned to a fate almost worse than death—living the same miserable day over and over again. Ask any person whose been there what that feels like. It's a special version of hell. Most addicts are jealous of the ones that die because they're finally free. I know I used to be. Angry and disappointed to wake up from my blackouts still breathing.

"You're not supposed to say all this to me, you know," Spencer said, and I sensed the tiniest smile peeking out of the corners of his mouth. Because he was right. Most people wouldn't tell an addicted person it was okay to get high, but I wasn't most people.

"What did I tell you on the first day we met?" I laid my hand gently on his shoulder. It was finally safe to touch him again. "I'm not like any other chemical dependency therapist you've worked with. I'll hold your hand throughout the journey no matter where it takes us." I shrugged and gave him a smile. "And, well, it looks like this is where it's taken us, so I just want to help you. Really, I just want to make sure you're okay."

And find out if he knew anything about Maddie. But that would wait. He needed to know I cared about him first.

He didn't push my hand off or run. All good signs.

We walked in silence. Heading down the hill toward the smoke shop. My phone buzzed in my pocket with notifications, and I ignored them even though I was dying to know what Gia had found out with Ethan.

"I just thought you'd be mad at me," he said when he finally spoke in a tiny voice that must've been exactly what he sounded like as a little boy.

"Mad at you? For leaving a really uncomfortable situation? Or for getting high again? Because, you know what? Both reactions are perfectly reasonable solutions to a tough experience, especially someone with your history. Neither of those things change how I feel about you." Unconditional love and acceptance. That was always my mission. Coupled with personal empowerment and accountability. "Do you know what? I still feel exactly the same way that I did about you now as I did two days ago when we worked on our vision boards during our session."

His body tightened at the mention of the vision board. No doubt overcome with a wave of guilt that his entire board centered around making it to one year sober. As the oldest of the bunch and with the longest history of using, he'd also been to the most treatment centers and detoxes. Twelve treatment centers. Twenty-seven detoxes. He'd tried all sorts of alternate therapies too. Used 5-hydroxytryptophan. Had acupuncture. Worked with a shaman. Two rounds of electric shock. It wasn't like he was never able to put sober time together. Just like the others, there'd been periods of sobriety. Thirty days. Ninety days. Ten months. And all the various spots in between, but no matter how long he'd been able to stay sober, he'd never been able to make it an entire year. That was his goal. From the very first time we met together.

We were introduced at his twenty-seventh detox center, and his face looked almost the same today as it did then. Sunken and hollow.

But it was the sadness in his eyes that hurt the most. Addiction would suck the life out of your soul, and his was already gone that quickly. Today was more than that, though. He also looked defeated. That was what happened when you put such an emphasis on the amount of time sober. As if the number of days you were sober was a measure of your success. It created such a toxic shame cycle too. That was why it was never my focus.

"There was so much blood everywhere and I just freaked out, Dr. Harlow. It's all my fault. I didn't mean to, Dr. Harlow. I didn't. Really. I didn't know. You have to forgive me." His voice sped up. He anxiously looked around us.

"Spencer, it's fine. I understand why you left. It's okay. We can get through this." I kept my voice calm and even. He looked like he wanted to run.

He pulled a cigarette out of his pocket and twirled it around in his fingers. "They told me to do it. She said to do it."

"Who told you to do it? Do what?" He sped up, and I hurried to keep in line. I didn't want to miss anything he might confess.

"Ohmigod. This is what I get. It's what I get, you know? They say karma. Karma will get you. Well, here you go. Here you go, Mama. Happening now. For your enjoyment." He dug into his pockets until he came up with a lighter. He lit his cigarette. He told us he didn't smoke. What else had he lied about?

"Spencer, what do you mean, they told you to do it? Do what? What did you do?"

He shook his head. "No. No." He pointed the cigarette at me. "I see what you're trying to do there. I see it. You think you're so much smarter than everyone else. Little Miss Doctor, you. But you're not smarter than the rest of us, you know. We're smart too. Real smart. All of us. Even them." He motioned down by the river, but there was nobody there. At least not anyone I could see.

I grabbed his arms to try to center him, but he pulled away.

"Stop touching me," he snapped. "I knew you'd come. This just proves it. Just leave me alone." He jerked his other arm from me and took off walking even faster. Chasing after him was the wrong idea, but I couldn't stop myself. I had to know what he knew.

"What are you so afraid of, Spencer? Just tell me. I can see that you're scared. Maybe I can help you." Was he scared of whoever Maddie was afraid of, or worried he was going to get into trouble? Or was he just really high?

"You're just trying to mess with my head now. I knew you'd do that. Stop. Stop it. Go away." He put his hands over his ears, growing more and more agitated by the second.

"I just came out here to see if you're okay, that's all. I just want to make sure you're okay," I said, trying to keep my voice as even as possible to counter his paranoia.

He shook his head. Eyes flared with anger. The color gone. All pupils. "No. No, you don't. That's not why. You want to know about the notebook. You want to know about Maddie. You don't care about me. Nobody does."

"Listen, Spencer, yes, I do really want to know what happened to Maddie. Would I be out here talking to you if she hadn't passed away?" I paused so he could understand I really did get where he was coming from. "Honestly, I can't say. I'm pretty sure that I'd be checking on you either way. And I will say this—if something had happened to you like it did to Maddie, I'd be working just as hard to figure out what happened to you. I can promise you that."

It took him a second to consider what I said before deciding whether he believed me or not. He worked his jaw. Eyes skittered everywhere. Ran his hands through his hair, super greasy now. Been on the streets for less than a day, but he already looked so rough. Covered in dirt and grime.

"I knew I shouldn't have done that. I shouldn't have done it. Something about the notebook and her mom."

"Whose mom?"

"Maddie. Her mom. That's what she said."

"Wait. That's what Hilda said? What do you mean, Hilda said?"

"No. No. No. She's the one that told me to give it to him. Said he forgot to get it. Then she was like, *Don't let anyone know*," he said, his voice pressured and hurried. "Right under the spot. She knows the spot. Should've been my first clue. Why me? Huh? How come?" He stopped for a second, his eyes searching mine for answers, but I didn't even understand the questions. His breath reeked of alcohol and burnt plastic. "She talked to me right under that spot. You know the spot. Everybody does. Coming out of the library." He rubbed his nose. Coughed twice. Spit the phlegm on the ground. "You can't hear anything. But you know that, huh? You know it all. The AC vent is too loud and right underneath that door—muffles everything."

"That's why everyone sits there?" I asked, trying to remember seeing anyone in that spot, but I couldn't pull up any memories. I didn't recall an AC vent, either, but it's not like I went around paying attention to those kinds of details in the house.

He nodded. "You didn't know?" He didn't wait for me to answer. "She knows. They know too. We all do. That's why we're always there. Everyone is. We all are. That's why."

"So, what about the notebook? Can you tell me more about it? Whose was it?" There was no way this was a coincidence. I hadn't even said anything about the notebook. He brought it up on his own, and I wasn't letting him go without an explanation. It was so hard to make sense of his tangential thinking, though.

He looked around like someone was following us. Paranoia oozed from every pore. "You can't tell anyone. You can't. Promise you won't tell anyone if I tell you?"

"I promise," I lied. There was no way I'd keep anything to myself that had to do with Maddie's death, but I wasn't about to let him know that. He'd stop telling me anything. He didn't look convinced. He looked like he was about to take off running again. "Whose notebook was it?" I asked again, knowing whose it likely was, but I wanted him to confirm it. To keep talking and tell me what he knew.

"Maddie's, I think," he said softly. His face crumpled like it hurt to say her name. "Pretty sure her name was on the cover, and those hearts in the corner that she drew on hers, you know? Those hearts she was always drawing?"

I nodded. She doodled two hearts on everything she worked on. "Who gave you the notebook?"

He shrugged and rubbed his face. Eyes still skirting around nervously. "I didn't want you to get in trouble. So you wouldn't get in trouble." He raised his head to look at me, waiting to see how I'd respond to what he'd just said, but I had no idea what he was talking about.

I took a step back. "You didn't want me to get in trouble?"

He nodded, looking like we shared a secret he didn't want to share. But he didn't answer. "Why would it keep me out of trouble?" I asked, unwilling to let it go.

"I don't know, man. I don't know. But she gave me Maddie's notebook, then she dies at the end of the night? Acting all secretive. I don't want any part of this. None of it. And now you're here? Coming out to find me?" He started walking again. His arms pumping fast at his sides. Head swiveling left to right like someone might run up on us at any minute. "Do you know what else? I kept the notebook. I read it. I've seen what's inside it. Those pages. I know." He walked faster. I had to practically run to keep up. "Where's everybody else at?"

"They're staying at Langham. Do you want me to take you there? You can come back there with me." He was getting more and more agitated every second. Maybe if I could get him there, I could get him settled. At least showered and in clean clothes.

"No. No." He frantically shook his head. Tossed his cigarette on the ground and didn't bother to put it out. I quickly stomped on it, then hurried to keep up. He was still talking.

"I'm not going anywhere near that place or those people again. That's got bad juju. I've never been around a dead body before, you know that? I stay away from all that freaky shit. I don't even like to watch scary movies. But a dead body? What if her spirit is like haunting us or something? I swear she's talking to me. Maddie's talking to me." He dropped his voice low. Clutched my arm. "I won't tell anyone what you did."

I pulled my arm away. I hadn't done anything wrong. Why was he looking at me that way? "What are you talking about, Spencer?"

"I know what it's like to be ugly inside. I see you."

HER
(THEN)

Slut.

Whore.

Bitch.

Everyone hates you.

Why are you still here?

She slammed her MacBook closed just as her roommate, Jasmine, burst through the door. Jasmine threw her volleyball bag on the floor along with her towel, wet from the shower. She wore her favorite bathrobe—the big fluffy white one from Victoria's Secret. Monogrammed initials. *JB.*

"Hey," she said like she did every time Jasmine came into the room. And like Jasmine had been doing for the past four weeks, she completely ignored her. Acted as if she hadn't spoken. Refused to even look in her direction. Jasmine just walked over to the mirror and started doing her makeup, like she wasn't even sitting there. She kept her head down and forced herself to try again, just like she did whenever Jasmine came into the room, which was becoming less and less often.

"You look pretty," she said to her.

Why did she sound so funny? And why did she tell Jasmine she looked pretty? What an idiot! What's wrong with her? How would she ever make this better if she couldn't act like a regular person?

She waited for Jasmine to speak. Even to just glance in her direction. Acknowledge she existed. She was so desperate for attention, she would've taken any crumb she gave, but Jasmine wouldn't even give her that.

She didn't know what was worse: being invisible, or them being cruel.

Jasmine hadn't even been there because Jasmine didn't like parties, and she should've just stayed home with her. But she'd wanted to be a part of it. All the pledges were going, so she couldn't say no. Besides, she wanted a spot in the house, and that meant showing up at all the functions.

UserND47012

She was being tortured by a number. They didn't even have a real name. Obviously, no profile picture. They could be anyone. Some old pervert still living in his mother's basement. Or someone she knew. The new chef in the dining hall. The barista who made her coffee at Romancing the Bean this morning—triple espresso with foam, no milk. The TA who graded her chemistry exam. Taryn's boyfriend. The possibilities were endless.

That's why it was so terrifying.

She eyed Jasmine suspiciously. Same way she looked at everyone now. That's what happened after you learned no one could be trusted.

UserND47012 could be anyone. Male. Female. Nonbinary. They were literally just a number.

They had other names too:

Jenn1008

Dontkillmyvibe

_3Hunna

Lovecats494

But the ones with just the numbers? The burner accounts? No profile pictures. Those were the worst. They said the most horrible things. And she just didn't understand. It wasn't fair. She'd done the right thing, so why was she the one being punished?

It wasn't an easy decision. They acted like it was. But she stared at the number for a long time before calling it:

NATIONAL SEXUAL ASSAULT HOTLINE: 1-800-656-HOPE

Sexual assault. That's what it was called. What happened to her at the party. And she could never get past those words. They were so huge. First page. First Google hit.

She couldn't bring herself to tap the numbers on her phone. Once she tapped the numbers, someone would answer, and once those words came out of her mouth—*sexual assault*—there'd be no taking them back.

It'd be real.

She still wanted to pretend like it wasn't. She might've been able to find a way to do that if she could just stop thinking about the other girls. But if you knew someone was evil and violent, you had to protect other innocent people, didn't you? She could bury her own truth, but what if it meant someone else got hurt? What if he did something worse to them? Boys like him didn't stop.

He'd already been going to other parties. Probably luring other girls into back rooms.

So, she had to do it. Even though her insides were shaking and her throat felt like it'd close up. Her pits sweat like they did before she took the mound at every one of her softball games. But finally, she made the call.

Saturday night. Exactly three weeks after it happened. She'd dialed the sexual assault hotline to ask them what they thought she should do.

Sometimes she wondered what would've happened if she'd never called the number. They were the ones, especially Carl—the crisis counselor who answered the phone—that talked her into going down to the police station and making the report. Without them? Without Carl? Who's to say she wouldn't have just buried the assault inside her, like so many other rape victims did? Tucked it away in the steel vault of college experiences.

Except it had wrecked her. She couldn't eat. She couldn't sleep. But at the same time she couldn't sleep, she also couldn't get out of bed. Do you know how torturous it is to lie there for days and not be able to sleep? It's like hovering between being dead and alive. And she was scared. Terrified as she watched him strut across campus. Post pictures of other parties. Other girls. Her sorority sisters.

What if he hurt someone else, and she hadn't said anything? It was all she could think about. What if those other girls couldn't stop him and he did something even worse than what he did to her? What was he capable of? She'd seen his eyes. Those big black eyes. Demon eyes always turned black. That's how you could recognize sociopaths. By their abnormal brain waves and their black eyes. She'd learned that in her general psychology class earlier this year, and it'd stuck with her.

Who could she call? She couldn't talk to Jasmine. Jasmine didn't even go to parties. Jasmine spent all her time studying in the library. Looking down her nose at her whenever she mentioned going out, so Jasmine would judge her for sure.

And her mom? It would crush her. She lived and breathed for her and her sister. She couldn't hurt her mom like that. She just couldn't bring herself to do it. She was incapable of putting that kind of pain in her eyes. Not after everything her mom had been through and how hard she'd worked to give them a good life.

Carl said all the things she knew to be true. She listened in class when they taught them about violence against women. She was a good student. So, all he did was confirm what she already knew—one in four girls experience a form of sexual assault by the time they're twenty-four.

Her worst fear was that nobody would believe her.

Never in her wildest dreams did she imagine they'd believe her and simply not care.

They were mad at her for telling. And not just mad. Furious. That was when she started getting the messages. That was when she learned there were worse things than what happened at that party. That was when she learned the world is full of evil people.

CHAPTER EIGHT

I flashed my ID at the security guard posted up at the celebrity entrance at the back of the Langham. The place was swarming with people, ever since it got leaked that the clients from Crystal Meadows were here. The front was taped off like they were having a huge event, and they weren't letting anyone inside without a registration number. It'd taken forty-five minutes just to get my clearance.

I hurried toward the front. The hotel lobby was massive and impressive—marble floors lining the entry. Gorgeous green plants spilling out of expensive pottery. The kind you only find at Rolling Greens. It smelled like rich people. This was more like what the clients at Crystal Meadows were used to. I'd texted Gia on my way, hoping she could meet me, but she still hadn't responded. I couldn't wait to tell her I'd found Spencer and what he said. Maybe she could help me piece together his nonsense. Even though most of it was paranoid gibberish, he mentioned the notebook, and that meant something. What had she found out from Ethan?

I was worried I wouldn't be able to find the clients and would have no way to contact them, because it's not like I had their numbers in my phone. But I spotted Javon as soon as I walked through the bar. She was curled up on one of the oversize couches, with her body draped around a man like a kitten. She saw me the moment I walked into the lobby. She froze just like Spencer had earlier, but there was no reason she needed to be worried about me—I wasn't her girlfriend. She wasn't cheating on me. I waved at her cautiously, doing my best to signal it was okay. She whispered something in the man's ear and quickly climbed off his lap. He hurried out of the bar looking embarrassed.

"I'm so sorry, Dr. Harlow. I'm so sorry," she gushed as soon as I walked up to her. "How embarrassing. Oh my God. I wasn't drinking. I just came down here to meet him. Rye has been such an asshole lately, and he wouldn't even come visit me last night to give me a hug. Can you believe that? I just—"

I grabbed her arm and interrupted. "Don't worry about it." I wrapped my other arm around her waist and brought her into a huge hug, squeezing her tightly. "Who doesn't like a good dopamine hit from a hot man?" I said, and it made her giggle, relieving some of the awkwardness of the moment. "I'm just so happy to see you, and glad you're all right."

"I'm not all right, though. I'm so sad about Maddie. I don't even know what to do. I haven't slept since we left the house. I keep seeing her sprawled out in the hallway, covered in all that blood. Every single time I close my eyes." She burst into tears. "Why would God let something like this happen to her? She was doing so good. She had another chance at life, and then—wham! Gone. Just like that." She buried her face in my chest and sobbed harder. I rubbed the back of her head while she cried.

"It's awful and so unfair," I said. Her tears wet the front of my shirt. I felt my own tears filling my eyes. "This is all so hard. People are feeling so many different things right now, which is why I wanted to come by and check on everyone. Do you think we could find a place down here to meet and give people a chance to talk about their feelings?"

She pulled back. Mascara left thick trails around her eyes. Her face was swollen. Eyes bloodshot. "Are you about to make us have a process group right now, Dr. Harlow?"

I laughed. "I am, and I'm going to need your help to do it. Why don't you go round up the others while I find us a room to meet in?

They have to have some kind of conference room that's a bit more private than this." I pointed at the bar, and she nodded.

She wiped her nose on the back of her sleeve and tucked her hair behind her ears. She straightened the front of her clothes. "Hopefully, everyone's still in Lyriq's room. That's where we all slept last night too. All of us piled on two beds."

I smiled despite the circumstances as she took off to get the others. I loved how sweet they were being. I was glad they all had each other, especially Javon and Lyriq. They were part of the same reality TV era and had kids the same age now. They'd been instant best friends since the moment they met on their first day at Crystal Meadows, and I really hoped they stayed close after this.

There was a small conference room near the elevators, and I started gathering chairs to form a circle, just like we did in group. We were relatively hidden behind the wall, so at least we had some privacy. Although they were all used to having therapy in front of the world, so I wasn't sure why I was working so hard to keep us away from anyone else.

It's funny how everyone had their drug of choice. Javon was addicted to men. Maybe more than she was cocaine. And not just any type of man—the terrible kind. The totally unavailable and abusive kind. She'd been on season twelve of *Teen Mom* when she was fifteen, and her case was one of the most tumultuous. Her dad and stepmother gained custody over her twin sons when they were two months old and had kept it ever since. It's what Javon still focused on all the time, even though it'd been over eight years and she'd had another four kids since then. But she wasn't alone in that. They all stayed stuck in the stage they'd been in when they fell from their prime.

It was true what they said about addiction stunting your development. It'd taken me a long time to grow up too. I'd gotten older while I was drinking, but I hadn't grown up. I was a twenty-three-year-old teenager when I sobered up. They all reminded me so much of myself. It was the entire reason I'd ended up in LA to begin with. While all my friends were getting engaged and starting families, earning their degrees and working big jobs, figuring out how to maneuver in the world as an adult person, I was living in my aunt's basement and barely able to hold down a job at the gas station on the corner. Answering an ad on Craigslist to be a sober companion had changed my life.

Every time Javon went into one of her spirals about her children, it took all my willpower not to give it to her straight.

"I just want to go home and see my babies," she'd cry during group, pulling her knees up to her chest like she was hugging herself. Huge alligator tears. Eyes filled. Rolling down her face. Wiping them off with her sleeve. Runny nose.

The truth was Javon could see her babies. Anytime. If she really wanted to be with her children, all she had to do was leave and go hang out with them. Her dad and stepmom had custody of them all, and they bent over backward trying to get her to play an active role in their lives. I'd never seen people be more accommodating, even when she treated them like trash. Whenever she was given the opportunity to see her kids, she never showed up. She missed more of her scheduled visitations than she ever made. Didn't go to any events at school that she could've easily attended. She still had yet to complete a single one of the parenting classes that were part of the conditions for getting custody of her kids back. And ever since Covid, they'd moved most of the classes online, but she couldn't even show up on Zoom. So it was a bit hard to feel sorry for her when she started crying about her children.

She'd only ever been famous for having babies, so it was like that's what she kept trying to be famous for. Her with her babies. She'd had six. By three different baby daddies. Her story was fascinating to me. As fascinating as they all were. How what they'd done as a teenager was so intrinsically linked to what they were doing as an adult.

Spencer was the same way with his skateboarding. He still hung out at the skate parks, even though he was one of the oldest ones there, swearing he was going to make his comeback. And he had a small entourage that believed him. Tripp had peaked in a punk band. A bass player, the youngest member in the group. They'd won on *America's*

Got Talent when he was seventeen. They'd toured for three straight years before a terrible accident killed the lead singer and derailed the band. But you could still find Tripp playing guitar on Hollywood and Highland, with a black top hat flipped upside down on the ground, living off the bills tourists tossed into it. He'd brought his guitar to Crystal Meadows and spent most of his days tucked quietly away in a corner, playing chords, his way of self-soothing.

They were all young too. Frozen in various periods of their development, like I'd been. I couldn't imagine what it'd have been like if I'd stayed frozen in mine. Maybe it was because there were no good memories wrapped up in mine. Just cold concrete floors. Detox or jail. That was where I always ended up. And it was detox that last and final time. The bucket next to my head—I'd apparently slept with my arms wrapped around it—but I had no memory of vomiting, just like I couldn't pull up any recollection of what I'd done to get there. None of it was unusual.

That was the thing that was so anticlimactic about my rock bottom—I'd woken up in that position so many times, scrambling to make sense of what I'd done the night before and feeling terrible. What kind of trouble was I in? What embarrassing thing had I done? Always on a dirty, pee-stained mat in clothes that weren't mine—if I was lucky enough to still be wearing them. I'd woken up naked plenty of times too. Most of the time there were bruises on my body, covering my arms and legs in various shades of blue and purple. Sometimes I remembered how I got them. Other times I didn't.

The best part of the AA meetings I attended in the early days of my sobriety was hearing members share about the awful and degrading things they'd done while they were using. People unabashedly shared about sleeping with sex workers while they were married, crashing cars, and leaving their children alone with no food while they went on the hunt for drugs, as if those things weren't morally reprehensible. They talked about waking up covered in their own urine or, worse yet, peeing on whoever slept next to them in bed. The fact that other people had done the most humiliating and horrifying things made me feel better about myself. It really did. Up until then, I'd pretty much just assumed I was a moral degenerate. That there was something seriously wrong with me. But we all had stories of complete and utter demoralization. That'd been the most surprising part, and also why I could relate to my clients so well.

I smiled as the elevator doors opened and all of them tumbled out. These were my people, and it was so good to see them. I hadn't expected it to feel this good. By the looks of it, Lyriq hadn't made it safely past the bar upstairs. She was swaying as she took her seat, trying to stay upright. Eyes at half-mast, heavily lidded down with alcohol or whatever else she'd managed to get a hold of while she was here. This was what happened when you put such a heavy emphasis on continual abstinence and the recognition of sobriety time. The cakes. The medals. The medallions. The awards. Speeches. Until you relapse and lose it all.

As if the moment you took alcohol or a chemical into your system, your body became possessed by some kind of devil and you lost all control. No. You made a wrong choice. You got drunk or high. Whatever it was. But your brain was still the same. Your brain hadn't actually changed. They called it the "phenomenon of craving" that developed and that once you started drinking, you couldn't stop. Even though the physiological experience of craving was real, there was no scientific evidence showing that it was true, but they'd been taught to believe that it was so, so that was the way they acted. Created a self-fulfilling prophecy. Just like Spencer, Lyriq had been programmed to believe she had a broken brain for so long that she acted accordingly.

I tried my best not to look disappointed, but it was hard.

Day twenty-eight.

One of our clients was dead.

One of our clients was back on the streets.

One of our clients was drunk.

My heart ached. That wasn't how any of this was supposed to end.

I took a seat in the circle and put a smile on my face. It didn't matter how I was feeling inside. They needed to see hope. They needed a voice that could lead them through this darkness, and I would be that voice.

"All right, everyone, let's take a few slow, deep breaths and see if we can't find our centers in all this grief." I raised my arms above my head and inhaled slowly, followed by an even slower exhale as I lowered my shoulders while they all followed suit. This was the same way we opened group at the house. Every day since day one. We took a few more deep breaths before we got started.

"It's so good to see each and every one of you. I was at Crystal Meadows last night, just in case nobody told you that, but the police wouldn't allow me to have any contact with you. I'm sorry. Really sorry. I wanted to check in with all of you then, and believe me, I haven't stopped thinking about you since I got the call about Maddie."

"I don't get it. The police wouldn't let us talk to each other either. We had to stay in our rooms like we were the ones who'd done something wrong. They've been here today, too, but they're acting even weirder than they were last night. Asking all kinds of questions like we're in some kind of danger or something, right?" Preston glanced around the circle, and they all nodded their heads in agreement, clearly having spoken about the things they wanted to address before they got down here. They used to do that back at Crystal Meadows, and I always thought it was so cute the way they'd designate a spokesperson to speak on their behalf.

"I wish I had more answers to give you, but I don't know what's going on either. And honestly, I've talked to the police twice, and I'm pretty sure they don't have a good idea themselves. They're still trying to figure things out. It's complicated, as I'm sure you can imagine."

"But we're safe, right? We don't have to worry about anything happening here." Javon searched my face for confirmation, but I couldn't give her the reassurance she was looking for with a clear conscience. It was possible one of them had something to do with what happened to

Maddie, given the police interview I'd left earlier. I couldn't say anything with any degree of certainty. Not anymore.

"Here's what I know—the detectives are working as hard as they possibly can to figure out what happened to Maddie, and I'm sure we're going to have some answers soon. Hopefully by the end of the day."

"But we're safe, right?" Javon pressed, unwilling to let it go without a definitive answer of some sort from me.

"Yes, you're safe." I couldn't look her in the eye while I lied, but I didn't know what else to say. Most likely they were perfectly safe. Definitely safer here than at Crystal Meadows. There was no security at Crystal Meadows, but there was security at all these doors and scattered around the hotel. Two in the lobby. Another standing watch behind the bar.

"I just . . . I just can't believe she's gone. My little sis." Preston burst into tears. He'd been the person closest to her. They'd been admitted during the same hour, and he'd taken her under his wing almost immediately. He was the only one who could get her to laugh when she was in one of her dark moods.

His tears created a chain reaction in the group, and within seconds, everyone was crying. I gave us a few minutes just to cry together before speaking. "Javon laughed at me when I sent her to get you, but I really want to give everyone an opportunity to talk about how they're feeling," I said. Which was followed by a sea of groans, but it was just for show. They all wanted to share, and opened up easily as soon as we got started.

"I'm going to miss Maddie so much. She made me remember what it was like to feel young. And you know what's weird? I feel really guilty even saying this, but Maddie's death has showed me just how much I've changed. For the first time ever, someone died around me and I wasn't jealous of them." Preston put his hand up to his mouth. "Oh my God. How sick am I? I know I wasn't supposed to say that, but it's the truth. I'm sorry, but it is. I've had this huge breakthrough, going through this. Just that I actually want to be alive. I don't want to die anymore."

Kendall reached over and grabbed his knee. She squealed, "Oh my God. Yes, me too. I'm so glad you said something, Preston. Seriously. I've been feeling like the absolute worst person for even thinking that way. But I have so much gratitude to be alive all of a sudden, and I'm so glad it wasn't me. I don't want to die as another statistic." She turned to look at me like she felt guilty for saying it. "I'm so sad she died, though."

I nodded at her reassuringly. "Both those things can be true. You can be really sad that Maddie died, but also happy and grateful to be alive."

Everyone in the circle nodded their heads in agreement, and I watched as they continued around the circle, sharing about their grief. Despite losing Maddie, I couldn't help but be proud of them as they described their experiences in the last twenty-four hours. They'd learned how to identify their feelings and separate their thoughts. Slow the thoughts down. This was why I loved what I did. Teaching people skills that made a difference in their lives. Things that helped them in the real world. I'd given them an emotional language in the same way their mothers had taught them their first words.

Tripp was the last person to go, and as he was finishing up, I had an idea.

"Okay, that was so beautiful. Thank you." I put my hands on my heart. "I really appreciate everyone taking the time to share. Not sure if you remember, but today is when we were going to write our goodbye letters to drugs and alcohol, and I realized while we were going around the circle that there's no reason we still can't do just that. We don't have to be at Crystal Meadows to write the letters or share them with each other. Hopefully you brought your journals, but even if you didn't, I'll find paper, or we'll just order a bunch of supplies and get them delivered. Either way, I say we make it happen."

"Yes." Preston jumped back in. "Maddie would love that. She'd want us to keep going, you guys. She would. You know she would."

"Why don't we close things up and then you go see what you have for journals and pens while I wait down here and make a few phone calls?" We all bowed our heads and closed our eyes, but unlike the prayers that ended most twelve-step therapy groups, I ended all mine the same way I started them—with a deep cleansing breath.

We were right in the middle of our closing when I felt a shift in the energy in the room. So did everyone else. We all opened our eyes and watched as a group of police officers walked toward us. Three of them. All in a line. In uniform. Their presence was the kind that made you immediately stand at attention. Everyone in the lobby and bar watched them make their way over to our conference room, straining to see what was happening.

I hadn't expected them to come up to me. So when they strutted over to me and announced, "Dr. Laurel Harlow?" I just stood there staring up at them and saying nothing. "Are you Dr. Laurel Harlow?" the one in the middle asked.

I found my voice. It was a nervous one, but I found it. "Yes, I am. How can I help you?" I asked, without any understanding of what was happening.

"We need you to come down to the station with us," he said, without so much as blinking an eye or cracking a smile. They'd never looked so serious before, or come in a group of three. Anxiety flooded my system.

"I'm sorry, what's this about?" I asked, like it could possibly be related to anything else besides Maddie's death. As if I had problematic cases that I had run-ins with the police about on a regular basis.

"We can explain all that once we get to the station," one of the other officers said. His face was set in a firm line. The others scanned the group. They all looked as nervous as I felt. Lyriq looked like she wanted to bolt the same way Spencer had when they found Maddie. No doubt she was thinking about her probation from shoplifting that forbade her from drinking or using any kind of drugs and the smell of whiskey permeating off her that would violate those conditions. But they weren't interested in her or any of the others. Their eyes were fixed on me.

I stood slowly. "Let me just gather my things, and I'll follow you down there. Is it necessary that we speak at the station?" I asked, glancing around. "Can we just pop into a room here somewhere?"

The officer in the middle motioned to the clients and the other people scattered around the hotel. "You trying to have all your business aired out in front of all these people?"

I made sure to look directly in his eyes. "I've got nothing to hide." I didn't like the way he was staring at me. I turned back to the makeshift circle we'd made. I couldn't believe how attached I was to them after such a short time.

This was it. Things would shift when I left the hotel. Almost like they'd been waiting on me to give them their next step, like I did every day. They wouldn't all be here when I got back. Maybe none of them would. A lump of emotion rose in my throat.

"Come on," the officer on his right said, like he was about to grab my arm, and I quickly stepped out of his reach. I didn't like being touched by strange men, especially not police officers.

"I'd like to say a proper goodbye, since we were in the middle of doing something when you showed up." I hated how the smallest bit of power went straight to some people's heads. I pushed all those angry thoughts away and focused on the five people in front of me. Our small team already down to five. It made me so sad. All the anger toward the police officers disappeared, and I struggled not to cry as the group looked up at me like eager schoolchildren, waiting for me to tell them what to do next. But I didn't know. Not any more than they did. But that wasn't good enough. I couldn't tell them that. Instead, I put on my bravest face.

"I just want you to know that I love each and every one of you so much. Today is technically day twenty-eight—graduation day, and I had to come down here and recognize that. That's the real reason I came. You all have made it through the most grueling and challenging twenty-eight days of your life, and I'm so proud of you." Lyriq burst into tears. I stepped next to her and rested my hand on her shoulder.

"Nothing takes away from the work that you did at Crystal Meadows. Nothing. And I'm not going anywhere. Well . . ." I motioned to the police officers behind me, angrily pacing to get moving. "Except for with these guys here," I said, trying to lighten the mood. And it worked. This brought laughs from the group, and most everyone's eyes were wet now. Even Kendall, and she rarely cried. "I never do this, but this isn't normal circumstances and you know it. I'm going to give you my cell phone number, and I expect a call from each and every one of you so that we can read your goodbye letters together. I want to hear from you. I don't care if you're sober. I don't care if you're making good choices. None of that matters except you being alive. So call me and let me know what's going on in your life." I blew them kisses. "I love you. I hope you know that."

Lyriq jumped up from the chair and flung herself at me. That was all it took for the others to abandon their chairs and join in on it. I hugged each of them, one by one. Marveling at how Tripp was right— we never actually knew what was going to happen in life. You could orchestrate your life down to the minutest of details, but at the end of the day, there was something else governing the universe. Or maybe it was totally random. There were days I thought that too. Either way, we actually had no control over our external circumstances. And now I was more worried about these people than I had been when they came into treatment. Definitely loved them more, and I knew too well that addicts were some of the most heartbreaking people to love. I dried my eyes and turned to the officers.

"Let's go," I said.

Everyone in the hotel lobby stared as I walked through. The police officers flanked me like they were my own private security detail, and I could tell that was what everyone was trying to figure out. Was I somebody really important, or was I in trouble? The doors opened, and one of them motioned to the first squad car parked in valet.

"You can go with Erik," he said.

I shook my head. "Oh no, I'm not going in that car. I'll meet you down there."

"We'd really like for you to come with us," Erik said, stepping forward.

I shook my head again. "Am I under arrest?"

They looked at each other, then back at me. "No."

"Then I'm not going with you. I'll meet you down at the station." I turned around and took off for my car before I lost my nerve or they stopped me. What was going on? Why were they treating me this way?

I called Noelle the moment I got in the car and brought her up to speed as quickly as possible while I drove to the station.

"What do you mean, they just busted into the hotel and said they needed to talk to you?" she asked after I finished. Her voice was frantic, immediately panicked.

"Exactly that. They didn't want to talk to any of the clients. Just me. Why me?" I asked before she could, as I slowed at the light before making a right. The closer I got to the station, the more nervous I got.

"How'd they know you were even there?" she asked.

Her question hit me hard. "I hadn't thought of that . . . I guess maybe they knew everyone from the show was staying at the hotel, so they thought I'd be there?"

I could hear the skepticism through the phone in the way she hesitated before speaking. "Totally possible, but it seems odd that they just happened to show up at the same time you were there. Do you have any idea why they want to talk to you again? This'll be the third time they've interviewed you. It seems a bit excessive."

"I know, and I have no clue why they're targeting me like this. I haven't done anything remotely connected to what happened with Maddie." I didn't like how they approached me. Not at all.

"Are you sure about that?"

"Yes, unless you know something I don't know," I said, slightly taken aback by her question.

She could tell she'd upset me. "I didn't mean it like that. All I'm saying is that they're going to be looking at every little thing, now that they think she was in some kind of danger or being stalked by some weirdo. You're going to be under a microscope. That's all."

"I haven't done a single thing that is in any way related to what happened with Maddie." I repeated myself.

"Don't be mad. I just want you to be careful. That's all I'm saying. They showed up unannounced to practically arrest you. Something's going on, so maybe don't go in there as trusting of them as you've been before. Think about what you're saying before you just go offering up information. How they might be interpreting it."

She was trying to make it better, but she was only making my anxiety worse. "I'm going to start looking for parking. I'll—"

"Laurel, don't be mad."

"I'm not mad," I said. "I just have to get my head straight before I go in there, and this conversation definitely didn't help. I'll call you when I'm through."

I ended the call before she could say something else. I couldn't have her paranoia or bad vibes seeping into my experience. I had to stay focused.

CHAPTER NINE

Wallace and Boone were in their usual positions. In their usual uniforms too. Her looking like she was going to leave and go to a black-tie event. Him looking like a middle-aged white man whose wife had just left him and he was sleeping on his best friend's couch. Such a strange match. How had they ended up working together? Maybe they didn't always work together. Maybe they were only working this case because it was so high profile, and one of them had been brought in from another city to help. The case was all over social media. The true crime people were going nuts. It had made national news. Vigils for Maddie started tonight. I was surprised it'd taken them this long.

I slid into the chair I'd been in last time we met, like we had assigned seats. Detective Wallace took his position across from me and folded his hands on his belly. Detective Boone was impassive. Her face as cold as the wall she leaned against. She spoke first.

"I don't want to waste any time on small talk, Dr. Harlow, because I'm pretty sure I'm the same as you in that I absolutely hate wasting time. Both of us have much more important things to do than waste each other's time, am I right?" Earlier, she'd acted like she might want to get a drink with me once the investigation was over, but now she was looking at me like she could barely tolerate being in the same room with me. "You know what I hate more than wasting time?" she paused, drilling her eyes into me, the way she did.

I stared back at her and crossed my arms on my chest, mirroring her. "What's that?"

"Being lied to. And here's something you probably don't know about me." She snorted, clearly enjoying this part of her job. Making people squirm. "I always assume people are lying. I never give anyone the benefit of the doubt. You've got to prove yourself to me. Multiple times. It's just how I am. I'm the least trusting person I know." She gave me a smile, half flirting. "Which obviously makes me a huge delight to be in a relationship with."

"I can imagine." I smirked back, refusing to be intimidated.

"Anyway, Dr. Harlow, I didn't trust you from the moment you walked into the conference room the first time. Not even a little. And then the way you prattled on and on about your approach to alcoholism, like you were so much more sophisticated than all the other great medical minds. So, by the time you left, I liked you even less." She winked. "I'm super direct too. Also, a big selling point in relationships." She laughed again. This time I didn't smirk back. She slowly moved from her spot on the wall, and even though there were only three steps to the table, she drew each one of them out. Her heels a distinct clink on the cement floor.

"I'm sorry you don't like me," I said, even though I wasn't. "But I don't think because you find my personality disagreeable, that it means I've done anything wrong."

"Dr. Harlow, you're starting to get on my nerves," she snapped, and Detective Wallace quickly gave her a concerned look and motioned for her to calm down, like her getting angry was scary. A perfect scene to their good-cop, bad-cop routine. But that's all it was. An act, and I wasn't buying it. Not tonight. It'd been too long a day for me.

"Look, Detective Boone, I'm sorry that you're so frustrated, but I don't know what you want from me right now." I really didn't. It appeared she'd decided she didn't like me, and I couldn't do anything about that.

She put her hands on her hips. "How about the truth?"

"The truth? The truth about what?"

She clenched her jaw, looking furious. "Maddie, Dr. Harlow. How about you start with telling us about your relationship with Maddie?"

"I've already told you everything about that. I don't know what else you want from me."

She strode over to the table and slammed her fist on it. "Knock it off."

Her intensity scared me. "I'm sorry I can't be more helpful." I raised my hands in a peaceful gesture.

Wallace gave Boone another look just like the first one before turning his attention back to me. "See, Dr. Harlow, I think the reason she's so upset is because we've found lots of evidence suggesting you were involved in what happened to Maddie, especially now that we know what happened to her. Because—"

I cut him off. "Wait! You know what happened to Maddie? Like, you actually know what happened in the bathroom?"

Detective Wallace nodded.

"What happened?" Had they made some sort of formal statement or announcement? I'd been so busy since the moment I got up this morning, I hadn't looked at any news or social media yet. I kicked myself for not at least checking on the way over. But I'd been so worried about things, it'd never even crossed my mind.

Boone piped up again. "We can't tell you that. It's not public information."

"I understand," I said, folding my hands on my lap. It was hard not to be nervous when, once again, they had all the pieces and I only had a couple. There were so many unknowns. What happened to her? How long would they wait to tell the public? Had they told Hilda yet?

"I'd like to get back to discussing why Detective Boone is so frustrated with you tonight. See"—he leaned across the table toward me—"you've done and been involved in some pretty alarming activity from the moment this investigation started. Things that have been concerning to our department. That—"

I was immediately insulted, and couldn't help but interrupt him again. "What do you mean? That's a ridiculous statement to make without giving some specific examples to back it up. You can't just go throwing around accusations like that."

He tilted his head to the side. "Fair enough. For starters, you lied your way into the house on the night of the incident." He held up one finger. "Then, you went and threatened Spencer. He—"

I jumped up from my chair, holding back the urge to slam the table like Detective Boone had just done seconds ago. "Are you serious right now? First of all, I didn't lie my way into Crystal Meadows that night. They just assumed I was part of the crisis response team because I said I was a therapist. Also, Gia was the one talking to the police. Not me. They wouldn't let me anywhere near the house at first. You don't know Gia. She's very determined when her mind's made up, and she also likes to get her way. So if anyone lied about who I was to get me inside the house, it was her." Detective Wallace opened his mouth to interrupt me, but I shook my head at him and continued. They needed to know exactly what I thought about this BS. "And second, the idea that I threatened Spencer this morning? Please. I never threatened Spencer. Not once. We actually had a great talk. All I wanted to do was see if he was okay and, obviously, check to see if he knew anything about Maddie. If he'd told me anything helpful about her case, I would've brought him straight down to the police station, and if I couldn't have gotten him to do that, then I would've relayed whatever information he gave me to you. But all he said was nonsense."

"So, you did talk to Spencer this morning?" Detective Boone asked, and just like that, I realized I'd stepped right into their trap.

I quickly backpedaled. "Yes, I talked to him. But I didn't threaten him." I looked into her eyes the same way she looked into mine. I wanted her to know I was just as angry with her as she was with me. "What would I possibly threaten Spencer with, anyway? He didn't do anything wrong."

"Oh, I don't know. Maybe the fact that he was the one who found the notebook and turned it in." She strutted to the other side of the room. Her back away from me.

"Wait. Spencer found the notebook? You said the staff found the notebook."

She shook her head. "I never said that. You were the one that told us about the protocol for the notebooks. You just assumed that meant we'd gotten the notebook from them." Her face was smug. She really didn't like me.

And then it dawned on me—it was because she actually believed I had something to do with Maddie's death. Like, really believed it. Suddenly, I felt sick to my stomach. I gripped the chair. I didn't have any idea what had happened to her, but I knew innocent people went to jail. It happened all the time, especially if you were Black. And even though I wasn't, it was still a possibility, and I didn't feel safe. I sank slowly back into my chair, officially squirming.

"The night of the incident, there was an officer providing security in the driveway on the property. Spencer gave him the notebook on his way out. Shoved it at him and said he needed to see it. That was the last thing he did before running down the street," she said with a pleased expression. And she had every reason to be pleased. Had she known this all along and not told me when we met before? What else were they withholding?

"Even if Spencer gave you the notebook, I don't understand how that has anything to do with me talking to him this morning."

Wallace raised his eyebrows. "You don't? Not that the person who gave the police the notebook implicating you just also happened to be the person you went looking for first thing this morning?"

"Implicating me? How does Maddie's notebook implicate me?" His accusations throttled me.

"You were the one monitoring all the notebooks, and Maddie had some very alarming content in hers. Do I need to remind you about what it said?" he asked, but it was a rhetorical question. Obviously, I hadn't forgotten something like that. "You either saw the pleas she made for help and ignored them for some reason, or maybe you decided to put them there yourself."

I shook my head. I didn't know which one of his accusations was more ridiculous. "Why would I do that?" I shook my head again. "No," I said, just in case there was any doubt of my opposition to all this. Whatever *this* was. "I had absolutely nothing to do with what happened to Maddie."

My blood raced through me. That's what every guilty person said, though. Everyone always denies wrongdoing, even if they've done it. What if I couldn't make them believe me? Had they been looking at me as a suspect this entire time? Was there anything I said that could be misinterpreted?

Boone cocked her head to the side. "You know, I might consider believing you if we hadn't found the biggest red flag." Boone turned around and walked back in our direction. She dug into her suit pocket and pulled out a phone. "This right here." She waved it in the air dramatically before handing it to Wallace. "We found Maddie's phone."

I shook my head. "They're not allowed on their phones. Most of them were as addicted to their phones as they were their drugs, so we took them away for that reason alone. We kept their phones with all the other belongings they weren't allowed to have in locked storage units by the nurses' station." I'd explained this to the detectives on the first night, but maybe they hadn't relayed the information to Boone and Wallace. "If Maddie was doing anything on her phone, then she or someone else broke in to those lockers."

"That's not the phone I'm talking about. I mean Maddie's phone." She pointed to the phone Wallace was holding. "The one she was using while she was in the house."

"Maddie didn't have a phone she was using in the house." Hadn't they listened to anything I'd just said?

"See, here we go again. What did I tell you? I hate being lied to. Not only did we find Maddie's phone. We found our way *into* her phone.

Hilda was more than happy to help us with it. Which, by the way, you were totally right about her. She's an absolute gem of a human. It takes so long to get phone records usually. I don't know if you know that. Maybe you do. Anyway, we would've been able to do it, but Hilda saved us so much time by letting us in to the phone. We got to bypass all the bureaucratic paperwork and just have a really great look into who Maddie spent her time talking to."

I pointed to the phone on the table. "I don't know whose phone that is, but it's not hers."

"Really?" Detective Wallace raised his eyebrows and smiled. He touched the screen, bringing it to life, then quickly tapped out a password. The screen lit up with an image of Maddie's face squished next to her puppy, Banks. Her little dog was as famous as she was. "We found the phone in with Maddie's things in her room."

Boone swiped open something on the phone and stared down at the screen for a second before she started reading out loud:

I miss you so much. I hate leaving you there at night.

Sweet dreams my little love bug.

I'm so proud of you.

"That's not you?" She held the phone up. "'My Love.' That's how she has your number saved in her phone. So cute. I love when couples have pet names for each other."

"What are you talking about?"

"Oh, Dr. Harlow, come on. Stop playing dumb." She glanced down at the phone again. "Let's see here . . . 323-555-4461. That's not you?"

"Give me that!" I lunged across the table and grabbed the phone from her, staring at the screen. There it was, just like she'd recited— my number. The same one I'd had since moving to California. Except instead of my name as the contact, it was "My Love." I stared at it in disbelief, trying to comprehend what was happening, what I was seeing.

I opened the text thread between "My Love" and Maddie. There were so many messages. I scrolled up. Hundreds and hundreds of them. Emojis. Memes. Cute little videos.

All the videos from Maddie were sent from inside the bathroom.

Her bathroom at Crystal Meadows. The hideous burgundy berry wallpaper that I wanted to redo because it was so ugly. But Gia insisted it would be perfect for the show. That it'd add character to the set. We weren't trying to be glitz. We were trying to be real life.

There was no mistaking the wallpaper. Or the shower. The mirror where she took all her selfies. Some topless. I broke out in a cold sweat. The room spun. Everything louder. A dull roar in my head. Waves. Like the ocean. Crashing into the side of my skull and leaving me reeling.

Wallace and Boone were watching my every move. All my reactions. It was just like the first time we'd filmed and I was so nervous to be on camera. I couldn't swallow now, like I couldn't swallow then. I felt like I was going to choke.

I slid the phone back across the table. My chest thumped, along with my head, so hard Boone had to be able to see it. My throat felt like it'd closed up, but I forced myself to look her in the eye. "I don't know what's happening here. Someone must've used my phone to make those texts or used one of those apps where you can assign it a number. You know those exist, right?"

"Right. Right. You're so smart, Dr. Harlow. Almost as smart as me." Wallace stared at Boone right along with me. He'd left all of tonight up to her, watching her like a proud father, even though he was probably younger than she was. "Here's the other thing . . . Maddie's Apple ID on the phone?" She pointed down at the device. Halfway between her and me. Sitting there, waiting to see which one of us would pick it back up. "That Apple ID is your email, and it's linked to your Verizon account. You pay the bill on that phone. You bought it."

Blink, Laurel. Blink. Now breathe. Speak.

I cleared my throat. "Am I under arrest?" I asked her, like I'd asked the police when they showed up at Langham.

"Not yet," Boone said, and Wallace nodded his head in agreement.

I stood up and pushed my chair into the table with my hands. "Then I'm going to be leaving. You can call my lawyer if you have any other questions for me."

CHAPTER TEN

My hands were still shaking as I gripped the wheel. They'd been that way since I left the police station. What just happened? I lied about having a lawyer. I didn't have a lawyer, but I had to get out of that room. I couldn't take one more question. I had to stop them. I didn't even know how you went about finding an attorney for something like this. But I was really scared I was going to need one, so it was only a matter of time before I found out. My heart thudded in my chest as I rounded the corner and got onto the freeway. Should I even be driving in this state? I felt like I was on drugs.

What was going on?

Nothing they said was true. Gia was the one who bullied our way into the house the night Maddie died. Not me. And Spencer? He'd been smoking crack since he left Crystal Meadows. The detectives couldn't trust anything he said. But my conscience tugged at me because he'd also mentioned the notebook, and that wasn't a coincidence. Obviously, something was going on with the notebook. Who wrote all those messages?

And why would Spencer say I threatened him? How'd they find him? I'd barely been able to do it. And he'd been spooked when I left him, so I doubt he'd stuck around Moorpark. Why would he keep the notebook in the first place? And then give it to the police? Their story didn't add up. Somehow, they'd managed to find him today in the middle of their second round of interviews. How'd that work? Besides,

I couldn't imagine he'd just talk to the police either. Like it'd be that simple for them. He'd barely talked to me.

Except how did I know anything they'd told me in there was true? Maybe they'd never even talked to Spencer. Maybe they were making everything up to see how I'd respond. Testing me. I'd seen the notebook, but I didn't actually know anything else about it. And police did all kinds of things to get people to confess details in murder investigations, which was what it felt like this had become. That was the most terrifying part.

It wasn't like the detectives showed me any proof linking me to what happened besides the phone. That stupid phone. I couldn't make sense of it. It was what made me question everything. I'd never sent Maddie a single text of any kind. Not once. There had to be some kind of explanation for it, though. There had to be. Maybe one of the clients or the staff members did it. But why would they want to make it look like I'd had a relationship with her?

I'd comb through my Verizon account as soon as I could, because there weren't any messages on my actual phone. But first I had to see Hilda. Seeing her was the most important thing to do, because she knew how Maddie died, and everything else hinged on that. I needed to be on equal footing with the detectives to have any chance of defending myself against whatever was going on, and against the bizarre accusations they'd just thrown at me.

I sped up and passed the car in front of me. If the detectives' intention had been to get under my skin with their questions and get me to second-guess myself about everything, then they'd succeeded. Because I was turned completely upside down, so much so that I almost missed my exit. I quickly swerved to catch it and get off the freeway.

If anyone knew about Maddie's phone, it was going to be Hilda. I'd texted her as soon as I'd gotten into the parking lot at the police station and asked if I could come by. It was late. Already past eight. It was an odd time to show up for the first time after Maddie's accident. But that wasn't what Detective Wallace had called it during the interview—he'd called it an *incident.*

I'd immediately noted when he called it an incident and not an accident, as they'd been referring to it up until now. That meant something. Everything they said and did meant something. Every move was intentional, and all their moves seem pointed in my direction. Why?

Had they been looking at me as a suspect since the very beginning? Were they looking at Gia the same way? Coming at her this hard? She'd finally texted me back about Ethan. Said he didn't live at the address he'd provided on the application. The woman who answered the door at the apartment said she'd never heard of him—which Gia had thought was super suspicious, and she'd told the police about it already. Gia was down at Langham with the others. Apparently, Lyriq was a total train wreck and had been drinking since I left the hotel. The stories she'd told in group about being a messy, sloppy drunk were true. She'd been locked in the bathroom, sobbing, for the last two hours, and everyone was trying to talk her out.

Gia texted me all her updates. I still hadn't had an opportunity to actually talk to her again, and honestly, part of me didn't want to until after I spoke with Hilda. Because I didn't trust anyone at the moment.

Guilt upon guilt stacked like bricks on my chest. I'd never felt like I was exploiting the clients at their weakest while they were at Crystal Meadows. But a tiny part of me felt like I was exploiting Hilda, and that wasn't okay with me. I wasn't that kind of a person, but I had to know how Maddie died because it was the only way to know what I was up against. It's impossible to fight an enemy with no face.

All the lights were on in the house when I turned onto Hilda's street, and I didn't know if that was a good or bad thing. People carrying signs and balloons flooded the sidewalks, spilling onto the streets and making it almost impossible to drive through. I'd forgotten about the vigil tonight. Candles were lit everywhere. I couldn't find a parking spot anywhere near the house, so I ended up two blocks away and walking.

The fresh air felt good, though, and the walk gave me a chance to practice what I was going to say to Hilda along the way.

I scanned the occupant list at the front gate of their complex until I found their last name and pressed the intercom button. Already feeling nervous.

"This is Dr. Laurel Harlow. I'm here to see Hilda. She's expecting me." I spoke into the intercom. All eyes were on me again, watching me from the street. Just like they'd been on the night of the accident when Gia had led me inside. I still couldn't believe the police had the nerve to act like I'd lied and forced my way into the house. Had I known going into Crystal Meadows would've created this drama, I never would've stepped foot inside that house that night.

"I'm Giovani, Maddie's cousin," the man who opened the door said, and he motioned me inside. "Hurry up before they start storming the courtyard and flashing all their cameras." He pulled me in and quickly slammed the door behind us.

The living room was packed with just as many flowers as people. Possibly more. The flowers were everywhere. On all the tables and shelves. They covered the floor. Lined the stairway. I'd never seen so many.

"They just keep coming," Giovani said, motioning around him as he noticed me taking it all in. His eyes filled with tears. "We've run out of room to put them."

"People really loved her." A lump of emotions rose in my throat. Her pictures from kindergarten through her latest headshot were proudly displayed above the fireplace along with the floral arrangements. I hated these types of situations. They always made me think of my dad. I already wanted to leave.

Maddie's manager, Tate, emerged from the living room and made a beeline for me like he knew I was triggered.

"Oh, honey, hi, hello," he said, taking me into his arms in one swift swoop. He kissed the top of my head, towering over me in his six-foot-four body. I leaned into him.

"Looks like you're in good hands. Let me know if you need anything," Giovani said.

"Thank you. I'm so sorry for your loss," I said. Because that's what you're supposed to say. But there're no right words for a situation like this. Losing someone you love is huge. Calling it *a loss* sounds so trivial. It's so much more than a loss. You lose shoes. Not people. And I used to literally cringe inside every time someone said it to me about my dad in the days following his death.

Giovani gave me a quick nod and then turned around, heading for the kitchen. The smells of the tamales they were cooking permeated the house. Relatives hurried back and forth from the kitchen, carrying plates of food. Other relatives and friends busied themselves with tasks and making sure people had drinks and knew where to find the restroom. The place was alive with the whispering hum of do-you-remember-when stories about Maddie.

I turned my attention back to Tate. "Have you seen Hilda?"

He nodded. "I pretty much didn't leave her side until Ricardo got here."

Ricardo was her husband, who'd stayed back home with their son all those years ago when Hilda and Maddie had come out to Hollywood after Maddie first got signed. He'd refused to follow. Said he wanted nothing to do with the Hollywood scene and wasn't going to subject his boy to growing up there too. So, they'd stayed behind in Louisiana, and even now, after all these years had passed, they still lived on opposite sides of the country.

"Do you want to meet him?"

I shook my head. That was the last thing I wanted to do at the moment. "I really just came to see Hilda."

He pointed to the stairs behind the living room. "Go on up."

He gave me another hug before I trudged up the stairs, preparing myself for whatever I'd find. The upstairs was in sharp contrast to downstairs, where it was filled with movement and people. Upstairs was quiet. Still. Barely breathing.

There were two rooms on each side of the hallway, with a bathroom in the middle.

"Hilda, it's Laurel. I'm here," I called out not knowing which door to go in, and not wanting to intrude on her privacy if she'd changed her mind about seeing me. That was perfectly understandable. I wouldn't force her to do anything.

"I'm in here," her voice called out weakly from the room to the right of the bathroom.

I walked to the door and knocked softly. "Okay if I come in?" I wanted to respect her grieving space and her privacy. I'd stand outside the door, if she wanted me to. Or leave. I was prepared for either.

"Yes," she said.

I slowly opened the door and let out a sigh of relief to find her in the master bedroom rather than Maddie's room. I didn't know if I could be surrounded by Maddie's things while we talked. It'd make this even harder.

Hilda sat in a rocking chair by the window, holding Maddie's baby blanket up to her face like she was trying to inhale her. The same one Maddie clutched in our first session and slept with every night at Crystal Meadows. I couldn't help but think of my mom. How it took her two years before she washed the clothes my dad left in the hamper. To this day, she'd never washed his pillow. Hilda raised her head to meet my eyes, and that was all it took for me to burst into tears.

"I'm so sorry, Hilda," I cried, feeling the weight of the failure and the loss pressing down on me. Her biggest fear had come to pass, and I'd promised her Maddie would be okay. How would she ever recover? How would I?

She nodded back at me. Her eyes cast a long shadow. I bent over and gave her a big hug. She didn't attempt to hug me back. Just halfheartedly patted my back. Simply going through the motions.

"I hope they're downstairs telling stories. Are they telling stories?" she asked after a few beats passed.

"They are," I said, even though I hadn't listened to the specifics. They hurt too much. Hit too close to home.

"That's what they were doing this morning when I came downstairs. Giovani and all his cousins. They grew up together, you know that? They really supported Maddie. They were invested in her success. Especially her youngest cousin, Liam," Hilda said.

I held back the urge to ask how she was doing, because of course she was doing terrible. Instead, I just said, "I know this is so hard and so devastating." I let out a deep sigh. Death is always hard. But the death of a child? Nothing compares.

"They told us how she died this afternoon. Did you know that?" Her voice, usually filled with so much emotion, was flat and devoid of all feeling. Almost robotic.

I nodded. Secretly hoping she'd tell me and holding back the urge to ask questions, then immediately feeling guilty for my feelings. But I couldn't help it. I cared about both of them, but I didn't want to get in any trouble and needed to get to the bottom of this.

"Anaphylactic shock," she said in the same empty tone, without me having to ask.

Her words fell into the room and landed with a quiet thud.

"Like an allergic reaction?" Nothing like that had crossed my mind, and none of the detectives had said anything hinting along those lines.

She nodded and returned her gaze to the window. I slowly took a seat on the edge of her bed, trying to fit what she'd just said with all the other conflicting information rolling around in my mind. Anaphylactic shock? Had Maddie used a different lotion? Changed soap? But that couldn't be it. Nothing had changed. We provided all their toiletries, like a hotel, because we didn't want them to sneak in drugs that way. We'd been using the same stuff since the day they'd arrived. Was it something at dinner? What'd they eat?

"Can I tell you something, Dr. Harlow? You know, like, between us?"

"Of course. You can tell me anything, and I won't tell anyone," I said. Normally I'd add the caveat of *Unless something you say leads me to believe you're a threat to yourself or someone else*, but I left that part off. This wasn't a real therapy session, and I actually meant it. I'd keep her secrets, especially if there was a possibility that she was going to have to keep mine.

"Part of me is happy about it. That sounds messed up, I know, but I couldn't stand the thought of Maddie taking her own life. I just couldn't. That's how I figured it was going to turn out, you know. That she'd been successful this time, and the thought of my baby still in that much pain . . . that she'd do something like that to herself . . . well . . ." She shrugged her shoulders, and her voice trailed off. Her throat bobbed with emotion as she struggled to talk. "I didn't want that to be the case, you know? I couldn't bear the idea of it. That her last moments would be so hopeless. Such despair." Another sob caught in her throat, but she didn't let this one escape either. "And I'm really happy that she wasn't high. I just . . . in a weird way, I like it a lot better that her death was an accident."

"That makes total sense, and your feelings are completely understandable. This allows her to hold on to her dignity." When it came down to it, the world still didn't have much compassion for those that died by suicide or drug addiction. There was so much stigma surrounding both. And nobody wanted to imagine their child in that kind of emotional turmoil.

It didn't make sense that the detectives were still coming at me so hard about Maddie, though. If she'd died from an allergic reaction, what did all those other things matter? Or did they just think I was doing something inappropriate with a client, so they were furious at me about that? Did they intend on filing a report with the psychology board? But they couldn't actually prove I had any kind of a relationship with Maddie outside our therapeutic one, could they? Still. Things weren't adding up, and whatever was going on with the phone scared me.

"They're doing a full toxicology report just to confirm, and they ran a bunch of other blood tests to see what she took to cause the allergic reaction. But I already told them what they're going to find—ibuprofen.

That's what she took, because it's the only thing she's allergic to. We got her tested for everything after her first allergic reaction in Sedona last year, and she's not allergic to anything besides ibuprofen. The whole thing terrified all of us. It was in the middle of the night, and we were on an RV trip in the middle of the desert. It took us so long to get her to a hospital. We almost lost her then. For a second, we thought we did . . ." She paused, at least in her words. She might still be watching the story unfold in her mind.

Maddie had been close to death so many times. Right on the edge. It was scary to think about how many times she'd dodged it. You couldn't help feeling your odds of actually dying increased the more near-death experiences you had, and it definitely felt weird. It wasn't lost on either of us that the first time I'd met Hilda was after one of Maddie's near-death experiences. And *near* meant she'd been as close as you can get. They'd brought her back. Narcan coupled with chest compressions.

And now, here we were.

Sitting in a dark bedroom after Maddie had died, Hilda clinging to Maddie's blanket the same way her daughter had done.

Hilda gathered herself and continued. "We wanted to make sure we knew everything she was allergic to so we were as prepared as we could be, and her tests only showed ibuprofen. But the detectives weren't listening to me today when I explained things." She sounded angry, and I was happy to hear emotion in her voice. So much better than detachment. "Why'd someone give her the pills? That's the part I don't understand. She couldn't take anything in that house by herself. Remember when she had period cramps so bad? We had to get special permission from the doctor just for her to take Midol. She didn't even have access to pills without staff giving them to her." Her shoulders sagged in defeat. She was still staring out the window. Processing her thoughts out loud. "I told them maybe she came into contact with it some other way. Because it wouldn't have taken much. She's really allergic. Could she have taken it on accident, you think? Gotten into something? That's what I asked the police, too, but they just think they know it all."

All my thoughts came to a screeching halt. It'd seemed so insignificant. It'd never even crossed my mind during all the police questioning. But I'd given Maddie pills that afternoon. Pills because she had a headache. Ones that Gia had given me in the hallway, on my way in to see Maddie for our session. She'd stopped me real quick and handed them to me in passing.

I'd thought nothing of it and given them to Maddie. What if they were ibuprofen? Did the police know that? Had they seen me giving her the pills? And even so, who made that mistake? Hilda was right. None of them were allowed to have any kind of medication without permission. Not even Tylenol. Granted, she could've gotten some ibuprofen on her own. But why would Maddie take something she knew she was allergic to?

Unless she'd done it on purpose? She'd smuggled in ibuprofen so she could die of shock? That seemed very unlikely. What seemed more likely was that someone had given it to her. And I was the only one who'd given her any pills that day. My stomach rolled. All I could do was stare open mouthed at Hilda while she talked.

"The detectives kept asking if she might've snuck the ibuprofen in herself, and I told them no way." She shook her head. "I'm not naive. I know how she is with drugs. How she gets. She's played all kinds of games on me before. I don't want you to think I'm under any impression that I can't be played by my daughter. I'm not. I told the detectives that too. But that Boone woman?" She cocked her head and gave me a side-eye, and I understood exactly what it meant without Hilda needing to say anything. She laid Maddie's blanket aside for the first time since I'd walked into the room. "That allergic reaction absolutely terrified Maddie, and she'd never do that to herself on purpose. Never. Do you know what happened to her during it? She was fully cognizant while her throat closed up. Can you imagine what that felt like? Not being able to breathe? She was in therapy for almost nine months afterwards because it gave her such terrible panic attacks. She turned into an agoraphobic and could barely leave the house for a while. She was terrified of ever feeling that way again. So there's no possibility she'd ever consider doing something like that to herself. No way," she explained. "The detectives kept asking me things like did she have any enemies in the house. Was there anyone who wanted to hurt her. Stuff like that." I leaned in closer, hanging on her every word. "I said no, and they kept acting like I was lying to them. But Maddie and I talked all the time. Every day. I don't know how she would've gotten through it without the phone. I'm glad she got to be part of the study. She—"

I put my hand up to stop her, interrupting her. "Study? What study?"

"You must've been part of the blind group. Gia said there were two groups, and you couldn't discuss the study or tell anyone what group you were in. She talked about how they wanted to make sure the study had good validity and reliability, so that's why they made it blind and placebo controlled, or something like that?" She shrugged. She sounded like my statistics professor in graduate school, when he was explaining experimental design in psychology. But his explanation had made sense. Hers didn't. "I don't know what group we were assigned to, but I'm just glad it was one that got to use the phone."

"And Gia gave you the phone?" I asked, my head whirling and spinning.

She nodded. "And I gave it to Maddie, like Gia had asked."

"Just curious about why you needed the phone for the study. What was it about?"

"She said they were doing important research examining the role that loved ones played in helping addicts recover from their addiction. Something to do with object relations theory and all that stuff you said to me before, about addicts lacking meaningful relationships? Anyway, they wanted to see if there was any difference in their recovery or their emotional stability when they had contact with a loved one. She said something about the theories of addiction starting to focus on the role that relationships play in recovering from addiction?" She said it like she wasn't sure. But everything she was saying about the research was true.

All the latest studies showed addictions partially stemmed from a lack of social intimacy and relationships. Having friends and being actively involved in a community of sorts made you less susceptible to addiction. All the findings were fascinating, and only further supported the way I'd viewed addiction for years. But as far as us being a part of that research? Or Crystal Meadows having any kind of secret experiment going on? Well, that couldn't be further from the truth. Even if there had been, Gia would be the last person to have anything to do with creating or managing it. Anything along those lines would have fallen directly into my court. And I'd never heard of such a thing. None of the other clients had said anything about it either.

"Yes, that's right. I'm sorry," I said. "There were so many different moving pieces of the show, and there were certainly things happening that I wasn't necessarily privy to. Can I ask—where'd Gia give you the phone?"

The Crystal Meadows house was full of cameras from the moment you walked in the door. But outside was devoid of any cameras—short of security cams in front of the door and over the driveway. That was one of the stipulations of the HOA allowing us to film on the property. We couldn't do anything in the neighborhood, and we'd easily obliged. We didn't want the viewers to know their location, either, and people online were practically novice detectives. They could figure anything out, and it wouldn't have taken them long to find an address.

"She gave it to me in the parking lot when I was leaving on that first day after we'd checked Maddie in. She stopped me when I was getting into my car. Told me about the experiment and asked me to give the phone to Maddie. Said the Wi-Fi was disabled and there were only certain numbers she could contact. Everything else was blocked." She smiled as she remembered. "I'm so glad Maddie was part of the experiment, because I got to talk to her that last night and tell her I loved her. That's the last thing I ever said to her, and I hold on to that.

Real close to my heart. She died knowing her mama loved her." And then it hit her. Full force. All she could do was weep. I held her as she let out the type of life-altering sobs you never forgot. Then she slowly pulled herself back from my chest.

"I'm so grateful she didn't do anything bad to herself. Not like the detectives were trying to make it sound like in the beginning. I know that's what everyone thought. Most people probably still do. But everything she said to me that night was about her future. How excited she was feeling. We talked about what we were going to do to celebrate her graduation. I'm just glad the truth's going to come out. So people can understand that what happened to her was just a tragic accident and she had nothing to do with it."

The truth? Is that what the detectives thought they were uncovering with me? What had Gia done? Was she so desperate for a number one show that she'd created this? Had she been doing the same thing we were afraid of the clients doing? But that didn't make any sense. The show was already a huge success. People loved it. We were up for an Emmy against *Queer Eye*. Was she trying to secure the award? Make sure she went out with a bang?

I was furious. How could Gia keep something like this from me? I had to get out of this room and figure out what was going on.

HER
(THEN)

The stars danced in front of her. Glittering. The release from her body as if her brain had actually popped from her head, followed by the blissful nothingness.

Her eyes slid open. The belt still tied around her neck. She let it slip out of her fingers. Fall to the floor.

Her mom called from downstairs. The thought of her mom finding her sent torrents of shame coursing through her entire body, and as quick as the good feelings came, they were gone. Replaced with disgust.

Her body wasn't covered in cuts. But it was covered in marks. Long thick ones, like she'd been whipped. And she had been. Just done it to herself. She wore sweatpants, and long-sleeved shirts pulled down tight around her wrists. Mom thought it was to hide all the weight she was losing, but that was just a by-product of not being able to eat. Her stomach refused food when she was stressed. Her clothing had nothing to do with her weight.

She'd never heard of anyone doing what she did to herself before. Have you? Slapping yourself with a belt? Tying it around your neck until you pass out?

That's the kind of thing she typed into Google late at night. But it always came back with stuff related to autism, which was fine, though she didn't think that's what she had. Nobody talked about tying a belt around their neck until they accidentally went unconscious or the way they slapped their face if they didn't have a belt to do it.

She wished she could talk to the loved ones of people who hanged themselves. She wanted them to know their loved one might not have meant to die. Maybe they just missed the mark. Maybe they just didn't let go of the belt quick enough. That happens a lot. More than you would think. Belts tied around your neck can easily go wrong.

It's just that maybe by doing it, you find out you actually like it. That your body responds to it. Wakes up. Feels alive. Lifeblood coursing through your veins. You never feel more alive than in the seconds after you've almost died. Ask anyone that's had the experience. She didn't put the belt around her neck because she wanted to die. She did it because she wanted to feel alive.

Has anyone ever thought about it like that? That's what she'd explain to people's loved ones if she could. Tell them they weren't trying to die. They were just trying to feel alive.

Anyway.

She missed life. Back when it didn't feel like she had to exist as a one-dimensional cardboard cutout of herself. Had she always been pretending to be someone else?

Truth was, hurting herself made her feel alive, if only for a split second. It also helped her heal. Not from him, but from their words.

Tell the truth, they said.

We're here to help you, they said.

He can't hurt you anymore, they promised.

Turns out.

He could.

And all his evil friends.
Who knew everyone would hate her?
That she'd be the one they punished?
Everyone hated her because she told.

Bitch.

That's how it started.

Whore.

That's the one that came next. Quickly followed by

Slut.

Their words marked her body. Like being hit. Slapped in the face each time. But it wasn't until they started threatening her life that it felt like getting punched. Hit so hard your teeth rattled and you bit a chunk out of the inside of your cheek, filling your mouth with the taste of blood.

Hope you get hit by a car on your way to school

It wasn't what they said. It was the hashtag behind it.

#rapid720

The metro line she took to campus every day. That's when she got scared for her life.
She'd never forget the way Jasmine looked at her that day. The day she told her she'd gone down to the station and given her statement to the police. Jasmine wore the same expression on her face as when she'd

told her about that night. As if she'd done something wrong. The one who should be embarrassed. But she was scared. Truly afraid they'd attack her.

She did everything right. Just like they taught in sixth grade. The day they separated the boys from the girls—boys in the gym, girls in the library. They all thought it was to teach them about periods and tampons. All the hormonal changes their bodies were about to go through. She knew all about periods because she'd been reading *Are You There God? It's Me, Margaret.* since she stole a copy from the library in fourth grade. That's what they were all prepared for. All the things that would happen to their bodies. They didn't know they were there to teach them about staying safe from bad guys.

They taught all the things. Not just about how to keep yourself safe, but how to keep your friends safe too. How to be an active bystander. That's what they called it. And she followed every single step. Exactly as they'd instructed. Carl's advice had been identical when he told her to report it.

Getting assaulted at that party didn't shatter her world in the same way their messages did. She knew she didn't live in a safe world. As a female, would you rather be alone in the forest with a man or a bear? Half the cis white men revolted when the majority of women chose bear. But as a girl, keeping yourself safe was drilled into your head from practically the moment you were born—that there's a world of bad men just waiting to take advantage of you. It's also how she knew, the moment the door closed behind her, that she was in trouble. That despite all her best efforts, she'd been caught in a trap.

And yes, that had been devastating.

But she still believed in a just universe. That, in the end, good would ultimately prevail over evil. That we live in a system where doing the right thing gets rewarded. Where doing the right thing matters. But their responses shook her to the deepest part of her core. He violated her body, but they raped her soul.

Her friends. Other women. Ones she was supposed to trust.

Turning their backs on her. Not just turning—stabbing her with the sharpest of knives. And they didn't thrust the knife into her back. Oh no. They stabbed it straight into her guts while they stared into her eyes with sweet smiles on their faces.

Alpha Kappa Alpha.

I hope you die.

CHAPTER ELEVEN

I pulled into the housing development at Crystal Meadows, hoping the key code for the gate still worked. I breathed a sigh of relief when it did and pulled in front of the house. I shut off the car and just stared at the building. It was still covered in yellow police tape. All the people were gone. There was no sign of any of the frenetic activity of the previous night. It hadn't even been quite twenty-four hours, but it already seemed like another lifetime ago.

Was the alarm set? Had they changed the code? The house looked so ominous and dark. What would they do with it now? Who would want it after someone had died in it? You were supposed to disclose that, but I wasn't sure anybody ever did, because how would you ever sell it?

I just wanted to go through the things in my office and gather as much important information to defend myself as I could before I lost all access to my clients' records. It was only a matter of time before it happened, so I wanted all my notes. Any video footage I could get my hands on. Any proof that Gia or someone else was setting me up for whatever happened with Maddie. And why. I was going for all of it. I was sure the police were doing the same thing—except when it came to me. I was going to do my best to see things through their eyes. It might be my only line of defense. As shocking as all this was, I was determined to think straight. I couldn't let my emotions dictate this. I had to be logical.

Our computers in the office were hooked up to monitors all over the house, the ones live streaming on YouTube around the clock. We were able to watch them from our offices at any time. In fact, they encouraged it. You could pick which screen you wanted to watch and focus solely on that one or have up all thirty-two at the same time.

I wasn't interested in seeing the accident footage again. I'd watched that so many times it was as if I'd been there myself. I wanted to study and analyze everything leading up to it. That entire day. There had to be some kind of clue.

The police were doing the exact same thing, but they didn't know what they were looking for. They didn't know how things were normally supposed to be. How the house and everyone in it functioned on a daily basis. There was no measure for them to weigh things against, to determine whether something was out of the ordinary or not. But I knew all the details. Every single one. Our program ran like a machine. The same thing every single day. It had to. That's the importance of structure. Teaching them how to live within predictability and structure. Ordering their outsides to help calm their insides.

There's no way Maddie wrote about feeling afraid for two weeks and neither Ethan nor Natalie flagged it for me to read. I would've made a note about it. Was it even her writing? I wished I would've looked at the notebook closer when they showed it to me, or taken a picture. But at least I had other pieces with her original handwriting. She was one of the clients who loved assignments. She'd insisted I give them to her, so I had.

"Five Ways Your Life Is Better without Pills." That's the one I kept because it came from her for sure. I remembered everything about that session.

It was the day I'd noticed the marks on her body. Angry red scars poking out from underneath her sleeve. I didn't say anything because Maddie was private. I knew she was keeping secrets. Unlike the others, who were dying to tell their own to keep America entertained, Maddie had no interest in exposing herself to the world that way. She still wanted to keep all her secrets, deeply tucked away and buried inside her.

I'd just assumed she was hurting herself, and I didn't want to draw attention to her cutting. For a couple of different reasons. I wanted to respect her privacy. Give her time to disclose what she was doing when she was ready. Equally important, I didn't draw attention to it because self-injury behavior can be so contagious among adolescents. Maddie's fans gave us two audiences. She was young enough to draw the teenage crowd, but also old enough to pull the twentysomethings as well. She was in the sweet spot. At least that's what Gia always called it. Both groups were highly influenced by cutting behavior. Had a weird competitive flavor to it, too, just like eating disorders in girls the same age.

So, I didn't say anything, and I'm kicking myself that I didn't. I looked around. Toward the end of the street, someone was out walking their dog. But besides that, everything was empty and still. Lights turned on. On nights like tonight, it felt like you could hear the houses humming. Everyone tucked inside, living their own story.

Neither the police nor the detectives said we couldn't go back to the house. Not last night, when I left after they questioned me, and not today at the police station. Nobody said *Stay away from Crystal Meadows*. They'd already done their entire investigation that night. The place had been cleared to be cleaned. That's why Aftermath Services was called. I'd been there for the whole thing. So there wouldn't be any additional evidence they needed to collect from the scene.

I just had to go. I couldn't give myself any more time to think about it or second-guess myself.

I slipped underneath the yellow tape, much like I'd done the previous night. I scurried up to the door the same way as before. Trying not to look obvious, trying not to hurry, even though I wanted to sprint to the door and barrel inside as fast as I could. I didn't want to draw any attention to myself or look like I wasn't supposed to be there.

What would I do if they'd changed the alarm code? Would I wait for the police? Take off? My heart pounded in my chest. Armpits instantly wet. It felt like there were a million people in the street, all with their eyes on me, even though, seconds ago, it'd been empty. I took a deep breath and unlocked the door. The alarm instantly screamed. I quickly punched the code into the keypad next to the door and held my breath while I waited for silence. Three beeps. That was it.

Off.

My entire body sagged with relief. I quickly shut the door and leaned against it, breathing hard. All the shades were drawn and it was difficult to see, but I didn't want to turn on any lights. Why was I so nervous? It's not like I was doing anything wrong. I was just trying to help the investigation. Bring Maddie and myself justice. She deserved that. So did I. So did Hilda.

Still. I wasn't sure the police would understand what I was doing and be okay with it. They might try to stop me. That's why I had to hurry. It felt so strange being in the house. I don't know if it was the dark or the dead body that'd been in the hallway the last time I was here, but it felt like being in a haunted house at a carnival. Walking through it like you used to do when you were a kid. Feeling your way through the darkness while you waited for the next jump scare. Never knowing which direction it'd be coming from.

I kept the light off even though I was afraid. My fears of the dark were irrational. The ones of the police, not so much. I felt my way along the wall, inching my way forward, my feet continually hitting the spots where they'd taken chunks out of the carpet because they'd been touched by blood. The holes kept tripping me up, but I continued until I reached my office at the end of the other hallway. My office jutted into the backyard, so nobody would see when I turned on my light besides the neighbors behind us. And I doubted they were looking or paying attention, especially this late at night.

I flicked the switch, and light flooded the room, making me squint. It felt surreal to be here, even though I'd spent the majority of my days here for the past month. Working at least twelve hours every day, even Sundays. Noelle hated me working so much and never would've allowed it if it hadn't been a temporary gig. It was the first time in my life I'd had any kind of a job like this, where I came into an actual office every day. I didn't usually work in the treatment centers. My job had always focused on afterward. Those difficult days back in the real world. Or the days before. Working with the ones who didn't want to go to treatment. Who insisted they could get sober at home. Those rarely worked out, though, and it was never long before we were taking them to treatment. I'd been surprised at how much I liked working at Crystal Meadows, and this afternoon's group at the hotel had only confirmed it.

I'd expected everything to be exactly as I'd left it, but that wasn't the case. The police had been in here too. My usually neat desk was a total mess. I still printed out hard copies of almost everything. I was old school and liked seeing things in front of me. We had electronic files, but there was something about having the paperwork in my hands. Being able to hold all the pieces. Touch them. Then, I could put them together like a puzzle. Rearrange them how I thought they belonged and as my hypotheses changed. The process didn't make sense to anyone else but me, and that was okay. My organized stacks of files and charts were chaotic and disheveled, though. I fought the urge to put them back in order. I didn't have time for that.

I quickly dug through my stuff until I found Maddie's file. Surprised they hadn't taken it. Or maybe they weren't worried about any of these paper copies because it was all online and they had access to it. I acted like I knew how a police investigation worked, but in reality, I had no idea. Maybe I was tricking myself into believing I was going to find something in here they hadn't, but I kept going back to the fact that I had a pulse on everything happening in the house. Knew every single routine. All their personalities. If anything was off, I'd find it, even if the police had missed it.

I grimaced at Maddie's day-one picture. The one we took with an old-school Polaroid when they walked in the door. We kept it taped to their file, on the front. She looked awful. Her tiny frame bloated and distended. Skin pale and blotchy, covered in picking scars. Long-sleeved shirts we thought hid lost weight from a secret eating disorder. But as it turned out, they disguised self-injurious behavior.

I quickly flipped through her medical file, but in comparison to the others, hers was the shortest. She'd only been hospitalized one other time aside from her overdose and suicide attempt. I tucked her file into my bag. I didn't know how much longer I'd have access to the computer with all her files, and I wanted as much information as possible to go over. The first thing I was going to do when I got home was to review all of it. Because I couldn't trust anyone—least of all Gia. She hadn't returned a single one of my texts since I'd left Hilda's. I still couldn't believe she might be involved.

I logged on to the system. The camera feeds took forever to load. They always did, even when the house was up and running, so it wasn't anything unusual. I wondered how long they were going to keep them going. Even though they weren't being streamed to the public, they were still hooked up, and they finally opened. Thirty-two tiny boxes on my screen. How the producers had kept track of the show during the actual show hour was beyond me. We aired the show weekly, and we always provided a recap. But you could watch it twenty-four seven, if you wanted. There'd been a producer there at night too. Not a full production crew, but there were some, because drama with addiction wasn't limited to daytime hours. We'd had plenty of crises at night, even though everyone had been tucked safely in their beds for lights-out at ten thirty.

It felt eerie staring at all the blank screens. Everything devoid of people. Like aliens had abducted everyone in the middle of the night. Every single client room was trashed. All of them had just thrown their stuff together and practically run out.

I moved the cursor backward and followed Spencer's movements in the days leading up to the incident. I couldn't find anything suspicious, so I shifted my focus to the day of the incident, carefully going through the footage. Part of me still thought he was just being paranoid and delusional because he was on crack. And if he hadn't mentioned the notebook on his own, I might've been able to let it go. I toggled between cameras and views. Rewinding. Pausing. Speeding up.

And then it happened.

At 10:43 a.m.

Spencer and Gia cross paths in the hallway. She has something tucked underneath her arm. Books and notebooks and worksheets. Which was already out of place, because she never carried any of that stuff. But the police wouldn't know that. That's why it was so important for me to look at all the footage. I could spot stuff like this right away.

She's smooth. So smooth. She gives Spencer one of her white-toothed smiles. Starts talking to him as they walk down the hallway. Slips her arm into his.

You can hear their conversation. Chatting away about what happened at breakfast, and if he's going to watch the Lakers that night. She puts her hand on his arm to stop him right when they're in front of the library. Right underneath the AC vent, like Spencer described. You can't hear what she says to him then. It's quick, just a few words. And he nods, staring at her, starstruck. He'd been smitten with Gia since he'd gotten here. She hands something to him, and it's so fast you'd miss it if you weren't looking for it. Seamless.

I froze the frame, zooming in and out, over and over again. But no matter what I did, I still couldn't tell what she was handing him. Until I switched to the last camera at the end of the hallway. For a brief second, you could see it. Scrawled across the screen: Maddie's tenth-step journal.

Oh my God. Oh my God. I leaped out of my chair and raced around the room in circles, running my hands through my hair.

I quickly grabbed my phone to call Noelle, but suddenly stopped. Were the cameras still on? Was everything being recorded? What if the police had access to this? Was it possible they were watching me right now? What if that's what they were doing? Just sitting back and waiting down at the station to see who entered the house. Had I stepped into another one of their traps? I felt as paranoid as Spencer.

I slowly sat back down, even though the adrenaline still raced through me at the discovery. I texted Noelle instead. Underneath the desk where no one could read the screen:

You're never going to believe this!!
This shit is crazy. Gia is involved in
whatever happened to Maddie. I
think she's framing me.

?!?!?!?!

Yes! I know. Sounds crazy but she is.
I'm at Crystal Meadows now and just
found a video of her giving Spencer
Maddie's notebook.

You're at Crystal Meadows?

Yes

What are you doing there? Aren't you
going to get in trouble? Won't that
look bad for the police?

That wasn't the important thing. It didn't even matter. But Noelle was always like that. She followed rules and hated getting into trouble.

Gia is involved!!!

Wtf??

Yes. I'll explain everything when I get
home but I just had to tell you

I'm so confused. Gia??

A series of confused emojis followed.

I'll explain soon

I instantly regretted telling her. I should've just waited until I got home. Because, of course, she was going to want to have a conversation about it. I couldn't make a statement like that and not expect Noelle to immediately want all the details.

I'm going to finish up and come
home asap

Ok . . . I'm worried

She should be. So was I.

What role did Gia play in all this? Could you tell she gave me the pills? I grabbed the mouse again and immediately went to work. Finding that footage was way easier than having to scroll through all the previous footage looking for Spencer. My session with Maddie was at four thirty, so it would be somewhere around that time. I moved the cursor to 4:28 and started watching again.

Watching myself felt strange. I didn't usually view any of the footage or weekly shows featuring me because I hated the way my voice sounded outside my head. Also, I picked apart every single one of my flaws on the screen, which assured that's exactly what I'd be thinking about the entire time I was on camera next. Reviewing the footage felt like an out-of-body experience similar to the one I had when I came into Crystal Meadows after Maddie died.

You can barely tell Gia gives me the pills. It just looks like we pass by each other in the hallway and briefly touch hands as if we're greeting each other hello. We smile and keep going. You definitely don't see the pills. But you know what you can see on camera? Crystal clear and in full audio? Just a few minutes later?

Me during my session with Maddie asking her if she still has a headache, and then proceeding to drop the pills like candy into her open hand. I even give her a bottle of water from my desk to wash them down. I never have water on my desk. Coffee always. That's one addiction I'm never going to kick, and it's the biggest joke with all my friends that I walk around chronically dehydrated. But I'd felt like I was coming down with a cold that day, so I'd been drinking water trying to flush it out of my system.

Gia gave Spencer the notebook.

Gia gave Hilda the phone to give Maddie.

Gia gave me the pills that killed Maddie.

Alarm bells went off inside me. Sending ricocheting panic coursing through my body. Gia set me up. I was fully convinced. Whatever this was—and I didn't know—she'd used me as a pawn. But she'd met her match in me. I wouldn't stand for this.

Every single computer in the house was encrypted with heavy-duty security, so there was no way to download the files. That part hadn't ever made sense because everyone could watch the videos. It's not like they were a secret. But I wasn't willing to let it go that easily. I needed these videos to show the detectives. I pulled out my phone and opened my camera. I recorded all of it. From my brief exchange with Gia in the hallway to me giving the pills to Maddie during our session. I recorded multiple angles so everything was as clear as possible. My hands shook as I fumbled with my phone, trying to work as fast as I could. It felt like any moment the police were going to burst through the door and arrest me, even though I hadn't done anything wrong. I quickly rewound the footage to yesterday morning when Gia gave Spencer Maddie's notebook, and pressed record. All my senses on high alert. Straining for the sound of anyone coming in to stop me.

The only thing left to do was check my phone records. Even if they'd deleted any call or texting history on my phone, if they'd been made, they'd be on my Verizon statement. I could do all that at home, where I didn't have to be looking over my shoulder every five seconds. I'd put it all together, everything I had, and then figure out exactly how I was going to present it to Wallace and Boone in the morning. I would be there first thing. Maybe I'd even go there tonight if it wasn't too late by the time I finished. I wasn't going down without a fight. No way.

HER
(THEN)

She opened her eyes to Mom's beautiful face in front of hers. Mom looked at her with an expression she'd never seen before and squeezed her hand so tight it hurt.

"Baby, I love you. Do you hear me? Baby, I love you." Mom grabbed her cheeks. Peered into her eyes. Mom's eyes were a deep muddy river. Tears stained her face. "Don't you dare do anything like that again! Ever. Do you hear me?!"

"I'm sorry." That's what she wanted to say to her mom. But she couldn't talk around the tube down her throat. She tried pulling it out when she woke up last time, but the doctors didn't like that. They'd stuck her with a needle after she did it, and strapped her hands to the side of this bed. Now she wore leather bracelets.

Mom turned to the doctor. The one with the tight green beanie wrapped around his head. That wasn't the name of it. But she couldn't remember what it was actually called. Her brain wasn't working right. Not after that shot of medicine they gave her. All her insides were swimming. Head warped and wobbly.

"You have to make her better. Do you understand me? Find out what happened to her. Find out who did this to her." Mom was talking in the shrieking voice. The same one she used when Grandpa had his stroke during Thanksgiving dinner. Sometimes she had it when her and Dad fought on the phone.

"Ma'am, we understand. We're going to do everything we can to help your daughter. Everything. I assure you," someone else said, but she didn't know whose face belonged with the voice because it came from behind her, and it hurt too much to turn her head. But his words only made Mom cry harder.

"Thank you. Thank you. I don't know what I'd do if anything happened to my baby. I couldn't live without my baby." She sobbed so hard she couldn't talk anymore. All the words gone. Taken over by her cries.

Mom curled her fingers around mine. Palms sticky. The bed rolled.

DEPARTMENT OF BEHAVIORAL HEALTH AND SCIENCES

There was the direction arrow again.

BEHAVIORAL HEALTH

There was nothing wrong with her behavior or her health—they all looked perfect from the outside—but there was definitely something wrong with her. They all knew it now. The secret was out. Written all over her body. She'd seen the horror in Mom's face every time she looked at the angry words cut into her daughter's flesh. She'd only just begun using the razor blade.

Wounds of the father. Wounds of the brother. Wounds of the man. Poetry carved into her skin. She liked it.

A sharp corner. Then another. Pushing through the double doors.

She wanted to stay downstairs in the ICU with the nice nurse. The one that hummed and smelled like palo santo. She didn't want to be admitted to this unit. Strapped to the bed like an animal. A tube down her throat. To keep her quiet? To breathe? Neither of which she had any desire to do. She didn't want to be quiet. She'd eaten too many of her words, and now she just wanted to throw up. She didn't remember what it felt like to breathe.

Funny how everything from before was gone that quick. Is that how they'll feel after she's gone? How long until they forget her?

Not long.

Nobody.

Ghost.

"You have to bring her back. Bring her back to me, please." Mom was crying again. The doctors gave her pitying expressions because they thought she was delirious. They'd already done their part. They'd saved her body. But that's not what her mom meant. She wanted her daughter to come back inside her body.

I'm already gone, Mom. That's what she wanted to tell her. *You've been living with my ghost.*

But there was just so much she couldn't tell her.

She couldn't tell her they made her do it.

That, for three straight days, she'd received hundreds of messages. One right after the other.

Why are you still alive?

Ur grandpa died because you were so ugly

U R the reason abortion should be legal

On and on it went. She tried not to look. Shut off her phone. Thought about throwing it out the window. But every time she turned her phone on, it was there. The vile hate.

They attacked on every platform. It didn't matter that she deleted all her social media. They sent her emails. Texts from hidden numbers faster than she could block them. Up until the final one:

What are you so afraid of? Do it

CHAPTER TWELVE

"Noelle! Noelle!" I screamed at the top of my lungs as I raced through the house. Running through the living room and into the dining room before she came flying down the stairs.

"What? Laurel, what? Ohmigod, are you okay?" She took one look at my flushed face and knew something was wrong. "What's going on?"

"You're never going to believe this. I can't believe it either. How did I never see this? From the very beginning, it was so obvious! So damn obvious." I whipped around her and stared out the window, scanning up and down the street for anything unusual or out of place. Our huge bay windows exposed us to the outside world. I quickly moved through the house, pulling down all the shades in every room. I didn't want Gia to see us, just in case she was spying on us. I was totally paranoid, but I couldn't help myself. Is this how Spencer felt? Why he was so scared?

"Gia is a snake. An absolute snake, and I can't believe I never saw it. How could I have never seen it?" I angrily rubbed my face with both hands. Still shocked. "Why is she setting me up? I just don't understand. Was she the one messing with Maddie? Trying to point the finger at me instead of herself?"

"Laurel, slow down. Settle down. You're not making any sense," Noelle said from her position behind me. And I wasn't. I couldn't. My thoughts were running faster than I could keep up with them. So were the questions.

"Come on," I said, grabbing her arm and hurrying into the kitchen. It felt like we'd be safer in there. I had no idea why. I quickly shut the curtains above the sink, like I'd done with the blinds in the rest of the house.

"You're starting to scare me. Why are you acting so weird?" She leaned back against the wall like Detective Boone did at the police station and eyed me cautiously.

"Because I don't know what she's planning next, and I have to clear my name before she does any more damage. Or something worse. I have no idea what she's capable of. You'll see. I promise you'll understand as soon as I tell you everything. You're going to be like, *What?*" My head was still reeling and spinning. I had all the videos. A bunch of random stuff I'd saved, too, just to have extra footage in case I'd missed anything. I'd transfer everything to a flash drive as soon as I got upstairs to my office. I just wanted to fill Noelle in first. I took a deep breath, desperately trying to settle. "Gia is setting me up. I don't know why, but she's definitely the one behind the notebook and Maddie's phone. She's trying to frame me."

Noelle stared at me from across the kitchen, doubt written all over her face. She looked to the back door and then at her phone sitting on the counter, like she was wondering if she should call somebody.

"That's okay." I shook my head at her. "I expected you to have that reaction. I never saw it coming either. Not in a million years. I was just as surprised. But then I watched all the videos at Crystal Meadows—the way she hands Spencer the notebook—and well, there was just no more questioning any of it. You can't deny what's right in front of your own eyes."

"What are you talking about? You're still not making any sense." She was looking at me like she looked at her mother, who had dementia. In a weird, pitying way. And if I hadn't been so excited about what I found, I might've been offended. Instead, I forced myself to slow down and start at the beginning so she could understand.

"Okay, this sounds crazy. I realize that. But I figured it out, and I'm telling you—literally every single thing makes sense now, and nothing did before. That's because Gia's been pulling strings from the very beginning. She made it look like I barged my way onto the crime scene, but that was all her doing. I didn't even know anything had happened, and I wouldn't have found out about Maddie until this morning if she hadn't called me." I didn't know why I was telling her all this. She was there when Gia called me. "She was the one who lied to all the officers at Crystal Meadows. But she told them that it was my idea, and it definitely looked like I forced my way in. Nobody knew it was her. It's basically my word against hers, and she told them first, so it already skews things in her favor."

"Why would you come back to the scene of a crime you committed, anyway? That's stupid. Who would do something like that?"

"I don't know, but the detectives are questioning me like I had something to do with it. Suggesting I found Spencer to intimidate him and get him to be quiet. But again—Gia was the one who brought him up to begin with. She was supposed to be talking to Ethan at the same time I was talking to Spencer. We'd decided to divide and conquer, but who knows if she actually did. I don't trust what she says anymore. Everything just looks bad for me. That's what I know, and she set it up that way."

Noelle wrinkled her face at me. "Did you have anything to eat today?"

"Stop it. I know this sounds ridiculous and impossible, but she set me up. And I don't know why, or if she intended for Maddie to die, but it's what happened." If my own wife was looking at me like that, how was I ever going to convince the detectives I was telling the truth? What if they didn't believe my version when I showed them the videos? That's why I needed the phone stuff too. As much evidence to counteract whatever version of events Gia was telling them.

"But why would Gia set you up? What's the point?" There wasn't any part of her face that looked like she believed me. I wouldn't have believed me either. It sounded ridiculous. Seemed impossible. She kept going. Her voice urgent and imploring. "And someone got hurt, Laurel. They actually died. Gia would never do anything to hurt someone on purpose. You know that. It's why you agreed to work with her. You know she's a good person."

I shook my head at her, just as baffled by the possibility. I was a therapist. I was supposed to see through people. How could I have been so duped? "I thought I knew Gia, but none of this fits with who I thought she was, and I don't trust her anymore. Not at all. There's no denying she gave Spencer the notebook, and she gave me the pills. The ones that made Maddie have an allergic reaction. She died of anaphylactic shock. I just—"

"Wait." She raised her hand to stop me. "Maddie died of an allergic reaction? To what?"

"Yes, that's what I've been trying to tell you, and those are the pills Gia gave me to give her. Gia's the one that told me she had a headache. She gave me the ibuprofen. That's what Maddie was allergic to." I gave Noelle a hard look.

She walked over to the table and slowly sat down, finally processing what I was saying, or at least beginning to take me seriously. She pursed her lips and rubbed her chin, "Did you know Maddie was allergic to ibuprofen before this?"

I shook my head.

"So how do you know Gia did?" she asked next, her eyes trained on me. "She might not have known she was allergic, either, especially if you didn't. She could've just been being nice."

"Why are you defending her?"

"I'm not." She raised her hands in the air. The concerned look hadn't left her face. "I love you and support you always, baby. You know that."

"I don't want you to support me. I want you to believe me and stop staring at me like I'm getting high again." I couldn't stand that look. The one everyone gave me after I disclosed my addiction history. It didn't matter how many years I'd been sober. Learning my background changed everything.

Noelle got up from the table and walked around the island to where I stood next to the sink. She grabbed my hands from my sides and gazed lovingly into my eyes. "Honey, let me run you a bath, and we can talk more about this in there, if you want. All about it. You can tell me everything. But afterward, I think you should really go to bed. Give it a rest for the night. Let the detectives do their job. Just try and get some sleep, because I can tell you're absolutely exhausted, babe. I know this makes sense to you, but it sounds a bit out there and . . ." Her voice trailed off.

"Crazy." I jerked my hands away from her and moved her off me. "That's what you want to say. I can see you trying to be polite."

"I'm not. I understand why you're upset, I just know you're tired, and sometimes when we're tired, we don't make the best decisions or think as clearly as we normally would. Plus, you've been through so much in the last twenty-four hours. Losing someone you care about is really hard." She brushed the hair out of my face and smiled down at me.

"That's what I mean. Right there." I pointed at her. "You're using your kindergarten-teacher voice. I don't need you to kindergarten-teacher-voice me right now, at all. I hate when you do that." But I didn't need to tell her that. I'd been telling her that since our first fight. That's what she always did. Turned into the teacher. She thought it was diplomatic and mothering. It felt patronizing and made me feel like a child. One of our oldest fights. The ones every couple has. "I don't have time to fight with you right now, and I don't need a bath." I threw her hands off me. I was so sick of arguing with her. She'd been intolerable since she lost her job, spending way too much time picking me apart. "And also, I'm not tired. I'm going into my office to work. If you would've let me finish my story, you would've learned I have an important video proving Gia had something to do with it. She's the one who planted the notebook and gave Maddie the pills that killed her." I said that last part with way more assuredness than I felt, but she didn't know that.

She wrinkled her forehead in confusion. "What do you mean, you have a video?"

"See, you haven't even been really listening to me," I snapped at her. I jutted my chin out defiantly. "And you know what? I'm over talking to you about it. I don't have any more time to waste trying to get you to take me seriously about this. But you know who's going to take me seriously about this?" I waved my phone in her face. "Detectives Boone and Wallace. As soon as I show them these videos from Crystal Meadows. Their jaws are probably going to hit the floor. I know mine did when I saw it."

"Let me see the video." She went for my phone, but I pulled it back out of her reach and shook my head.

"Oh no," I said. "I already tried to have this conversation with you—except you weren't interested, and now I've wasted too much time. Because you're right, I *am* exhausted. But I've got a few more big pieces of evidence to put together for the detectives in the morning. I'm not going to bed until I've done it."

I walked past her without giving her a chance to respond and hurried upstairs to my office. I'd meant what I said. Yes, I was tired, but I wasn't resting until I finished this. It was too important. She might not realize that, but I did.

I sat down at my desk and jiggled the mouse, bringing the computer to life. I went straight to my Verizon account and pulled up my phone history. I'd searched through my phone quickly during the interrogation, and there wasn't anything there. But it could've easily been deleted from my actual phone. I wanted to prove to them that it'd never been there to begin with. Someone must have used a different phone and one of those apps to make it look like the number contacting Maddie was mine. And if I had to bet, I'd say it was Gia.

There it was. On the first page of my Verizon statement. Maddie's number. Right there. Added to our family plan. My stomach sank. Irked up the back of my throat. This had to be a mistake.

I pressed the link to this month's call log. It took a second for my brain to process what was on the screen. All the numerous calls. A huge amount of data used—probably FaceTimes. Texts. Hundreds of them, back and forth between Maddie and me, just like the detectives said. It was all there in black and white. No way it came from a burner-number app. But wait . . .

Lots of the calls were late at night. Some after midnight. Long after I'd fallen asleep. Times when my phone was plugged in next to me on the nightstand. How? What?

The air tightened. Then thickened. Noelle was behind me. She put her hands on my shoulders. My insides chilled at her touch.

"What'd you find?" she asked, peering over me to look at the phone records too. Her hot breath on my neck. Tickling the hairs.

The silence stretched out between us.

I'd never made any of these calls. None of the texts or FaceTimes either. Hadn't taken a picture, and definitely hadn't sent any. There was only one person with access to my phone besides me.

I forced myself to turn around and look at her. "I don't understand." Goose bumps rose on my arms. "What have you done?" The question came out high and frightened.

"What do you mean?" Noelle batted her eyelashes and tried to look innocent, but she wasn't fooling me. We'd been together too long for that nonsense.

"I never made a single call or text to Maddie, but there were all kinds of texts and calls to her made from my phone. They've been deleted on my actual phone, but they're right here on this statement." I pointed to the monitor, but she'd already seen what was on the screen. I could tell by the way she averted her eyes. How she was still breathing hard.

"That's really weird," she said with a puzzled expression on her face, still trying to feign surprise. "How would that even happen?"

"I don't know, Noelle. Why don't you tell me?" I pushed my chair back against my desk as far as it would go. I didn't want her anywhere near me. I fought the urge to shove her away from me. Angry tears filled my eyes. "Why are there calls on my phone to Maddie I didn't make? Most of them are in the middle of the night, when I was asleep."

She just shook her head. The confused look hadn't left her face. But she wasn't confused. She was stunned into silence. She hadn't expected to get caught tonight, and now she didn't know what to do. I spun around and started gathering my things as quickly as I could.

"What are you doing?" she asked from behind me, in a voice filled with pain, like I'd been the one to betray her instead of the other way around. I just kept throwing things together and ignored her. I stuck the flash drive into my computer and transferred the videos onto it from my phone. "What are you doing?" she asked again, unwilling to let it go. "Will you just stop what you're doing and talk to me?"

I couldn't even shake my head. I was too twisted up with emotions and confusion. "I'm going down to the police station."

"You're going down to the station?" she asked, in the same caring voice she'd been using since I walked in the door, but I didn't trust her. My brain refused to accept she'd played a role in this, even though it was right there in literal black and white.

"They need to see all this." And I needed to get out of here. I couldn't breathe. I couldn't think. I didn't dare feel all the feelings threatening to heave their way to the surface.

"Honey, I really want to figure out what happened to Maddie, too, but sometimes your mind creates explanations that aren't true simply because you need one so badly. And you're so tired, love. Why don't you just go to sleep, and we can talk about all this in the morning?" She put her hand on my shoulder again, and I jerked away.

"I'm going down there. I don't care what time it is. It's a police station. Someone is there and will let me in. They'll call Wallace and

Boone. They might even still be down there themselves. Who knows." I refused to look at her. It hurt too much. I just kept downloading the videos and statements in case I couldn't get them to come up at the station, with their spotty Wi-Fi.

"You can't go to the police station tonight. At least not without an attorney. Do you hear me, Laurel?" I didn't respond. "Laurel?" She let out a frustrated sigh. "Let me go grab my phone. I'm going to call the name of the attorney that Kesha gave me last year. I just think you should be careful about this. You need to get an attorney. You can't talk to the detectives again without one. This is way over our head, and I want you to be protected." She turned and rushed out of the office before I could stop her.

How could she stand there and want to protect me when it looked like she was part of setting me up? Was it possible that a burner number would still link up with my phone? End up on a statement? That's what I wanted to be true. I couldn't stomach the alternative. Please, no.

Noelle thundered back up the stairs. It sounded like she was running. Why was she running? I turned around as she reached me, carrying a bat in her left hand. She raised the bat high, and my scream caught in my throat just as the aluminum cracked against my forehead.

CHAPTER THIRTEEN

I turned my throbbing head to the side. Pulse-pounding pain shot through my entire body, leaving me nauseous. I fought the urge to turn my head to the other side and throw up. Instead, I just let the waves of nausea throttle me and the vomit move up and down my throat, leaving a burning trail behind it.

There. The sound of Noelle's voice. Soft. Muffled. Close.

It's so dark in here. I can't see anything. Am I dreaming?

I wanted to open my eyes to see her. But my lids were so heavy I couldn't lift them. Like someone had taped them shut. They didn't budge, no matter how hard I tried and willed them to move. I wanted to try harder. Fight. But all the effort just made my head hurt more, and I was so exhausted. I'd never been so tired.

The pain. So intense I couldn't stay awake.

There was Noelle's voice again. So angelic and sweet. I'd recognize it anywhere.

Just for a minute, and then she was gone. Or maybe I was.

I couldn't tell. Shifting in and out . . .

I slowly opened my right eye. Just a crack. Barely a slit, and it took so much work. But I did it. And there she was again. Noelle. She was still here. Of course she was. She would always take care of me.

I squinted, trying to see her better, bring her into focus. But she was so hazy. Like she was standing behind a row of flimsy white-cotton clouds. I could still make her out, though. Dipping a sponge into a bowl and bringing it to my lips. My love. I smiled. My lips cracked. Pieces of them stuck to my teeth. I didn't know I was thirsty or how dry my lips were until the water hit them. Suddenly, I was so thirsty that I couldn't swallow or breathe.

I wanted to yell for help, but the words couldn't get past my lips. They were stuck somewhere deep in my throat. Everything was frozen. Heavy. Hurting.

Please. I want more. Give me more. I'm so thirsty.

I couldn't keep my eye open, but soon I felt the water again on my lips. The trickle of it as it made its way inside me. But then it just stayed there. In my mouth, doing nothing.

Swallow, Laurel, I instructed myself, but you shouldn't have to tell yourself to swallow. That's supposed to happen automatically.

I'm not okay. Something's wrong with my brain. What happened?

I couldn't panic. It was over if I panicked. I had Noelle. *Noelle will take care of you. Breathe, Laurel. Breathe.*

I counted the seconds in and out. Just like I had in my early sobriety, when everything about being sober sent me into paralyzing fear. I'd felt this before. I could get through it. The mind-bending anxiety slowly drained from my body, only to be replaced by the pain, erasing the lingering adrenaline with shearing, hot stabs to the back of my head.

I just wanted to go back to sleep.

This time it was easy. I was so tired. Being awake was such a struggle.

Both eyes. Awake. No more singular vision. *What's happening? Where am I? Did we get into a car accident? Was this the hospital? Am I dead? Still dreaming? Where's Noelle?*

Every movement hurt. The worst migraine of my life, splicing down the entire left side of my brain. Splintering in the back and shooting all the way down my spine. I moved my eyes instead. Back and forth. Like a doll who couldn't move its neck.

It was so dark. Everything was so hard to make out. Was that a dresser? A desk? It was impossible to tell. Where had Noelle gone? Had I imagined her before? What would I do if she didn't come back? What's happening? How'd I get here?

Just when my mind started to spiral, the sound of a door opening snapped me out of it. Brought me straight back into my skin. Reality. Then footsteps. Closer. Soon, they were right next to me. It's her. My love. I'd recognize her smell anywhere. Earth.

She was back. Thank God she was back. Of course she wouldn't leave me here alone for long.

I instinctively reached for her, but my wrists wouldn't give. I tried again but just got snapped back to the bed. I rolled my eyes to the left. Panic rose in my chest. There were ropes tied around my wrists, strapped to the bedposts behind me. I was terrified to look farther down my body, but I had to.

Belts.

Wrapped tight around each one of my legs, so I was lying spread-eagled on the bed like a human sacrifice. I tried to scream, but I couldn't. I thrashed back and forth, trying to wake up, hoping this was a nightmare. My head slammed against the headboard. Skull crashing against the wood. Spots danced in front of my eyes. I couldn't move more than a few inches off the bed. It felt like someone was choking me.

Noelle! Help me! Please help me! What's happening? Tell me what's happening. My brain screamed the words that stayed stuck in my throat.

The terror brought my vision into focus.

Noelle's face finally came into view. Crystal clear and sharp. Like the best digital camera. She put her fingers to her lips as if to shush me. Why was she telling me to be quiet?

Noelle, help me! I willed the words to come. Harder this time. What was wrong with me? Why couldn't I talk? Am I brain-dead? *Noelle, help!*

The air shifted. I felt her. Sensed her before I saw her. Another presence coming out of the shadows and into my view. The clunk of her combat boots on the wooden floor.

Gia.

And that's when I remembered. Everything came flooding back. My insides went cold as I remembered the bat.

HER
(THEN)

Her heart throbbed in her head. Each beat pulsating. All her senses on high alert. She couldn't see him. The blindfold wrapped tightly around her eyes. The one that'd been wrapped there since the moment she woke in the back of the trunk. She knew immediately she was in a trunk because of the thrum of the tires underneath her. The small space. Like being in a coffin.

How could she have been so stupid? Why'd she say yes to Jasmine? She should've known better.

She'd screamed until her throat was raw. The taste of blood dripped down the back of her throat, but the duct tape across her mouth assured no one heard her, which only made her scream louder and flail harder.

"Shh . . . shh . . . sweet baby girl," he cooed when the trunk unlatched, and she toppled out, her hands tied behind her back. With nothing to break her fall, she landed on the ground, knocking the wind out of herself. Her lungs roared. The blindfold loosened and fell from her eyes. Lights danced in front of her. Spotty. She couldn't pass out. Not again. She had to stay awake.

And she did.

Struggling against them while they carried her down to the creek. Eyes searching. Ears straining. Terror accentuating every sense.

This was supposed to be over. The worst of it done. Monsters only attack once. But these weren't like regular monsters. These were vicious creatures.

They dragged her, kicking and screaming, underneath the railroad bridge. Down by Dodge Creek. Nobody could see you when you were out here. They'd come in two cars. That's how many there were. She was outnumbered from the start.

They'd been so mad when the police arrested him, Aaron, during physics class. Right in the middle of the lecture. In front of everyone. The cops had stormed to the front of the classroom. "We wanted to make an example of him," the police officer wearing the bulletproof vest said on the news the night of the arrest.

And they had. Assuring everyone else saw it, too, and felt the same way, which only made them hate her more than they already did. They didn't say her name on the news—just kept referring to her as the nineteen-year-old female victim—but they didn't need to.

She should've been immediately suspicious when Jasmine brought coffee and asked her to go down to the commons. It'd been weeks since she'd spoken a single word to her, but she was just so happy Jasmine was speaking to her again that she'd jumped at the opportunity without thinking. Plus, she never for one second thought Jasmine could be involved in something as sinister as this. Except she should've known better than that by now.

Nothing's more powerful than the desire to belong. Jasmine might've been the one that drugged her. They had to get her high to force her in the trunk. She'd started feeling funny fifteen minutes into their coffee.

Jasmine wasn't anywhere now, but she couldn't see anyone's face. They all wore ski masks and circled around her on the ground. Until one of them stopped and kicked her in the side with their boot. Right in the ribs. That was the only signal they needed.

They grabbed her hair and pulled her into the shallow water, shoving her under. Then circled around her. Chanting and laughing like the kids in elementary school used to do on the playground during recess, when they were playing Monkey in the Middle. They pointed and laughed. Called her ugly. Whore. All those things. The same things they said in the comments online. She knew it was them, even though they wore masks.

ND43791 was definitely the ringleader.

At some point, she just closed her eyes and drifted away. To that special place she'd learned to go to. Before long, she was on the ground. She couldn't tell you who hit her first. She wrapped her body into the fetal position and covered her head. Their kicks coming hard and fast. One on top of the other. But that was the part where she smiled, even as she choked on her own blood. They didn't know she'd grown to like it. That the searing-hot pain of broken vessels made her feel good. She let them kick her, hurling their insults at her, and hoped they'd kill her when it was all over.

"Just let this be the end, please," she'd silently begged the universe.

She was so angry when she opened her eyes in the dirty water on the edge of the creek and discovered she was still breathing. Very much alive. That's how you knew you really wanted to die.

She would've if the farmer hadn't found her. At least that's what the doctor said. She was bleeding internally. They brought her to Saint John's Hospital. Twenty miles in the opposite direction of Providence, where nobody knew her or her family. It felt like a special blessing they'd given her without knowing it. So, when the nurses asked who her parents were, she gave them fake names to match their fake numbers. She told them her parents were out of the country on business and that's why they were having such a tough time reaching them. She let them treat her until they started becoming suspicious. Then, she slipped away quietly in the middle of the afternoon, when nobody was looking. She would take her chances with the internal bleeding.

Because nobody could ever know about what happened underneath the bridge.

CHAPTER FOURTEEN

My chest ached. It was so heavy, like someone was sitting on top of me. A scratchy blanket rested against my face. The faint smell of broccoli coming from somewhere. Tears leaked out of the corners of my eyes. I'd been crying in my sleep again.

I was tied to the bed in this room. There was no light. No sound. No air. I couldn't tell if it was day or night. How many hours had passed. Whether I'd been trapped for a few hours or a few days. It was impossible to figure out, when I was cut off from all sensory cues.

I wasn't home. That much I knew for sure. I'd smell home. Feel it too. This bed wasn't any of the beds we purchased for our house, and we didn't have a room with an east-facing window like this. I had to be at Gia's. Was I in her guesthouse? Her guesthouse was huge. I'd only had time to glance at it while I was there the other day, but it was big. Probably two bedrooms. I could be in there. Where else would they have put me?

Or maybe I wasn't at Gia's. Maybe I was somewhere else. Anything was possible. What would it mean if I was somewhere else? How'd they get me here?

Most importantly, why were they doing this to me?

Noelle knocked me out. I still couldn't believe it.

Every time I closed my eyes, I saw the way she came into the room carrying the baseball bat. The one we'd bought when we swore we were going to join a summer softball league but never did. That was the scariest part. Her violence wasn't impulsive. It's not like we kept the bat hanging out in the living room or in one of our closets, where she could've just grabbed it because she was mad. The bat was buried deep in the garage. It'd been there for over three years. That meant she'd gone downstairs to get it while I was on the computer looking up the phone records, or—and this possibility was the most horrifying to me—she'd already gotten it out of the garage before I got home because she'd planned on attacking me.

Her eyes were so determined as she rushed into the room. Completely laser focused in a way I'd never seen them look before. And she'd charged straight at me. It all happened so quick. One minute she was in the doorway, and the next minute, she was raising the bat over her head and racing toward me.

Noelle! I—

And then the crack.

Straight to the middle of my head.

I could feel the imprint on my face, all through the center. It wasn't that I couldn't open my eyes because they were taped down with something, like I'd thought before. No, they were swollen shut. I still couldn't open my right eye all the way. What if it stayed like that? Everything was blurry out of my left one, even though I could open it. I'd never had a broken bone before, but my nose was definitely broken. I could barely breathe through my nostrils and, coupled with the tape over my mouth, I never got enough air. It was a constant battle to keep from panicking.

The door opened. My body froze, like it did every time now. The two of them walked in together. Side by side, like a team. I didn't know what to do, so I closed my eye and pretended to sleep, like I had before, hoping maybe they'd talk to each other about their plans and give me some sort of clue as to what was happening. And why. How come they attacked me? What were they planning on doing to me? How was all this connected to Maddie? Was everyone at Crystal Meadows still okay?

They might unknowingly answer some of my questions if they thought I was asleep. That's what I'd been waiting for. Some kind of tangible information about what was going on. I've never felt so lost. Or scared. I fought against the urge to attack them when they got close, and kept my body still instead. It was so hard not to move, but I forced myself to do it.

Energy radiated off them as they stood next to the bed, and I didn't have to open my eyes to feel them staring down at me. Was this how they'd hovered over me while I was knocked out? The thought of it was so creepy it made my entire body itch, but I couldn't scratch, which only made the feelings intensify. Who would do something like this? Why would Noelle ever be a part of it? Whatever this was.

I kept my eyes closed, even though I desperately wanted to peek, and willed one of them to say something. Anything. But nobody spoke as the empty air stretched out between us. What were they doing? Just staring at me like a couple of weirdos?

A few more minutes passed before I heard the sound of soft footsteps pattering away. Noelle was leaving. She walked soft. On the tips of her toes, always, from spending her entire childhood in ballet. I listened for the sound of the door closing, but it didn't latch. Did that mean she was coming back?

Gia's slap to my face stunned me like a Taser gun, interrupting my thoughts. My eyes snapped open. Body tense and pulling against the straps. Gia grinned down at me while excruciating pain surged through my entire body, making me woozy.

"Hi, there!" she said in a chipper voice, like it was the morning and she was waking me up for an important day.

I flattened myself up against the bed, desperately trying to get away from her, but there was nowhere to go. I didn't want her to touch me. I didn't want her to even look at me. Terror coursed through me along with the pain.

"Here's what we're going to do, my sweet." She opened with one of her favorite pet names for me, talking to me the same way we talked to each other on set. Just like I'd done to her the other day. However long ago that was. The world had flipped upside down since then. "You have to eat something if you want to start feeling better. But that's going to require us taking this tape off your mouth, and as you can imagine, we're a little nervous about it. You're going to have to behave if we do that. Do you understand me? I need you to promise me you're going to be a good girl if we take this off your mouth. Can you do that?" She peered down at me, and I nodded my agreement, even though I didn't know what I'd do once the tape was gone.

"Here's what being a good girl looks like." Gia dropped her voice low, to nearly a whisper, to make sure Noelle couldn't hear her, wherever she'd gone. "You're going to be quiet. And what I mean by quiet is that you're not going to say a word. Not to me, and definitely not to Noelle. This isn't the time for conversations, understand?" She peered into my eyes. Her breath stank of old onions, and I wanted to gag, but I gave her a brief nod instead. Forced my eyes to look serious. She nodded back at me and continued, "And here's the other thing it's not time for: yelling for help. You might not have realized it yet, or maybe you have . . ." She paused to gaze at me pointedly again. Studying my face for clues to my state of mind. This time I held my breath when she came close. "But you're in a bit of a dangerous situation, and once you realize that, well, you might be tempted to start screaming for help. But I'm going to stop you right there." She gave me a big smile. Just like the one that'd been on her face when I opened my eyes after she slapped me. "I know you've only been to my house once—and it was clearly not under the best circumstances, given what happened to our poor little Maddie—so I imagine you weren't paying much attention to the surroundings." She paused, pretending to think, like I'd pretended to sleep seconds ago. But I wasn't fooled. "I have a recording studio in the back, you know . . . Did you see it during your visit? Tucked away in my guesthouse? It's super private." She watched as I recalled the building, and smiled again. She was enjoying this. "Yep, and it's soundproof. Completely up to code too. We've had bands record entire albums back here, and you can't hear a thing. We've never had a single complaint from the neighbors." She straightened as we heard the sound of Noelle's footsteps returning to the room. This time she was carrying a tray of food and beverages. Just like she used to bring me whenever I was sick or on the days when she served me breakfast in bed. Gia turned to her and smiled, flipping her long dark hair over her shoulder.

"We've gone over the rules while you were gone," she said, and Noelle gave her a small smile back. She was trying to look brave, but I could tell she was nervous by the way she was fidgeting with the things on the tray. "And I'm happy to report Laurel is on board with all of them. She's aware of how she needs to behave." Gia turned her attention back to me, giving me a pointed look. "Aren't you, Laurel?"

I nodded my consent again, but the only thing I was on board with was getting free. I'd agree to anything. I just wanted to breathe.

"Well, let's do it, then!" Gia exclaimed, giving a small clap. She leaned over and started pulling the tape off my mouth, in one slow, torturous movement, so every tiny hair on my face clung to it while she pulled. I lay motionless and didn't make a sound, even though it hurt. I refused to give her the satisfaction of seeing me in pain. I gulped for air when she finally removed the last corner. Breathing heavy, like I'd just finished a workout.

Gia motioned to Noelle, and she moved to the other side of the bed. They each grabbed a hold of one of my arms, and without speaking, they worked together, grunting and pulling me up to a half-seated position against the wooden headboard. My muscles cried out in agony after being released from the same cramped position for so long, but it felt so good to be sitting upright instead of flat on my back.

Gia picked up the spoon and started feeding me, dipping it into the bowl and bringing it to my lips. I opened my mouth like a baby bird and let her. Nothing else mattered at the moment except getting sustenance into my body. I needed it to fight. She didn't have to worry about me being quiet. I'd shut my mouth as long as she fed me. Besides, it gave me time to study Noelle and get my bearings.

The soup was the cheap kind from a can, with the funny aluminum smell, and it reminded me of childhood. But I didn't care. It tasted gourmet. I couldn't stop staring at Noelle in disbelief as Gia robotically fed me. Noelle being violent was so far removed from any concept I had of her. It just didn't fit. She was the most sensitive of souls. The only time she ever reacted aggressively was when someone she loved was threatened or some sort of injustice had occurred, especially if it involved children. But nothing like that had happened here. Far as I knew, at least.

I wasn't supposed to speak, but I couldn't help myself. "What's going on, Noelle?" My voice so dry and sore it came out as a raspy whisper.

"Hey!" Gia snapped, jerking her hand away from my mouth like she was going to stop feeding me. "What did I say about talking?"

I ignored her. "Please, Noelle, just tell me what's happening. Why are you doing this to me?" I jerked on my ropes, emphasizing the fact that, in addition to being cracked in the head with a baseball bat, I was now tied to a bed.

"Shut up! I told you the rules." Gia interrupted me before Noelle had a chance to speak, but I raised my voice louder and spoke over her, drowning her out.

"Did she make you? Is she forcing you to do this? Noelle—look at me!"

Gia shoved Noelle aside and towered over me again, like she'd done when Noelle wasn't in the room. She gripped my face and squeezed my cheeks, making me bite the insides of them. The taste of blood was instantly on my tongue and in the back of my throat.

"What part of shutting your mouth and being quiet do you not understand?" Gia practically growled. Her eyes filled with venomous hate as she peered down at me helpless on the bed.

Her eyes were fixed on mine, but my gaze was glued to Noelle and the way her body leaned ever so slightly into Gia while she spoke. Her hand rested on Gia's lower back. Fingertip touch. That was what gave it away.

My heart lurched, and my hands jerked against the ropes holding them in place. "Oh my God. That's what this is about?" Gia hadn't let go of my cheeks, so I had to speak through clenched teeth, and it hurt, but I didn't care. "You're sleeping with her?"

"We're not having sex," Noelle flung back. But they were. It was written all over her face. Gia looked smug. How had I missed it? How long had it been going on?

"You couldn't just run away? Or leave me the old-fashioned way? You had to send me to prison? Is that what you were trying to do? Or just ruin my entire career by making people think I slept with one of my clients? I mean, Jesus." I tugged on my restraints. "Why this? What have I ever done to deserve anything like this?" I shook my head. "Nothing."

"You sure about that?" Gia asked at the same time Noelle spoke.

"Because you're a liar," Noelle said, her lower lip quivering. She was doing her best not to cry, and her entire body trembled. Gia put her arm around her shoulders, whispering something in her ear. I wanted to fly off the bed and shove her off my wife.

"I'm a liar?" I struggled against my restraints, forcing myself to ignore Gia and focus on Noelle. "What are you talking about? Seriously. I have no idea what's going on. Please. Help me. Whatever is happening or has happened, we can figure it out together, Noelle." I was lots of things. Full of mistakes and flaws, but being a liar wasn't one of them. She'd been brainwashed, or misinformed. Something. I had to find out.

Gia shoved Noelle behind her, hiding Noelle from me with her body. I skirted even farther back on the bed. "You don't even know who I am, do you?" She asked it like I should know exactly who she was, but I didn't. My insides churned.

She grabbed my chin and forced my face up toward hers, squeezing my cheeks together again until I winced from the pain. "I should've known." She snorted with disgust and shook her head at me like she was scolding a small child. "I'm Georgia Mathews."

She announced it like a big reveal, and I searched my brain for some type of recognition of her. But I couldn't match her name with anyone or anything. No event. Except that didn't mean anything, because my brain wasn't working right now. It was mush. Sinking sand. Thoughts fell right through it.

"I just . . . I can't . . ." I stumbled over my words, wrestling with the desire to lie, but I didn't know what I was lying about or agreeing to. Which was worse? What I'd done, or not remembering?

"Alpha Kappa Alpha," Gia sang out in a singsong voice. *"Show them why that Southern spirit will never die. Banners high and we will fight! Fight! Fight!"* My alma mater song. The University of Southern Mississippi. Black and gold. The place where I'd spent the majority of my drinking days. My hardest ones. In a hazy blur of small-town college dive bars buried in the Deep South. Was she one of the pieces of time I couldn't remember? What had I done to her?

I was glad I was tethered to the bed, because it felt like I was going to come undone. A part of me had always known this would happen. Someone. Something. Somewhere. Would come back to haunt me from those days. Here it was. Worse than I ever could've imagined, given my current circumstances.

"You know who else was an Alpha Kappa Alpha?" She scowled. She hadn't taken her eyes off me yet. I wanted to shift my attention to Noelle—peek at what she was doing, how she was responding to the way Gia was treating me and the things she was saying—but I didn't dare break eye contact with Gia. A few more uncomfortable seconds passed before she announced, "My sister."

I swallowed hard, searching my memory. "Your sister?"

Mathews. Georgia Mathews. She said that was her name, but was it her real name? Everyone in Hollywood had pseudonyms. Had she been married? Did she change her childhood name? Was it the same as her sister's? And what did her sister have to do with what happened on the show?

"Yes, my sister. Her name was Paris. Georgia and Paris. Cute, huh?" She gave me a fake smile, followed by an even faker laugh. "And yes, my parents were obsessed with geography. Also, yes, Gia is short for Georgia. Can you imagine me as Georgia, though? It sounds so Southern belle–ish. And as you know, there's absolutely nothing Southern or belle-ish about me." I quickly shifted my eyes to Noelle. My breath caught in my throat. She had her hand supportively around Gia's waist. It was still just as shocking. All the soup I'd just scarfed down felt like it was going to come back up.

How could Noelle do this to me? What had she been a part of? I willed her to look at me, but she wouldn't.

Gia kept talking, spewing forth the words like they'd been bottled up for years. "My sister wasn't at all like me. We're from Detroit, you know, and I hated the South. Everything about it. But her? She was the only thing that made it tolerable. Really, she was the one that ever made anything okay in my life. She was my person."

USM.

A piece of information I could work with. Something to help me figure this mess out.

Gia had gone to USM. Apparently, so had her sister. Why had she never mentioned that to me before? She knew I was an Eagle. She'd been in my office numerous times and seen the degrees lining the wall behind my desk. Why didn't she say anything then? Everyone, especially fellow alumni, always commented when they noticed where I went to college. Pride for your alma mater runs deep in the South.

And then it hit me—what if she'd been planning this from the very beginning? What if it started four years ago, when she came to me for help getting sober?

Suddenly, everything felt incredibly more serious. Like I was standing in the middle of a spinning vortex. Everything blurred, whipping around faster than I could keep up.

She gave me a calculated nod. "I think it's disgusting that you don't remember the person whose life you destroyed. It makes you even more vile." She narrowed her eyes to slits. Nobody had ever looked at me with that much disdain, and it made my insides shrink. "Paris Mathews."

Hearing her full name jolted my memory. Ignited the vague recollection of Paris Mathews from the sea of eager pledging faces that night. As eager as mine had been the year before. I remembered meeting her in the bathroom. Her putting on that bright-red lipstick in front of the mirror. So nervous. I'd given her a swig of the vodka from the bottle I'd been carrying in my purse for just as long as I'd been at the school. A flask carried over from high school.

"Come on," I'd said, grabbing her arm and pulling her back out to the party with me. Some abandoned trailer they'd found at the back of the athletic fields, where we'd been the last few weekends. Tonight, there was going to be a huge bonfire. "You'll be fine. Everyone's nervous their first time."

It was my most vivid memory of her. She stayed in the dorms during rush week, but she didn't ever say much, and we weren't on the same floor. I barely even saw her. Except at the parties and the other functions, but I was always drunk at those events, so they were blurry. Most of my nights were like that back then—fading in and out.

"I'm sorry," I said to Gia, even though I didn't know what I was apologizing for. But whatever had happened to her sister was terrible or we wouldn't be in this situation. Whatever was at stake here—it was huge. Big enough to hurt people. Innocent people like Maddie.

She gave a sarcastic laugh. "Oh, you have no idea how sorry you're going to be."

CHAPTER FIFTEEN

I couldn't miss the sharp intake of breath from Noelle after Gia threatened me. Maybe she'd been as unprepared for this as I was. But I quickly pushed those ideas away since she was the one who'd hit me in the face with the bat. Apparently, my wife had no problem resorting to violence.

"Please, Gia, I'm sorry. I really am. I don't know what happened. I don't know why I'm here or what I did to you and your sister. But I'll tell you this, whatever it was, I'm so sorry. I understand that you must be so hurt or you would never be doing this to me. I get that. I do. You—"

"You get that? Do you? Do you really get that?" She flicked my chin with her hand, sending searing-hot pain to the back of my head. I grimaced. She did it again. Harder this time. "We were only eleven months apart, you know that? Practically twins. Our mom used to dress us alike when we were younger, and we'd pretend we were. We loved fooling people that way. We were so worried about her when she started hanging out with the wrong crowd." Gia leaned closer to me. Stabbed her finger into my chest. "You were the wrong crowd. The bad influence. It's why I always thought it was so funny you'd turned yourself into a sobriety coach." She rolled her eyes and laughed at me. "You know you're really just a glorified babysitter to all those rich people, right? An expensive handbag for them to carry around."

I barely remembered Paris from that week. It was such a blur. Between the booze, the pledging, and the parties. Not to mention I was working just as hard to please the sorority president, Haley, as all the other pledges. They were working to get into the sorority, and I was desperately trying to get a spot living in the actual sorority house. "I wish I could make this better, Gia. Really. I'm so sorry." I just kept repeating myself and my apologies, but she wasn't hearing any of it.

"You left her at that party with that animal. Do you know what he did to her? He tied her up in the back of that trailer and then called in his buddies. She was tied to a bed, just like you right now. But imagine four or five drunk frat boys surrounding you." She motioned to the bed. Her face dark with rage. The kind that poisoned your insides. "She remembers you going out the window. You know that? She thought you were going for help. That's what she told me. How she stared out the window the entire time she was being assaulted and kept telling herself that at any minute, the police were going to break down the door and rescue her. *Why'd she leave me, Gia? How could she leave me there?*"

"I shouldn't have done that, and I'm so sorry. I didn't know that's what happened to her." My heart hurt. Not from the pressure or the injury, but from the memories pushing their way to the surface, and the pain of what her sister must've gone through. How hard it must've been for Gia to find out about it. "Please forgive me."

"Stop saying you're sorry. I don't want to hear it. Do you get what it's like for a freshman to be invited to a party, with all the upperclassmen of the sorority that you're desperately trying to get into? You ever been there, Laurel? Or how about, once you go to that party, then you get assaulted by one of the members of the brother fraternity? You ever been there? Had to fight someone off you? Run back to your dorm room scared to death and hide in your closet the rest of the night?"

"Yes," I said, and it stopped her in her tracks. All her forward momentum gone, just like that. The energy zapped from her words. "I got raped during pledge week my freshman year too. My big sister—you know, the person assigned to watch over me during pledge week, kind of like the one assigned to watch over your sister during hers? Yeah, that one. She's who took me to the party. She's also the one that left me once I drank too much and started throwing up in the bathroom. So yes, Gia, I do. Unfortunately, I do."

The details from Paris's assault were disjointed, but I clearly remembered mine. It's funny how your brain processes certain traumas and forgets the rest. It either remembers every single minute detail, down to the number of tiles in the floor, or is completely blank. Sexual assault of women on college campuses was highest during fall semester—orientation and pledge week. Fifty percent of all sexual assaults on women during college happen then. The Red Zone. I was part of the statistic. Same as her sister, apparently.

"You're just saying that so I feel bad for you," Gia said, glaring at me.

I shook my head despite the ache and forced myself to keep looking at her and not at Noelle. I couldn't make this about Noelle. It had to be about Gia and what I did to her sister.

"I'm not. I'm saying it because it's true. And that wasn't the first time for me either." I motioned toward Noelle. "Ask her. She knows. I told her all the stories." My undergraduate college career was littered with unwanted sexual advances and assaults. They happened to me and to everyone else I hung out with back then. It went with the territory. I'd spent years unpacking it in therapy.

Gia shifted her eyes to Noelle, but she just stared at the ground, refusing to make eye contact with either of us. At least she'd kept my secrets. My heart swelled. That meant something. Gia knew it, too, and she was flustered. I pounced on the opening.

"I still don't get it. Why me, Gia?" I asked, my eyes sending a desperate plea into hers. "I was at the party, but it was a huge party. The entire sorority and all the pledges. Not to mention all the others from the fraternity. And you know how it gets. You end up with half the campus. That's the main reason things got so out of control. There were a lot of people in that trailer that night who ended up in the back room. Not just me. I know you want a target. Someone to place this on.

But it doesn't have to be me. Let's go after whoever raped her. Get her the best attorney around. There's not a statute of limitations on sexual assault. Not anymore. Or let's go after USM. We can do something. Something besides this." I motioned down to me, hoping I could talk some level of logic and sense into her.

She shook her head at me. "Too late."

"But it's not. It's never too late. We can find a way to make them pay for what they did to Paris. Let me talk to her. Victims are always terrified to come forward, but I can help her feel safe. I've done this before with other people, so it's not like it'd be the first time I walked someone through it. It's the least I can do for you. For her." I talked fast. Almost every female I worked with had some form of sexual assault in her background. Women struggling with alcoholism are at a much greater risk of experiencing sexual assault. Even higher on college campuses. "I'm so sorry. I never should've left your sister alone in that room. I didn't know what was happening when we first opened the door. I thought the guy on the bed was her boyfriend. She looked like she was sleeping and he seemed so nice. Really, I just remember all those drunk fraternity boys chasing after us girls and waving around those handcuffs like they were going to lock me up. I reacted out of sheer panic. I was terrified of what they'd do to me, and I didn't know what was happening with Paris, I swear. Please, Gia, let me help you make this right. It doesn't have to be like this."

"Do you wanna know what happened to her? To Paris?" Her face was in mine now. Her lips close enough to kiss. She cocked her head to the side. "Ask me." The vein in her forehead throbbed. "Ask me what happened to her."

I shook my head. I didn't want to know. Nothing happened. That's what I told myself that night—she was okay, just like I tried to convince myself that I was okay too. All my memories from the party were so fragmented. That's how my blackouts were. I never lost the whole night. Just pieces. That's the kind of drunk I used to be. It could be true. And since it could be true? Well, then, it practically was. I'd cataloged it in the sea of blackout nights. It wasn't even the first troublesome night that came to my mind when I obsessed about my past. There were so many more alarming ones to worry about. I spent more time worrying about the car I'd sideswiped coming out of the alley behind Schleck's Bar after last call, or the night I hit a garbage can leaving Saint Vincent's. That was my greatest blackout fear. That the garbage can had actually been a real person and I'd killed someone.

What if it was? My conscience must've whispered that question hundreds of times over the years. But Paris? She was just another girl like me. Struggling to make it through college, and desperately trying to find her way and make friends. I was so lost in my alcoholism and grief that I couldn't see outside myself or my pain. I didn't dare say that to Gia, though. It'd make her want to hurt me more than she already did.

Her breath was hot in my face. "She killed herself. You know that? Even though we're not supposed to say that anymore. *Died by suicide,*" she said sarcastically. "That's what we're supposed to say now. Like, what does that even mean? You know why we say it? Do you?" Her face was twisted in pain. Lined with grief. All I could do was shake my head. "It's supposed to take the responsibility off the victim. You know? Remove the blame from the victim and put responsibility on their mental illness. But you know who's responsible for Paris's death?" She shoved her face even closer to mine. "You are, Laurel. You."

HER

(THEN)

After Dodge Creek, she assumed all the bullying and harassment would be over. Wasn't that the point of her punishment? To flog her publicly for what she'd done to Aaron? She'd been so relieved. Because that's what she'd thought. She'd finally reached the end. They'd made her pay. There's nothing left to do after you've been punished for your sins except go free.

She could've taken the bus from the hospital, but instead she walked the four miles to the neighboring town, even though she was still bruised and beaten. Her steps were slow, but it gave her time to think about how much she'd liked giving a different name and pretending to be someone else while she was in the hospital. She'd slid into the role so effortlessly. Like trying on different-size shoes and being shocked to discover they fit so much better than the ones she was wearing. She didn't know it'd be so easy to just be a different person. That's where her head meandered while she walked. To other people and different lives.

Somewhere past Johnson's farm was where she decided that's what she'd do. Be one of those people that just walked away from their life and was never seen or heard from again. You know the ones.

You hear about them on the evening news. Watch their stories play out on *Dateline* and *20/20*. The lady shopping at Walmart who walks into the parking lot and is never heard from again. The man that leaves for work in the morning, like every other day of his twenty-two years at the same factory, and disappears without a trace on his way home. The bride who vanishes from her own wedding during the reception.

She could do it, too, if she wanted to. Just disappear from her life. There was nothing saying she couldn't. Nobody holding her in place. Just imaginary walls and boundaries. But what if she really could just leave? Start over and become someone else. If you got a different start, another beginning—would things end up differently? Would she be the same person in a different environment? Nature versus nurture. What was it?

She was about to be her own living experiment.

In the days following the assault, she was in pain and could barely get out of bed. Getting beat up is like getting into a car accident. You don't realize the full extent of your injuries until the next day. And she was torn up. But part of her liked it. The final beatdown. She'd taken the punches. The sharp blows to the stomach. The hands around her neck. And something about those hands around her neck had taken away her desire to use the belt. It'd been thirteen days since she hurt herself. The longest period of abstinence since she started.

Newly sober. In recovery, or whatever it was they called it.

Walking through the world without any skin on is what it felt like. But she was doing it. She already felt like an entirely different person. And she was.

That's the thing about trauma. You never get to go back to who you were before it happened. It doesn't matter how badly you might want to or how hard you try. That person is gone. Along with that life. It's a marker that forever changes you. And if it doesn't? Well, then it wasn't real trauma. Because real trauma? You're altered forever. Anything else is just a hard time.

If she was going to move forward—and for the first time in forever, she actually considered it—she was going to have to leave this place behind. She needed to blot all this from her memory and become someone else. It was the only thing left to try.

She barely had any friends, but she loved her family, and it was going to be hard leaving them behind. They were going to be so devastated at first. That was understandable. But as time went on, they'd realize how much better their lives were without her around. Once she was gone, they'd be able to really mourn her loss instead of sitting in the room with her dead body for a second longer.

At least that's what she thought.

It gave her a reason to live another day, and you need purpose to give your life meaning or it gets dark really quick. And if things got any darker in her life, the light was going to go out completely. So, that's what she clung to. And much to her surprise, it was enough to get her out of bed in the morning. There were a couple of days when she even showered.

Until Saturday. The first one after Labor Day.

A note slipped underneath the dorm door. That's what happened when you'd wiped all your social media and tried to exist in an analog world. You got notes slid under your door like it was fourth grade all over again.

It hurt to admit it, but she thought it was going to be the apology note she'd secretly hoped for since the assault. One of her sorority sisters—just one of them—writing to say they were sorry for what was happening to her. Out of all the girls, there had to be at least one of them that felt guilty for how they'd treated her. At least one. Or one of them that had been assaulted too—although it felt weird to hope for that. But she did. It meant she wasn't alone, and statistically it was impossible. There had to be someone besides her.

She hurried over to the floor and grabbed the paper, unfolding it and opening it as fast as she could. Her heart raced in her chest. *Could this be the one?* It's what she told herself at night, when it was really bad. There had to be somebody else besides her. She was finally going to meet her. They could share their stories. Help each other get through this.

Die stupid bitch

CHAPTER SIXTEEN

Betrayal trauma. There's a word for it. I remember the first time I saw a video about it on TikTok. I hadn't really understood it at the time. I'd never been cheated on before, though. But this was more than being cheated on. This was the appearance of an entirely different person. Like Noelle had been possessed by an alien. Who was she, and what was she capable of? How did we get here?

Noelle wouldn't do any of this if she hadn't been pushed or coerced in some way. She was the most law-abiding and rule-following person I'd ever met. She'd never even skipped a class in high school. Hadn't been to detention. No speeding tickets—not because she was extra careful and cautious but because she didn't speed. She wouldn't even sneak water into a movie theater. I teased her about it all the time. Yet there she was tonight. The woman who'd never gotten a speeding ticket, slapping duct tape across my mouth and yelling at me to be quiet.

I couldn't fault her for it, though. The being-with-Gia part—yes. I hated that, and it crushed me. But being a part of a revenge plot against someone after they'd done what I'd done to Paris? I would've wanted to hurt me too. It'd all become clear once Gia derailed. And it hadn't taken her long once she started talking about Paris's death by suicide.

"I was the one who found her dead, you know. It wasn't the first time she tried it either. I found her in the bathtub once before that. She didn't just slit her wrists—she shredded them. I still have nightmares about it. Anyway, we shared an apartment: 612 Crown Street. Right next to the Jiffy Lube. She moved in with me after she moved out of the dorms because they were torturing her so badly. I made her show me all the messages. The awful things you and those people said about her. That's what killed her, you know. Being relentlessly bullied every single day after she'd lived through the worst trauma of her life." Her voice shook as she struggled to control her emotions. "That first time she tried to die? Before she attempted, she took black Sharpie and wrote the monstrous, vile things they said about her all over her body. Hundreds of them. Their insults covered her. It must've taken forever. Do you know how hard that was to get off? But I did it. I scrubbed that filth off her once the paramedics bandaged her wrists. I refused to let them take her to the hospital until I erased every last one of those words. The ER doctor kept asking us why her skin was so pink."

I gulped, struggling to find the right words. Ones that wouldn't set her off but still showed a level of responsibility and understanding about the situation.

"That's awful, and I'm so sorry. There's absolutely nothing I can say to make any of that better. But Gia, I was a kid myself. Just a really messed-up girl, and I was so drunk that night. Not to mention terrified those boys were going to do something to me. And I kept telling myself Paris was fine because I was desperately trying to convince myself that I was fine too. That none of us were in trouble. I know that doesn't help. God, I know that doesn't make it better. Nothing ever will. But even though I was there that night and failed to help her, I never bullied her afterward. I swear I didn't. I was too worried about staying out of their line of fire myself. Please, Gia. Trust me—hurting me is not going to make this better. Nothing will make this right. No matter what you do to me, it won't bring her back."

Gia's face was stone. Like she hadn't even heard me. Nothing had gotten through to her. Had she meant to kill Maddie or just to ruin my career? It was the most important question. Because if she meant to kill Maddie, that changed everything about this.

She finally spoke. "Do you know what we never told anyone about that last time? The time she ended her life?" I didn't want to know. I really didn't. But she was going to tell me. She wasn't really asking for my permission. "We found her with her phone on her chest. Isn't that the saddest thing you've ever heard? She died reading all those terrible things people said about her. Those were the final words in her head before she passed. I'll never get over that. Do you know what that last text message said?" I closed my eyes like it would block the words from reaching my ears somehow. "The night she did it, she got a final message, and it said *Kill yourself, bitch*. And do you know who sent her the final message? You, Laurel. You." She stabbed her finger in my chest. "But you probably don't remember that, either, do you?"

"Please don't hurt me," I begged, but it was too late. She lunged at me like she was going to claw my eyes out. Her hands instantly tight around my neck and squeezing hard.

"No!" Noelle screamed as she reached for Gia. "No!" Noelle wrapped her arms around her and started pulling Gia off me, but Gia wouldn't let go without a fight. She struggled to hold on to me as Noelle wrangled her away.

"Stop it, honey! Just stop!" Noelle screamed as Gia flailed against her. She whipped Gia around to face her. She grabbed Gia's cheeks the same way Gia had grabbed mine seconds ago, and forced her to look at her. "Look at me. Listen to me. We're not doing this. You understand? Stop! Just stop it."

Gia's shoulders heaved up and down. Her fists were clenched at her side. Her entire body rigid. Noelle just stared at her for what felt like minutes while Gia struggled to control herself. Suddenly, she threw Noelle off and charged at me again. But Noelle was much stronger, and she'd worked with plenty of children having meltdowns so she easily wrangled Gia. She dragged her, kicking and screaming, out the door, without so much as a backward glance at me, then slammed the door behind them.

I meant what I said to Gia. I didn't recall sending any messages to Paris, but that didn't mean anything. I was obsessed with the sorority, and the president, Haley, since she was the one who called all the shots. I was young, lost, and desperate to belong. I would've done anything they asked me to do. I hated that fact, even back then when it was happening, but I couldn't stop it or make it less true. I'd never felt so alone and disconnected from people around me. It'd been that way since my dad died, and for whatever reason I'd gotten it into my head that living in the sorority house would be the thing that grounded me. Gave me the feeling of home I'd been missing out on for so long.

The girls in Alpha Kappa Alpha were always torturing someone. It was their favorite extracurricular activity. I thought women were supposed to grow out of the mean-girl phase after high school, but it hadn't happened yet. There were so many of us they picked on. It's not like I was exempt. I never really paid attention to their current target because it was constantly changing. The only thing I felt when they showed me any texts or videos they'd sent to someone or passed around in their group text was pure relief.

Waves of gratitude that it wasn't me. That they hadn't caught me on one of my hard days, hunched over and sobbing into my hoodie in the last stall of the bathroom, like they'd done with that one girl. Because guess what? There'd been plenty of days when I had been that girl. Those women were supposed to be kind. They were supposed to be my sisters. Just like they were hers. That was the point of the sorority. But they weren't kind. Only on the outside. On the inside, they were vicious wolves, ruled by Haley, the alpha. Everyone vying for position. I didn't realize any of that at the time, though. It wasn't until I got sober that I saw things for how they really were—and not how I wanted them to be.

I didn't doubt for one minute that I'd sent Paris a message, even if I had no memory of doing it. Because I would've done anything to belong. *Anything.*

Did I deserve to die for that?

Gia's eyes sure said so, and I couldn't blame her. If you'd done something like that to one of my sisters, I'd wish the same thing on you. Whether or not I'd carry it out was an entirely different story. I wasn't sure I'd be able to, but I understood Gia's pain and her desire for revenge.

But Noelle? She had no reason to be involved in this. For what? To keep Gia? Prove her love? Because she was under her spell? How had she justified and rationalized any of this? The questions were endless. How did we end up here? Things like this didn't happen to people like us.

When did it start? And at what point did they decide to destroy my life? What was the plan? Had they always intended to kill Maddie, or was that an unfortunate accident? Either way, it didn't change the fact that Noelle had been pretending to be me and texting Maddie. How had she done it? She must've erased all the history every day. But it would've had to be so strategic. Methodical. It wasn't just that she'd done it—she'd lived a double life.

I scoured my brain for a sign that something had changed, because there was nothing to do alone in the dark except think. I kept coming up empty handed. Literally nothing seemed out of the ordinary. Not our routines. Not our sex life. Our conversations. Finances. We'd been together long enough to have had some rough years. Every couple that had been together for any length of time had them. But we were in a good stretch. A really good stretch. We haven't even had a yelling-and-stomping-and-door-slamming fight in a couple of years. We had a trip planned to Greece. One to Rome next summer. A shared 401(k). Retirement. We even had our burial plots picked out. Cute matching headstones. If you'd asked me two days ago what the most stable thing in my life was, my answer would've unequivocally been her.

How could I have missed so much? Was I so wrapped up in myself and my own life that I didn't see what was happening right in front of me? Was that even possible? I have a doctorate in psychology. I worked with other people. I should've been able to see this coming, but I didn't. How could I have been so wrong about my own wife?

Yet here she was. In love with another woman and keeping me tied up like a prisoner. How long had she known about Paris? How did she sit across from me at dinner and not want to stab me with the fork? To cry? Or scream? To tell me that she'd found one of the missing pieces from my past. It's not like she didn't know my history. She met me in early sobriety, back when I was riddled with guilt and shame over the things I'd done while I was drinking. I was obsessed with my past, reliving it over and over again to try to put all of it together like it was one gigantic puzzle I needed to figure out so I could go on with my life. It had been one of the main topics of conversation with my first AA sponsor.

"How do you live with all the unknowing? With the guilt? And all the shame?" I'd asked her after I finished going over a detailed list of all the horrible things I'd done to myself and other people as the result of my drinking. It was part of my twelve-step work, and it'd been a tough piece to get through.

"You've got to just let it go. You can't live in the past. Eventually, if you want to have any kind of meaningful life, you have to forgive yourself and move forward. There's nothing else you can do. You'll torture yourself forever and live in agony if you never stop trying to figure out what happened in that other life," she'd said. More than once.

So, eventually, I did.

But it's not like I ever forgot my past or the fact that I'd hurt so many people. I'd certainly never forgiven myself or thought it was okay. Much like other addicts, I was someone I didn't recognize when I was using. It was one of the reasons I'd gone to school to study addiction, because I wanted to understand how rational, decent people could do such abhorrent things while they were under the influence. Also, why I'd spent so much of my adult life helping other people get sober. It made something beautiful out of something so dark, and in a way, I felt like I was paying back my debt to the universe. I'd never forgotten how fortunate I was.

Noelle doing anything like this was more of a shock than if she'd died. Or gotten sick. Or any of the other awful scenarios you tortured yourself with when you really loved someone. Because when you really loved someone, there was nothing scarier than losing them. So, I'd thought of all those things, and what I'd do. All the hypotheticals.

If she died, would I remarry or stay single forever? Would it even be possible to live without her? Or what if she was wounded in a terrible accident and on life support until the end? Could I pull the plug, like she wanted me to? Was I capable of that? All those scenarios had run through my head because that was how my hamster-wheel mind worked. But this?

Something like this? Whatever this was. I still didn't know.

The urge to pee pressed down on me. I'd been trying to stave it off. It was as if my senses had been knocked out, too, and were slowly coming back to life along with the rest of me. They'd pumped me with fluids, and I had to pee. It was one of those things where as soon as I noticed it, that was the only thing I could pay attention to. The urge grew stronger.

How had I been going to the bathroom? Had they gotten me out of bed? There was no way they'd gotten me out of bed in a concussed state. The two of them weren't strong enough to lift me off the bed in a dead sleep and carry me to a bathroom. They'd barely been able to pull me up to the top of the bed to feed me. Had they used a bedpan? The thought of it was so humiliating, my cheeks instantly flushed with fiery-red heat. Noelle and I had been together for over ten years, and we still gave each other our privacy in the bathroom. So embarrassing.

I pushed myself up onto my elbows and glanced down to see what I was wearing. I hadn't paid attention before. I was in a long black T-shirt. One that wasn't mine. What was I wearing last night? It definitely wasn't this. Funny how that night seemed so long ago already. I still had no idea how much time had passed. How long they'd had me in this room. It was incredibly disorienting on top of everything else. Where were the police? Gia and I couldn't just disappear without them coming to look for us. Despite her role in things, she was still at the center of the investigation, right along with me.

I scooted over to the side of the bed. My head hurt a bit less—or maybe I was just getting used to the constant excruciating pain. I moved down to where I could pull up my shirt and looked down again to check myself out.

Thinx period panties. Black, just like my T-shirt.

My stomach rolled. They had me in period underwear. And the moment my mind saw them, it made the connection with my body that I was also wet. I was lying in soiled period underwear. They basically had me in diapers. That's how they were handling me going to the bathroom.

There was no more questioning what this was. I'd do anything to get out of it.

CHAPTER SEVENTEEN

They were always together, ever since I'd become cognizant again. Noelle was never alone with me. Not like she'd been before, when I was drifting in and out of consciousness. Or maybe Gia had always been there, lurking in the shadows, and I just hadn't been able to see her. They'd only been in the room twice since the altercation. Once to feed me more soup, and once to change my underwear.

Up until yesterday, I hadn't been scared for my life. Even when I woke strapped to the bed with tape on my mouth, it still just felt surreal. Like we were playing some kind of weird game. But I was in period panties, and Noelle wasn't being forced or coerced into keeping me tied up. She was doing it on purpose and of her own free will. She might've kept Gia from hurting me yesterday, but she hadn't stopped her from keeping me tied up, and she hadn't tried to help me escape.

And earlier? When they'd come in to change me and I tried to kick Gia in the face? Noelle was the one to slap me and shove me back on the bed. She'd also been the one to wipe between my legs before sliding on a fresh pair of Thinx. I'd never been more scared or mortified in my life.

I'd been desperately hoping for an opportunity to get Noelle alone, so when she opened the door and walked in by herself seconds ago, it was like winning the lottery. I just needed a chance to talk to her without Gia. Nobody else needed to get hurt. We could make this right another way.

I studied her as she came into the room carrying a tray of food, just like she'd done before. She bustled around in the exact manner she always did whenever she was taking care of me. Her shuffle was the same. All her features. It felt like she should look like a different person, too, but she didn't. She was still Noelle.

She looked everywhere but my eyes as she slowly worked the tape off my mouth. She did it with a tenderness that wasn't there when Gia did it. She held down my skin with her other hand while she took off the sticky strip, trying to minimize the pulling and the pain. She tossed the tape into the trash can next to the bed. They used a new piece each time, ripping it off the roll with their teeth.

"Noelle," I said to her, my voice rough and raspy. I'd screamed until my throat went raw yesterday after they'd left me alone, desperately trying to get them to come back into the room or get one of the neighbors to hear me, even though Gia said the studio was soundproof and I had tape over my mouth. "Baby, please, you have to untie me. Just for a minute. Please, just untie me, and we'll talk." But she kept refusing eye contact. Just busied herself sorting the items on the tray, though everything was already in perfect order. "Please think about what you're doing. This isn't you. You're not this person. You have a heart of gold. You don't hurt people or do these kinds of things. We can end this. Right now. You and me. We can figure it out together. I know we can. Please."

She ignored me and set the tray on the nightstand next to the bed. Crackers, water, and bread next to a bowl of Campbell's soup. Like, did they suddenly not have food in the kitchen? This was ridiculous. Rationing out my food like I was some weird prisoner of war. They couldn't bring me leftovers from whatever they'd had for dinner? This was all Gia's doing.

"Look, you have every right to be angry and hurt over what happened with Paris, Noelle. You do. I can't imagine what it must've felt like to find out what I'd been a part of. And yes, I was at that party. I was in the room. But you have to believe me that I didn't know what

176

was actually happening that night. Not that it makes it okay. It doesn't make it okay. Nothing makes it better. It's like I was saying to Gia. But there are other ways to make what happened right. Even to punish me." I was talking as fast as I could—Gia might walk into the room soon. "What I did was wrong. I don't want you to think for one second that I think my behavior was okay or acceptable. You know how I've agonized over these things, Noelle. You know that. But this isn't going to make anything right. It's not. Another person died—Maddie died, and she had nothing to do with what happened to Paris. Nothing."

She pulled the spoon out of the cellophane wrapper. She was wearing one of her favorite dresses. The red one with tiny white flowers on it that hugged her body in all the right places. Made her feel sexy. That's what she always said, every time she wore it. The other thing she always said was how wearing dresses made her get in touch with her feminine self when she was falling in love. It's practically all she'd worn while we were dating. Where had she and Gia spent the day? Or the evening. For all I knew, it was the middle of the night. Wherever it'd been, they'd been busy falling in love. Her face was flushed with it. She probably still tasted like Gia.

"How did she get to you?" I asked, staring at her in disbelief. Getting her on board with punishing me for being a part of what happened with Paris didn't mean she had to fall in love with Gia. The two weren't synonymous. Or were they?

She ignored my question and just started shoveling the cheap chicken noodle soup into my mouth. Feeding me like I was a sick child. The same way she'd done it after I got horrible food poisoning on our flight back from Bali two winters ago. I didn't want to take the soup. A protest against all that was happening and everything she was doing to me. But my body wouldn't listen. I was too hungry and so thirsty, and it tasted *so* good.

"Please untie me. Just for a minute. Please, Noelle." I spoke in between the spoonfuls. "I need to sit up. Or even just move my arms. You can leave my legs tied up. Something. Anything, please. I need to stretch. You don't know how this feels. It hurts. Like, my entire body aches."

She shook her head and put a cracker in my mouth. Not so much to feed me as to shut me up. I chewed and swallowed fast. Every minute unattended mattered. "Just do my wrists, please. You can untie them and stand across the room while we talk or something. This makes me feel like an animal. And I might've done some terrible things in my life, Noelle, but I'm not an animal. You know that. Please. I just want to stretch. Please." Her posture shifted. Her eyes moved to the right—a tell that I was penetrating her emotional resolve. I kept pushing. "It's not like she'll even know you did it. And then we can talk. Really talk. Like two adults. You owe me that, Noelle. You at least owe me this. You know that."

She glanced at the door and then back at me. She was scared of Gia. She'd never been scared of me, and I was supposed to be the bad one. She spoke in a rushed voice. "Okay, I'm going to untie one arm, but that's it. Just one arm. Do you understand me? I'll give you five minutes to move around and change positions. Work the kinks out of your muscles." She held up her hand like I was one of her students that required visual representation. "Five minutes. That's it. That's all you've got."

"Thank you, oh my God, thank you so much," I gushed as excitement and adrenaline shot through me.

She bent over the bed like she was going to untie my right hand, then suddenly changed her mind and walked over to the other side of the bed to untie my nondominant hand instead. Smart move. She wasn't stupid. Her fingers hesitated on the frayed rope. I could practically see the second thoughts spinning in her head.

"I'll close my eyes and turn to the side so I can't see when you've done it," I said quickly before she changed her mind. She was seconds away from it. She kept glancing at the door behind her, like Gia could sense Noelle was about to do something she'd told her not to do. "Or, you know what? Blindfold me while you do it. Put that tape over my eyes. Then you'll know for sure I can't try anything while you're untying me, because I won't even be able to see."

She rolled her eyes at me. "I don't think we need to do all that, but turn around and look the other way while I do this."

I closed my eyes and rolled to the side as best I could in my position. This was it. This was my chance. I might not get another one. I had to be smart. Play this right. I couldn't underestimate her.

"Okay," she said within seconds, and I jerked my arm free immediately. The pure joy I felt when I could move it without restraint was indescribable. I shifted my body. My lower back cramped from being in the same position for so long, but I didn't care.

"Thank you so much. You see this?" I waved my arm around. Wiggled all my fingers in front of her before she moved across the room. "This is you, Noelle. Helping people. Being kind. Compassionate. That's who you are. This other person? Whatever you're doing? Whatever you've gotten yourself involved in? This isn't you, Noelle. Baby, it's not."

"Laurel, stop. I didn't untie you to argue with you." She shook her head, picking up the spoon like she was going to start feeding me again. But I wasn't having any of that. I'd had enough. Time to focus on what was important. I might not get another opportunity.

"What are you doing, babe?" I gave her the most pleading and pitiful look. The one she always said melted her.

"Be quiet," she hissed as she eyed the door behind her. "I'm going to put your tape back on your mouth if you can't sit there and be quiet."

"Noelle, seriously, what are you doing?" I asked again, ignoring her. "You could've killed me, hitting me with the bat. Do you know that? I probably have some permanent brain damage. How do you know my brain isn't bleeding as we speak? I need a doctor. Noelle, I need to see a doctor. You don't want to do this. What if I die?"

My words just bounced off her. They meant nothing. What was I going to do if I couldn't reach her? I had to, though. I'd counted on being able to reach her. Like if I just got a second alone with her outside

Gia's spell, I'd be able to connect. I still believed the Noelle I loved and the one that loved me was in there somewhere. But what if she wasn't?

Suddenly, there wasn't enough air to breathe in the room. My body pulsed with the desire to move. To run. To flee. But I was strapped to the bed. Which only made the awful feelings intensify.

I dropped my voice low, just in case Gia was close and could overhear. Or maybe to keep it off camera. This place probably had cameras. Why hadn't I thought of cameras before? What if they'd seen me working on the ties? I forced the questions down.

"Please listen, and think about what you're doing. There is no way that you don't get caught for this. Whatever this is. Whatever you plan on doing to me. You're screwed. The police are literally watching every single thing I do right now because they think I'm a murder suspect. You realize that, right? You don't think they've noticed I'm suddenly missing? Just disappeared. Overnight, without a trace? I mean, how suspicious does that look? Did you stop to think about that part?"

"Shut up, Laurel. Just shut up," she snapped. "You can't—"

"You have to help me. You can't let her do this to me. You just can't. You know I would never do anything to hurt someone else. Not on purpose. I'm a good person. I was just super messed up in college. I mean, I lost my dad. I wasn't coping well. But I was barely an adult. Please. You have to see that. You know me. You know I'm not a terrible person."

She ferociously shook her head. "I don't know who you are. You've lied to me our entire relationship. You never told me about Gia's sister."

"Lied to you? Come on, Noelle. That's just her putting nonsense in your head. Changing the entire narrative. You know I told you everything about my past, and part of that history was big chunks of time I didn't remember." I drilled my eyes into her, even though I could barely see her in the dimly lit room. She'd held me while I sobbed about the missing pieces. Rubbed my back while I told her how guilty I felt living such a good life when I'd hurt so many people. She told me to forgive myself, just like my sponsor had done all those years ago. "You don't remember when we got stranded in the airport over Christmas in Iowa during that snowstorm? How we watched that documentary about the father who'd killed his son in a drunk driving accident and had no memory of doing it? How hard we both cried when he received his community service award for all the hard work he'd done creating drunk driving legislation and sharing his story?" I paused for a second. I wanted every single one of those memories to come back, because I'd fought against the idea of my forgiveness as hard as she'd fought for it. So deciding to punish me now went against everything she'd always stood for. "You brought me into the bathroom and told me to look in the mirror. And what did you tell me to say to myself, Noelle?" She refused to answer, but I knew she remembered exactly how she'd told me to forgive myself. I gave her a few more beats before continuing. "You can say whatever you want and rewrite history however you see fit, but there's nothing I've hidden from you, and I've always felt awful about my past. You know that's the truth. I never had a single sober interaction with Paris. You think I wasn't just as horrified to find out about her as you must have been?"

"I don't care what you say, Laurel. I would never be able to say those kinds of things to another person. Ever." She shook her head again. Tears streamed down both cheeks. She always cried when she was upset. "I don't care how drunk I was. If I'd drank all the alcohol in the liquor cabinet and shot heroin afterward—I couldn't tell another person to take their own life." Her voice caught in her throat. She looked away, desperately trying not to break down. "People who can do that are sociopaths. You're an animal."

I shook my head. "You know that's not true. You know I'm not a terrible person."

"If you can say something like that, then you have that kind of evil inside you. Period."

"That's not fair. It just isn't. You can't act like I was just some regular college kid. I was an emotional wreck. I started drinking the day of my dad's funeral. The actual day. Do you know that? I had my first drink—a shot of whiskey that my cousin gave me on the way to my dad's burial plot—and never stopped until the day I sobered up. Eight straight years. Not a sober breath. Never a day. Do you understand me? Do you have any idea what that was like?" I'd shared my story with her before, but maybe she'd forgotten the seriousness of it. The way I used to live. But more importantly, how it ended. "And I almost died. In case you forgot that part. It got really, really dark. So terrible that I almost pulled a Paris. So don't you think for one second that I was ever okay with any of my behavior back then. And don't you dare pretend you have any idea what it's like to lose your dad at sixteen." She hung her head in shame, and I hoped she felt bad. But I kept giving it to her. I had nothing to lose at this point. Maybe this would reach her. "You want to know something else? The thing I never told anyone about my dad?" I'd never told anyone what I was about to tell her. I spent my days helping people dispel their secrets, but I'd kept my worst one. I was a bad therapist. Like a dentist with bad teeth.

Noelle held up her hand. "Laurel, don't. Stop."

I shook my head at her. "Oh no, you're going to hear this. You know how I told you that my dad worked all the time? So once a month, he'd take turns and meet one of us kids at the 7-Eleven on the corner, with coffee? Right after he finished his shift, and he'd walk us to school? It was his way of making us feel special and giving us individualized attention. We each got our turn. Morning coffee with Dad, and he always brought us a glazed doughnut. Of course, we all cherished it, since we barely ever got to see him and almost never got one-on-one time." Memories of that day rushed to the surface, and I tried not to cry. But telling the story after all these years made everything heave. It still hurt so bad. "The day before our coffee date, we got into a huge fight over a party I wanted to go to that weekend. He wouldn't let me go and refused to budge no matter how hard I begged. I was sixteen and furious. You know what it's like when you're that age. Everything is such a big deal, and I was so mad at him. So, you know what I did? To punish him? Really hurt his feelings?" I paused for a second, struggling to control my emotions. "I stood him up the next day at our coffee date. I didn't go. I took the bus instead. Didn't tell him or anyone else what I was doing. Didn't leave him a note. Just left him standing alone on the corner, with his coffee and a glazed doughnut for me. He had a heart attack on the driveway that night, and I never saw my dad again. Do you know what that does to a kid, Noelle? Because don't forget for one second—sixteen is very much still a kid."

"Stop talking," she snapped, finally having had enough. She raced over to the bed, waving her finger at me. "She said you'd try to flip things in your favor. That you'd say all these things to make me feel sorry for you. Anything to get me to let you go. To turn against her." She folded her arms across her chest. "But guess what? There's nothing you can say that's going to change the way I feel about her or about what you've done."

"What I've done?" I pointed to myself with my free hand. "How is what I've done—and I'm not saying what I did was right—but how is that any different from what you're doing to me, Noelle? What happened to the kindergarten teacher who used to tell her students that two wrongs don't make a right? Do I need to remind you how many stories you have where you used that line? You don't see the parallel?"

"Maddie was never supposed to die. We were supposed to give her an EpiPen in time." For a brief second, I saw the guilt creep onto her face. But as quick as it'd come, it was gone. Back to stone. "How were we supposed to know that was going to happen? Nobody could've predicted that."

"Okay, well, it did happen, Noelle. Someone died. An actual person with a family. An entire future and life ahead of her. One that she'd just spent a month desperately trying to put back together. A mom who's absolutely devastated. Everyone at Crystal Meadows is affected. You didn't just wreck my life. You wrecked so many other innocent people's. How is that any different than what happened with Paris? Seriously. I just—"

"Enough!" She cut me off. "You don't think I know that? You don't think I've been up every single night since it happened, unable to sleep?"

"No, Noelle." I shook my head wildly at her. "I don't. I don't think you've been up at night. I think you've been sleeping just fine. I bet Gia makes sure of it. Probably makes you c—"

She interrupted me again before I could finish my sentence. "You don't have to be crude."

"Crude? I'm in diapers." This had gone far beyond whatever punishment they'd been trying to inflict on me. We were at complete humiliation and actual harm.

"The overdose was just to get them to look through her things and find the phone. I told you, we didn't plan on actually hurting her. None of this was supposed to happen."

"Oh my God. I know you're not that naive. Gia knew. She knew exactly what would happen. There was probably never even supposed to be an EpiPen. She's the biggest—"

She cut me off. "I don't want to talk about this anymore. I'm finished." She hurried over to the bed. Carrying keys in one hand and the rope in the other. "Your time's up. You've had your five minutes to talk. Roll over like you did before." She motioned to me as she got closer. "Come on."

It happened too fast for her to register. My free hand shot out, grabbed her hair, and smashed her face down against the bed frame as hard as I could. Her eyes wide with horror and surprise. Teeth cracked against the wood. She yelped. Blood gushed from the corners of her mouth. She didn't have time to cry before I gripped her hair and brought her head down again. This time smacking her forehead. Even harder than before. The bed shook. Her entire body went limp, and she slid to the floor, landing with a harsh thud.

Jesus Christ. I just smashed Noelle's head open. But there was no time to think or feel bad. Or anything else. I just had to go.

Run.

Terror roared through me. Gia could walk in the door any moment and see what I'd done to Noelle. I wasn't strong enough to fight her in this state. I had to hurry. My head throbbed and spots danced in front of my eyes as I worked the knots on my other wrist as fast as I could. My fingers shook, but within seconds, my other hand was free, and I let out a squeal of delight.

My body cried out in agony as I bent down to free my ankles from their restraints. They were nothing compared to my wrists. The belts came off easily and effortlessly, and I flung them aside. I leaped off the bed, jumping up so fast I almost passed out. I grabbed the bed to steady myself. My legs were weak. The room moving and spinning. Adrenaline thrummed through me. Noelle was on the floor. She let out a deep, slow moan.

I scanned the room. Should I tie her up? I could use the belts. Tie her up to the bed, the same way I'd been. But that would take too much time, and I was so weak. I could barely stand up. There's no way I'd even get her on the bed.

I bolted for the front door and pummeled through it, falling onto the sidewalk in front of the guesthouse. The roar of the alarm quickly followed. A shocking surprise. Blinding security lights pierced the night sky and my eyes, making me squint in revulsion. They must've been holding me for the entire night. Or had I been trapped in there another day?

Where was I?

I desperately tried to orient myself, but I felt like I was upside down. Everything woozy. I shuffled forward, trying to run but limping despite my best efforts. My legs wouldn't cooperate with how fast I wanted to move. They kept folding underneath me like they could no longer hold my weight. I couldn't go through the main house. I didn't want to be seen on the cameras. I was going to have to go over the privacy fence.

My body screamed at me as I threw myself over. Someone grabbed my leg. I whipped around.

Noelle.

I kicked her in the head. She let go, and I pitched myself over again. But my arms were too weak, and she grabbed my ankle before I made it, pulling me back over to her side. I landed with a hard thud. Knocking the wind out of me.

I scrambled to my feet, running toward the gate, but she caught me within seconds and throttled me, sending me sprawling onto the concrete walkway. Flat on my stomach. Skinning both knees. She jumped on top of me. She grabbed my hair and snapped my head back. Much like I'd done to her seconds ago.

"Now, why'd you have to go and do something like that, Laurel?" Her voice quivered with anger. Her knee dug into my back. My lungs crushed against the sidewalk. Face flat.

"Help! Somebody help me!" I screamed as loud as I could. She slapped the back of my head, but that didn't stop me. I just kept screaming louder. "Help!" Then quickly remembering you were never supposed to yell for help when you were in trouble, because people wouldn't come. Yell *fire*. Always yell *fire*.

"Fire!" I screamed so hard it tore my throat, and in the next second, her hand slapped, sharp and stinging, straight across my face. The smack. Just like she'd hit me with the bat.

"I told you to shut up," she growled. She smashed my head into the ground and hoisted me up by my shirt, desperately trying to wrangle me back inside. But I wasn't giving up. Not without a fight.

Black combat boots.

Long, lean legs standing there, unmoving. Right leg slightly bowed out at the knee. One step. And then another. Frozen. Standing there watching us. I couldn't see enough to recognize the face because my head was smashed into the ground, but I didn't need to—it was Gia.

"Help me!" Noelle screamed at her, and then Gia came running, like it'd taken her a second to process what was happening.

She pounced on me with Noelle. Slamming me back against the concrete so hard my teeth rattled and I saw stars. Gia grabbed my arms and twisted them behind my back. Yanking me up.

"Fire!" I tried to yell again, but it came out almost a whisper because I was so out of breath. Noelle grabbed my legs while I kicked and flailed about, trying to get the pair of them off me. But they quickly overpowered me. I swung at them blindly. Screaming and yelling. Not words. Just sounds. Loud enough for all the neighbors to hear. Biting and clawing at them like a feral cat whenever they came near me, desperately trying to stop them. Connecting with any part of them I could find. Back. Neck. Hands. Stomach.

"Get her inside," Noelle said through gritted teeth. Her nostrils flared in and out, heavy with exertion. Blood dripped down her face. Stained the front of her dress. She needed stitches.

"I'm trying," Gia snapped back. Her face was covered in slick sweat. Her breath hot and panicked in my face as she held my hands behind me and shoved me through the back door of the guesthouse. Noelle slammed it shut behind us.

I let out another violent scream, my throat raw and burning. But somebody had to hear me. Somebody heard that. I gave Noelle a satisfied grin. She didn't smile back. With her face bloodied and bruised like mine, she just threw me on the floor and kicked me in the side like I was a stray dog that had just tried to bite her.

HER
(THEN)

It didn't stop with the first note. They just kept sliding them under the door. Slipping them into her bags. Sending them in the mail. Throwing them at her in the cafeteria. And it wasn't like she could just stop going to the cafeteria. She had to eat, and she was on a meal plan, so that was her only option.

Those first few days after she got the note and it started happening again, she tried really hard to keep her spirits up. Telling herself that she'd be gone soon and it wouldn't matter. People wouldn't do this to her in her new life. Nobody was going to treat her like this again.

Then she found the fake accounts all over Instagram.

Imagine what it's like to be scrolling on social media—on her own fake account, of course, because she didn't do anything with her actual one anymore—and coming across yourself. It's like getting kicked in the teeth. Someone had taken all her old pictures and created an Instagram account: *Attention Whore*. That's what they called it. Thousands of hateful comments about her. Some having to do with what happened. Others having nothing to do with it at all. People just spewing viral hate.

That wasn't the only account. There were multiple fake accounts. And not just on Instagram—on all the platforms. Spam accounts. Accounts others had created. That was when she realized her tormentors were worldwide and there was no getting away from them. Some of them were her classmates, sure, but there were hundreds from neighboring schools that had never even met her. People from other countries weighing in. She became a target. An anonymous dumping ground. A dirty toilet. A graffiti wall that got tagged, over and over again, with their insults.

Hurting other people made them feel good. That's what this world was full of. People that preyed on others' misery and enjoyed it. She just wasn't sure if she wanted to be here, around such bad people, anymore. She could leave everything, just like she'd been planning to do since the hospital. Pack all her bags and go. Load up the car and drive far, far away until she found a place to become a different person.

But even if she became a different person, somehow beautiful again, she still lived in a world that was so ugly. Hideous. Social media had inflicted humanity with a terrible virus that turned people's brains into mush and made them vile creatures. It was only going to get worse. Not better.

That's when she knew it didn't matter. That even if she left and went far, far away, she still lived with these people and in a world that hurt her heart too much to exist in it. She wasn't alone in her reasoning. People were starting to decide what quality of life was considered worth living in their opinion. Like Jolanda Fun, the thirty-four-year-old woman from the Netherlands who died by euthanasia on her birthday because of her depression and other mental health issues. She'd even prepared her own funeral, with handwritten notes to the guests where she described being born in love and choosing to let go of her hard life in love to gain the peace she'd been searching for.

She wasn't sure that's what she'd say in her note. But if she did it, if something like that was what she decided to do, then she was definitely going to write her own eulogy.

There were so many other people like Jolanda. Some physically ill. Others tortured by mental illness. All with the same decision. Other people just like her. They'd asked similar questions. Found alternative answers. Maybe she didn't have to drive away and become a different person. Maybe it was okay not to want to live here at all.

CHAPTER EIGHTEEN

My stomach seized with another cramp. It'd been doing that all night long. Ever since they tied me back up after I tried to escape. I'd been in agony ever since. My insides rolling and twisting. I didn't know if it was from dehydration, getting kicked in the side so many times, or being stuck in the same position for so long. Either way, I'd never been in so much pain.

I wanted to wrap my arms around my stomach, but I couldn't. They were strapped to the bed again. They'd upped their game and had me in four-point restraints, with zip ties instead of the rope. Panic blurred the edges of my vision as another sharp spasm gripped my stomach. This one so painful it made me nauseous.

What would happen if I got in real trouble while I was here? Like, what if my appendix was bursting right now and leaking poison throughout my entire body? And they didn't check on me until the morning. Or tonight. It could be day or night. I had no idea. There wasn't an ounce of outside light getting into this room.

What would I do if something was seriously wrong with me and they didn't come back for hours? That was entirely possible. It already felt like they'd been gone forever. What if they never came back? Just left me here alone in Gia's guesthouse? How long would it take someone to find me?

Gia had been screaming at Noelle when they left.

"How could you untie her? What the hell were you thinking?"

I couldn't make out Noelle's response. All I could hear were her sobs. Great big hiccuping ones in between her apologies. I've never heard her cry like that, and it would've broken my heart if I wasn't so angry with her.

I meant everything I said to her earlier. She didn't get to come at me like she was the great purveyor of social justice when she'd just literally killed a person herself. Her actions, whatever part she'd played, had destroyed an entire family. How was she any different than I was? And how did she not see it? It was just like I told her earlier. She was the same as me.

Sending those text messages to Paris wasn't all that different from Noelle messaging Maddie. And she remembered doing it. She'd been in her right mind. I'd never tell anyone to hurt themselves any more than she would. And if I'd sent a text to Paris, it was out of the age-old desire to fit in and because I didn't want the other girls to turn against me. Life was all about self-preservation back then. Paris wasn't the only one they bullied.

Even though I knew Noelle had done it, part of me still couldn't believe she'd sent Maddie all those messages and pretended to be me. Because that part had to be her. She was the only one that could've in the middle of the night. How had Maddie never seemed weird in any of our sessions?

Maybe Maddie didn't know it was me on the phone. She never called me by my actual name during all our exchanges. Who did Maddie think she was talking to? I hadn't had time to scroll through all the messages from that night. My investigation had been cut short by the blow to the head with a baseball bat.

There was no way Noelle would do something like this if she didn't think it was justified. Or would she? Because never in my wildest dreams did I imagine Noelle would leave me for somebody else. Yet here we were. I literally never thought about it. I worried about a lot of things, but not that. She'd always loved only me. Not that she hadn't had other partners or been in love before. But she was just like me—only getting married once. That's why both of us had waited so long to do it. We'd wanted to make sure we were with the right one.

And she was my one.

In the same way I thought I was hers. Our connection was instantaneous. That lesbian imprinting on each other's soul that happens almost immediately with certain people. She'd been like that. From the moment I spotted her from across the bar, in her white T-shirt and high-waisted mom jeans, sipping on an IPA. We still argued over who saw who first. But I'd definitely been the one to make the first move. Leaving my friends behind and strutting across the bar to introduce myself. All I'd had to do was make her laugh once, and I was a goner.

She grew up outside Chicago and spent most of her childhood in trailer parks. Her dad drove a semitruck, so he was never around. And her mom worked two jobs—one as a waitress and another as a security guard at night. Noelle raised her brothers and sisters, just like mine raised me. She was the oldest, and their babysitter, but she didn't care. Creating elaborate summer camps and game nights for them at home. The things she did with them were so much fun—water balloon fights, tag, detailed costumes—that it wasn't long before other kids from the trailer park joined in. And she welcomed them with open arms. Instead of being bitter and resentful about being robbed of her childhood and forced to be an adult way too soon, she turned it into something beautiful—her love for working with children.

What would the parents of her students think, when it came out that she'd held her own wife hostage with her . . . what, lover? Girlfriend? What were they to each other? I was obsessed with how it started. How Noelle ever crossed that line. I thought I knew her better than anyone else, but I might not have known her at all. It was a terrifying thought.

People talk about grief being like an invisible string. Like there's a string connecting you and your loved ones that can't be severed, even by death. And I'd always felt that string. That was the thing about Noelle. I felt her with me always, even when we weren't physically together. She was as natural to me as breathing. Our love was supposed to transcend time, distance, and space. She'd always been mine.

Turns out, I was never hers. Whatever that invisible string was—some people called it a cord—ours was broken. Severed. Just like that.

This. Me. Right here. This was the plan. It wasn't about Maddie or Spencer or even Gia's sister. It was about me. Getting me in this exact spot. And doing what? Torturing me? How did this end?

Noelle stopped me from getting away. She could've let me go free, and she didn't. She didn't have to chase me or tackle me. She actually stopped me and forced me back into this room, where she tied me up all over again. I still couldn't believe I'd bashed her face in like that. But I had to be sure I knocked her out, otherwise I hadn't stood a chance of getting away.

Another cramp seized my stomach. Followed by another. I couldn't breathe in between the waves of nausea, coming and going faster and faster with each spasm. I didn't know how much time had passed since I woke up in pain. It could've been minutes. Days. Hours. The one thing I knew was that if I was going to be here, I was going to need to figure out a way to measure time. Did I just count? What if I lost track? How would I know? It was so disorienting. This was why sensory deprivation was used as a torture technique to get war prisoners to talk.

Gia was the one controlling this. Orchestrating the entire thing, like it was another one of her famous shows. She was a director, which meant she thought about all the things, considered every angle. So she didn't just happen to accidentally fall in love with Noelle. She'd strategically roped my wife into this. How had she done it? Noelle might be in love with Gia, but Gia's love had a purpose.

She'd plotted every single step. Thought of every single scenario.

She needed Noelle, or Noelle wouldn't be here for this.

I shifted in bed, sitting up slowly. My body already so stiff. Like I'd been on an airplane for hours. Gia didn't need Noelle for anything that happened with Maddie at Crystal Meadows. She could've easily done all that herself, especially the phone. In fact, it probably would've been safer and easier to do it that way. None of her plan hinged on having someone help her. Or be in love with her. The realization continued to settle into my bones. Having an accomplice, and then subsequently falling in love with said accomplice, was extremely risky. It was a huge liability. She would never take that chance.

Unless it was part of the plan. A much bigger plan. One that went way beyond this.

If any of this was an accident. That's how I'd been perceiving things until now. A revenge plot gone horribly wrong.

What if it wasn't? What if that was just Noelle's experience, and what Gia wanted us to think? Maybe she actually needed Noelle for the next step. If Gia had meticulously plotted and planned out everything, did she set it up so that I would discover her the way I did? Was all this actually part of it? Had we been playing into her hand all along?

I had a sinking feeling deep in the pit of my guts that this was only the beginning. There were multiple parts to her plan, and Maddie might've only been a tool to get to me. If Gia had intentionally killed Maddie—and every cell of my being fought against the possibility that it might be true—then she probably didn't have a problem killing someone else. If she'd ended Maddie's life, she could just as easily end mine.

The next wave of agony gripped me and sent explosive diarrhea down my legs. The foul smell immediately filled the room. Another cramp. Another mess. What was wrong with me?

And then it hit me with startling clarity—what if they weren't just feeding me soup? What if they were poisoning me? Gia hadn't needed Noelle's help prior to this. But she needed her for whatever happened next, and I was pretty sure the next part included getting rid of me forever.

CHAPTER NINETEEN

I was in my thirties, so I'd lived long enough to have all kinds of stomach flu strains, a couple of bad bouts of Covid, and the occasional food poisoning over the years. But I'd never experienced anything like the torment happening in my stomach. My cramps felt like dull knives cutting through my insides. Maybe worse. I was certain the next wave would kill me.

Everything was wet and foul smelling. My hair stuck to my forehead. T-shirt clung to my body, damp with sweat. Diarrhea. Vomit. Sweat. All of it puddled around me.

They weren't just feeding me soup, and this had nothing to do with my injuries. They were poisoning me. Trying to kill me. The smell alone was enough to convince me something toxic was in my body. What was the plan? Say that I'd overdosed? And then what? How would they explain all my injuries? They'd have to explain theirs too. They might've overpowered me, but I'd made plenty of good skin-to-skin contact with them. Enough to ensure they were marked and bruised too. Noelle probably had a matching broken nose. What was she going to tell people about that? And I'm certain I knocked a few of her teeth out. Her mouth was so bloody, it was hard to know for sure, but her front teeth might even be gone.

I didn't feel bad. Not for any of it. Especially not now.

They hadn't been back to check up on me. Not once since the fight. They might never come back, and I was trying not to let that freak me out any more than it already did. I just had to hold on long enough for someone to rescue me. There's no way one of the neighbors didn't hear us screaming and fighting. No way. You couldn't just ignore that, and this wasn't the kind of neighborhood where things like that normally happened.

I kept reminding myself about Detectives Boone and Wallace whenever I'd start to spiral into complete panic—they were looking for me, and they wouldn't stop until they found me. Detective Boone was a pit bull, and she'd sunk her teeth deep into me. No way she'd just let me go. She'd find me. It was only a matter of time. I just had to stay calm. Not lose it until then. I could fall apart afterward, when I was safe.

Noelle's plan was simple. Help it look like I was having an affair with Maddie while she was in the treatment center under my care. Maddie was young and vulnerable. Neither of which would've looked good for me in the court of public opinion, which was really the only résumé that mattered. They both knew that. Probably why they'd taken it a step further as if that wasn't bad enough. Made it look like Maddie was scared of me and my feelings for her. That she felt threatened by all of it. Lastly, create a scenario where I tried to kill my younger mistress by giving her medication I knew she was allergic to.

I believed Noelle when she said they were supposed to give her an EpiPen and intervene on time. And maybe that was right. It was hours after I'd given her the pills that she had the allergic reaction. It was entirely possible they'd been planning for her to have a reaction almost immediately, and it happening at night instead was unexpected.

This could have all accidentally fallen in Gia's lap.

Ultimately, did it matter, though? I was here. Trapped. And by the feeling in my stomach, Gia was trying to kill me, and it was working.

This was hard. The barely breathing. The pain. My insides being shredded. The foul smell of diarrhea making me sick.

Noelle would kill to keep Gia. As much as I wanted to stay alive, I couldn't help but burn with anger and resentment. She'd never loved me enough to kill for me. Maybe I was as sick as Noelle was, because it made me so jealous.

HER
(THEN)

Once you decide to let go and make the conscious decision to leave, the most peaceful process takes over. This was how hospice patients must feel, especially the ones that were in a lot of pain. Knowing she didn't have to live a second longer in a world full of cruel and horrible people brought her so much comfort. Her life had been out of her control for so long that she'd forgotten what it felt like to not be a victim. To have her life in her own hands again felt indescribably wonderful.

It motivated her to get out of bed in the morning, and she started planning Leaving Day like you'd plan any other big event—a wedding, birthday, engagement party. Like any big day, she wanted it to be perfect. She started thinking about what she wanted to eat that day and the night before, which led her to make a list of all the restaurants she wanted to eat at before Leaving Day. There were so many foods she'd never tried, and others that she loved so much she wanted to make sure she tasted them one more time.

She picked Saturday, June seventh, as the day. Exactly one week after finals. It was important to finish the semester. Which felt weird. Like, what did it matter? But she didn't want to look like a quitter. That's not how she wanted people to see her. She didn't want to waste her parents' money either. They'd sacrificed a lot to get her to college.

So, she had sixteen days. Sixteen days to eat at all her favorite restaurants. As soon as she'd put all that on paper, it brought up other activities and things she wanted to do or see one final time. Before she knew it, she was ferociously scribbling a bucket list. She stayed up all night doing it, and by the end, there were fifty-four things on her list, ranging from restaurants to roller coasters. That was a lot to get done in sixteen days, but she could do it.

That's what she started doing in between classes and homework. Crossing things off the list. She went to Six Flags for the last time, and took along with her a childhood best friend that she hadn't seen in years. Seeing her again had been on the list, too, and she got to cross two items off at the same time. Not to mention she had the absolute best day. It was wonderful.

They went on all their old favorite rides and tried all the new ones. Screaming until their throats were raw on all the scary parts, and laughing so hard at each other that their stomachs hurt. Melting the cotton candy on their tongues and staining their teeth blue. They even took a picture in the old-fashioned photo booth. Both of them grinning so wide, ear to ear, with their superhero capes on.

"Today was truly perfect, and so much fun." Mary thanked her as they walked back to their cars at the end of the night. "I can't remember the last time I had a day like this, and didn't realize how much I needed it. So thank you so much. And seriously, when can we do it again?"

She'd given Mary a huge hug, holding on to her friend much longer than she usually would. Trying to soak in every piece of her. Remember what she felt like. What she smelled like. That's all she was taking with her when she left. All her favorite things. None of the bad.

The hardest part was writing the letters to her family. At first, she'd started writing each of them an individual letter, but quickly changed her mind. Writing out the explanation for her choice over and over again was too much work, but she couldn't skip it because she had to let them know why she'd done it. She was going to hurt them forever, and they deserved to know why she felt it justified. Her sister would never forgive her or understand, but at least she'd try to make her. She didn't want any of them to think they weren't reason enough to stay. If their love were enough to keep her here, she'd stay forever. But it wasn't. She had to make them understand that. Which meant she had to explain herself in each letter, and it would've taken her forever to finish. Gobbled up so much of her time, and she needed to maximize every minute.

So, she wrote one big letter to her family. Starting with an explanation at the top, then going through each of them one by one, saying the special things she wanted to say, like the people who wrote multipage Christmas letters and tucked them in with the family holiday cards. Except instead of listing all the important milestones and achievements that had happened over the year, she described what she loved most about them and her favorite memory of a moment they'd shared. It was surreal writing the introduction, knowing they'd read it at her funeral because she specifically requested it in the letter she left for the coroner. She wanted people to understand her choice. The thought of them wondering if they could've done anything to prevent it was too much.

Writing the family letter was the hardest step, and making the funeral arrangements a close second. She hated that part, too, and that her parents would have to pay for her service and burial, but at least it was cheaper than what they'd pay for three more years of college. She took care of the hard decisions for them. She didn't want them to think about whether she wanted to be buried or cremated. They'd never had those conversations before, and she didn't want them worrying about what she'd want at a time when they'd be so emotionally distraught. Her mom would second-guess herself no matter what she chose, and she couldn't do that to her mom. It had been tough to think about those things, but she'd signed off on the last sections of her will yesterday. The hard parts were done.

Now she could just focus on her list.

CHAPTER TWENTY

The door creaked open.

"Oh my God, what is that smell?" Gia's voice first. Quickly followed by Noelle's.

"That's so awful. I don't know if I can come in here."

I wanted to tell her to stay. *No. Please. Don't leave me alone with her.* But I had to save all my strength. Every single ounce of it. I wouldn't fight. Not until it was time. Not until I was ready.

There might've been a gag from one of them as they walked over. I wasn't sure. I kept my eyes closed. I couldn't imagine what I looked like on the bed, but I was too far gone to care about my appearance or even be embarrassed. Their plan was to kill me. At least it was Gia's. That much I was sure of, and I wanted them to think I was nearly dead already. Maybe then they'd move my body.

That might give me an opportunity to get away.

Or maybe by then I'll have been rescued by the detectives. I've definitely been gone long enough for them to be looking for me now.

I wasn't giving up hope.

But I wanted Gia and Noelle to think so. That I was close to death. Then I could see what they were planning next. Whatever they'd given me was pummeling my kidneys. There was a dull ache in my back. Like I'd strained the muscles on both sides. But I'd put my body through hell before. There was still a chance as long as I didn't stop breathing, and there was plenty of energy left in my breath. I held on to that chance.

Funny—I'd spent so much of my life wanting to die, but now that the possibility was right in front of me, the only thing I wanted to do, more than anything else, was live. I kept hearing my dad's voice calling out my name.

Laurel. Softly. Gently.

A few seconds later, again. *Laurel.*

At first, I thought it meant I was already dead and he was coming for me. Then I realized I had a fever. A super-high one. I was delirious and shaking, alternating between feeling boiling hot to feeling ice cold. I shivered so hard I bit the inside of my cheek. Noelle and Gia hovered over me now, like they'd hovered over me so many times before.

"Rise and shine, sleepyhead," Gia called out like she used to do in the mornings at Crystal Meadows. She loved waking the clients up. She always said it was one of her favorite parts. That, and the meditation in the late afternoon. Crystal Meadows felt like another lifetime ago. Where was everyone? How were they doing? I missed them. Would I ever see them again?

Of course I would. I was getting out of here. I needed to stop thinking that way.

I kept my eyes closed. Made my breathing purposefully slow and labored. I wanted Gia and Noelle to think I was really struggling and having a hard time. I was, but they needed to *know* that. They had to see it was serious.

"Is she supposed to breathe like that?" Noelle asked, noticing immediately. Her voice filled with concern and maternal care.

"She's fine," Gia snapped. It was the first time I'd heard her take a tone other than loving and kind with Noelle. She obviously didn't like her being worried about me, or maybe the stress was finally getting to her. Either way, it felt like progress and made me happy. But I forced myself to keep a straight face.

"I don't know, Gia," she said, and there was no mistaking the sound of nerves in her voice. "Why is she so sick? What's all this? I don't understand."

The way she asked let me know she had no idea about the soup. Just like I'd suspected. Things might feel like they were spiraling out of control for Noelle, but that was only because Gia intended things to feel that way.

"Probably because of her concussion," Gia said without a second thought. "That's what happens when you get hit so hard in the head, and she got really jostled around yesterday when the two of you were fighting. There's a good chance her brain is swelling."

I might've had a fever, but I didn't miss the concussion-and-fighting comment pointed right at Noelle. Making it feel like this was her responsibility. That she'd put me in this condition. Which wasn't exactly true, but it would work to make Noelle feel guilty and easier to manipulate if she thought she was responsible for what was happening to me.

Cold water splashed my face, and I instinctively flinched and opened my eyes.

"Wake up, sleepyhead," Gia said again. The sadistic smile she always wore whenever she looked down on me plastered across her face. "How you feeling?"

I glared at her. With as much hate for her as she had for me. But then I quickly remembered my plan and forced myself to look somber and sick. I couldn't show emotion or that I had any fight left in me. They had to think I was weak. Totally nonthreatening.

"After the events a few days ago, we thought it was time for a little family meeting. Now, I'm not sure how much attention you were paying when I explained how things would work. So far you haven't done a very good job following along, but hopefully, you'll be able to figure this one out. They left Paris in the back room for sixty-two hours before the construction crew found her, and you've got about three hours left to go for yourself. She sat in the same, you know." She pointed to me and wrinkled her nose in disgust. "Her own filth. But in the meantime, we have an assignment for you. Here's what you're going to do for us." She walked over to the chair sitting underneath the window with blackout curtains taped over it. They still had yet to turn on a light in this room.

Noelle stood behind her, slightly hidden, but I could tell she was holding Gia's hand. Gripping it tightly. Even though it was dark, I could still see part of her face. Unlike Gia, who looked smug and satisfied, Noelle looked anxious. She was trying not to be, but I knew her well enough to know. I recognized the rigidity in her neck. The way her shoulders were all hunched up. And if I could see her feet, I'd bet her toes were tapping against the soles of her shoes.

Good. She wasn't all gone.

Gia pulled a notebook and pen out of a red backpack and walked over to me. She waved them in the air as she strode back across the room, like she'd found something important that'd been missing.

"Remember these?" She flicked on the light. My eyes flinched in horror. The brightness physically hurting them after having been in the dark for so long. But that didn't matter. I quickly scanned the room.

The window had been taped down with darkening blinds. Guitars were stacked against the other corner. A small fridge. A flat-screen TV.

I could break the window. It wasn't like it had bars. But it wouldn't be as easy to get out of the zip ties around my wrists and ankles. They'd upped their game this time. And I wasn't going to be able to do anything without them noticing, because the red light in the corner of the room told me they'd started recording me. Watching me the same way we used to watch the clients at Crystal Meadows. Where were they now? How would they respond to all this?

Gia waved the tenth-step journal in the air while she smiled. She had a black eye from the fight, and a bunch of scratches on her left cheek. How would she explain that to the police the next time she saw them? Noelle looked gruesome. Her face was as bloodied and beat up as mine. There was no way they had Noelle out in public like this. What explanation would they give? She clearly looked like she'd been beaten. And there was no mistaking it—I'd knocked out her front teeth. She was barely opening her mouth.

"I just thought there was nothing more appropriate for you to write your letter in than one of these tenth-step journals." Gia opened the notebook, flipped a few pages, and then handed it to me, as if my hands were actually free to take it from her and read it. She pointed to the page she'd found. "Right here." She tapped it. Her fingernails loud. Click-clacking on the page. "Right here, where it says *'Have you kept something to yourself that should be discussed with another person at once?'* This is where you're going to tell them exactly what you've been keeping to yourself."

I shook my head. Shook it again, ignoring the pain thrumming through me.

"Oh yes, honey. That's exactly what you're going to do. You're going to write down that you're a horrible person. That you've been living with just as many secrets as all the clients you treat." She tapped the pages again, just in case I'd forgotten where she wanted me to put all the things she was describing. "You'll tell them it goes all the way back to when you were drinking in college. That you helped kill one of your sorority pledges and you've never been able to live with the guilt. How you left her to be raped. That you continued to torture her with your friends afterward. Bullying and taunting her. How you sent her the text telling her to kill herself months after the assault. You're going to write all that right here." She pointed to the paper. "But that's not where you're going to stop. You're going to tell them you had an affair with Maddie while she was at Crystal Meadows. That you were the one she was scared of, and that you gave her the ibuprofen because she threatened to expose you."

Gia was determined to take everything from me until there was nothing left. She wouldn't stop until she'd destroyed all I valued, including my dignity and my respect. She'd left nothing untouched. She'd ruined my love. My career. My legacy. It would be forever tarnished from this incident, even if I managed to clear my name. People wouldn't look at me the same way ever again. And the fact that I'd had an affair with a client who was barely an adult? She ensured my personal reputation would be just as badly damaged.

She wanted to torture me first. It wasn't enough to end my life. She wanted me to suffer too. The worst part was that I couldn't blame her for it. As awful as it was for her to do all this to me, it was even more awful what they'd done to Paris, and the part I'd played.

Still. I wanted to live.

"Gia, listen to me. I can still tell people what I've done. I can take accountability and responsibility for my actions. If that's what you want. Someone to take responsibility for what happened to Paris—I'll do it. I will. You have my word," I begged.

She shook her head. Maybe at some point she'd wanted that and it would've sufficed, but not anymore. It'd been too long. The wound had too much time to fester and grow toxic. She didn't just want me to take responsibility for her sister's death. She wanted to punish me for it too.

"I can't sign this letter, Gia. I can't."

She sneered at me. "Oh yes you can, and you will."

"And if I don't?"

She motioned to the corner where Noelle stood arranging the food on my tray. She was wearing a dress again. An actual dress, during this moment. Their outfits kind of coordinated. Gia bent down next to my face so Noelle couldn't hear what she was saying. She pointed at Noelle and whispered, "I'm going to hurt her. Right in front of you. And I'm going to make you watch."

"No." I shook my head hard. "No," I said again, just to emphasize the point.

Pleasure radiated from her eyes. She'd been waiting for this moment for years. Probably played it in her mind a thousand times. "Oh, I'm going to hurt her if you don't. You can believe that. In the most painfully slow way possible." She leaned even closer. Her lips brushing against my ear as she whispered, "I'd probably start with a little bit of boiling water sprinkled on her body. Just drip. Drip. Drip. She has such sensitive skin, you know." I writhed against the bed, desperate to make her stop, but she was too far gone; drunk on revenge. "Next, I'd move to slicing her skin open . . . or you know what? I changed my mind. Maybe we stick with the theme and I'd just burn her with a cigarette. I still have like half a pack out there on the patio somewhere, I think." She motioned behind her, flashing me another smile.

I jerked my head to the side. Away from her face. Her awful words. "Please stop. Don't hurt her, Gia. Please, Gia. She didn't have anything to do with this. Do whatever you want with me. Just please, leave her alone. I'm begging you."

She gave a casual shrug. "Like I said, all you have to do is write out your confession exactly as I instructed and your little wifey will be fine." She lifted her head and raised her body before calling out to Noelle in the sweetest of voices, "Honey, are you almost ready with that soup? I think our little prisoner is really hungry tonight, but I don't think I blame her. Do you? She's had a long, emotional day, and we've just given her some tough news to handle."

My blood froze in my veins. She wouldn't hurt Noelle. She couldn't. But she would. I could see it in her eyes. The way she was looking at me while she spoke to her. My grandmother used to babysit us a bunch when we were kids, and she was super religious even though my parents weren't at all.

"You know why I believe in God, Laurel?" she'd say every Sunday, after she'd dragged me to church with her and made me sit through the entire boring service. "Because there's pure evil in this world. I know that because I've seen it, and, well, everything in this world runs by the laws of science. If there's pure evil, then there's got to be pure good. That's God."

I'd never really understood her words before, but that's because I'd lived a life free of evil. Until now. But there it was. Staring me in the face with a smile.

There was no doubt in my mind that Gia would hurt Noelle. I'd never believed her love for Noelle was real. Noelle had always been a pawn in this. She'd just gotten lucky that Noelle cracked me upside the head with a baseball bat. Gia probably hadn't seen that one coming when she'd devised her master plan to exact her revenge on me for my role in her sister's death. But it'd only worked in her favor. Gia was a brilliant mastermind.

Noelle had played right into her hand. Showed her just how committed she was. I wasn't going to be able to reach Gia. That was a given. I furtively glanced at Noelle. How would she feel if she knew their plan included killing me, or that Gia had threatened to hurt her if I didn't do what she wanted? Had she told her that part? Or did she just think this was where it all ended? Where I wrote out a confession to everything I'd done after Gia had her time to punish me? And then what? We all just go back to our lives like none of this had happened?

What about Maddie? The other clients at Crystal Meadows? That whole situation is just brushed under the rug? How would that even work? How was Noelle not thinking about any of this? What happened to my anxiety-ridden queen? Who overthought every scenario ten thousand different ways. She'd suddenly lost her intelligence with this one?

This was the love. The crazy love. The delusional kind. The kind you read about in the major headlines. That made middle school teachers fall in love with their students and send them completely inappropriate pictures. That made Gypsy-Rose kill her mom. Husbands murder their wives. Mistresses poison their lovers. How did you do that? How'd you cross over from regular love into delusion? Into sickness?

Because this? Right here? This was la-la land.

But no matter what, Noelle was still my wife, and I loved her more than any person on this planet. I couldn't let Gia hurt her, and I knew that she would if I didn't do what she asked.

"Untie me, and give me the pen," I said, staring her straight in the face so there was no mistaking my seriousness. "I'll write the letter. I'll do whatever you want me to do. Just please don't hurt her."

HER
(THEN)

She pushed through the heavy wooden courthouse doors and stepped onto the sidewalk. The sun beamed down on her. The wind brushed against her face as she walked toward her car. She'd just left the district attorney's office. Meeting with the attorney definitely wasn't on the list, but she'd gone anyway, just to see what she had to say. And the district attorney was fired up.

It was nothing like she'd expected. The DA greeted her in the reception area and thanked her repeatedly.

"I know this is so hard and difficult for you," the woman said, placing a hand on her back as she walked her down to the hallway and into her office. "But I'm going to help you get through this in the least traumatic way possible. And I'm also going to make sure that asshole never gets a chance to do to another person what he did to you."

She was determined to hit Aaron with the stiffest penalties. The woman shared her own story with her. She was one of the statistics too—one in four. She kept saying "I wish I'd been brave enough to come forward."

Over and over again. Turns out, it's one of the reasons she does what she does.

For a second, she almost told the woman. Not about the second attack, but about what she was planning to do—Leaving Day. The district attorney was practically a stranger, but she felt safer with her in that office than she had in a long time. But she couldn't bring herself to do it while she was there. Now she couldn't stop thinking about what she might've said if she had. Would the DA have been disappointed? She'd been so proud of her.

The attorney was convinced she could throw the book at him. Usually, in situations like this, it's just his word against hers. But even though it'd been weeks since the attack, she still had the clothes she'd worn the night it happened. She'd balled them up and thrown them into the back of her closet. Unwashed. His DNA all over them. Carl had been the one to tell her to take them when she went to the station and made the initial report. Turns out being anemic was lucky in this case. She'd been covered in angry bruises from the attack, and still had fading bruises in all the spots he'd grabbed her. Spots that corroborated her story.

They'd gotten another girl to come forward. A junior. The same thing had happened to her last year. Seeing another girl's story on TV had given her the courage to share what he'd done to her too. She'd been too afraid before, but she wanted to help now. She'd said thinking about him doing it to somebody else had enraged her.

Outside the DA's office, she opened the car door and slid into the driver's seat. Everything felt different. The world had shifted. Or come back to alignment, like the GPS on her life had finally recalculated.

She couldn't leave.

In any way.

She had to stay. A girl had come forward to help. What would it do to that girl if she ceased to exist? She knew how much courage it took to share what had happened to her. What an emotional journey she must've gone through to walk through those police station doors and ask to speak to someone. She wanted it to mean something for her. She wanted the girl to get her justice. She wanted her own.

And it looked like they might actually get it.

It was more than that, though, she realized as she drove away from the station. It'd been fourteen days since she started working on her bucket list. She only had two items left on it. A double-fudge banana split from Tangoes on Third. She'd planned to do it tonight after she made dinner. She was meeting Mary again. It was the third time they'd hung out since Six Flags. She'd unknowingly done eight items on the list.

That was the thing. Even last night. She'd thought about how she was almost done with the list, and instead of being excited for the big day, she found herself wondering if there was anything else she'd forgotten that she wanted to do before the day got here. She had this overwhelming panic that maybe she wanted to go to Six Flags again. Ride the Superman ride one more time. What if she wanted to have Bob's Sirloin or the banana split again? It'd all been so good, and Mary and she had so much fun watching all the dogs play in the park afterward.

As the sun faded behind her along with the courthouse, she felt the turn. The final shift. Not just in the world, but inside herself.

She was still here. And maybe that meant she was supposed to be. Maybe it meant there was still a place for her. Another side to the pain. More people that were good than bad.

She remembered an influencer she'd seen once, and the thought made her laugh out loud. Because no matter how hard she'd fought against it, the virus had gotten into her mind and rotted it from the inside too. But anyway. Her name was Amy or Andy—or maybe it didn't even start with an A. But she saw her talk about her last attempt.

About the EMS worker who found her that night as she sat next to the road fighting the help she so desperately needed. Wanting to throw herself off the balcony, and at the same time wanting to throw herself into his arms. He'd held out his hand to her, to pull her up, both from the ground and the bottom of her soul, and asked her, "Can you get up just one more time?"

She'd felt that one in her guts the first time she'd watched it. She felt it more even now. And her answer was the same as the influencer's had been—yes.

She would try again. Another time. She could do it right here. Get up again. Create another list. She could always save the date.

CHAPTER TWENTY-ONE

I'd been frantically trying to loosen the ties around my wrists. So far, nobody had been in since I wrote out my confession, and I hadn't heard anything except the sound of my own breathing. I was scared that meant nobody was watching me anymore either. That maybe I'd been completely abandoned. But they couldn't just leave me back here to rot. Even if the neighbors hadn't heard us struggling outside—which I couldn't imagine that they hadn't—but if for some reason they hadn't, they had to notice the smell by now. I smelled like a dead rat trapped inside the walls of a house.

Gia and Noelle hadn't thought this through. They weren't criminals. They were amateurs. They hadn't planned for any of this. For Chrissakes, the belt around my ankle was Louis Vuitton. They'd probably ordered these zip ties from Amazon.

I'd been working on them so long, my fingers ached. There was no need to duct-tape me anymore. Not only was the studio soundproofed, but they were also playing music on all the speakers outside it now too. I could scream as loud as I wanted and nobody was going to hear me.

My heart sank when Gia walked into the room alone. She flicked on the switch, filling the room with light and making me squint. I didn't feign sleep. I wanted her to look right in my eyes and see how sick I was.

"Hey, you," she said as she got closer. Her right eye was rimmed in black and purple. There were big scratches on her cheek and her neck.

I'd made sure of it. I wanted their skin underneath my fingernails. As much DNA as I could get. She was going to have a hard time explaining all that. I hoped the detectives showed up at her house unannounced.

It was an eerie thought. Imagining them up in the front of the property having conversations about the case while I lay captive back here. Just a few feet from them. Whatever scenarios they were creating to explain Maddie's death, none of them included this. That much I was sure of.

I stared back at Gia lifelessly. Letting spit puddle in my mouth, then drool out the corner of my lips and dribble down my chin. I shivered without even having to try. I willed her to feel sorry for me. To have some kind of compassion, but her eyes were stone.

She carried a red Popsicle like she was bringing me the most delicious treat, and I clenched my jaw instinctively. I'd starve to death or let whatever she'd already fed me kill me before I took anything else from her. She walked straight up to the bed and leaned down, placing it on my lips. I could feel the cold on my lips, but I kept them tightly closed.

"Open your mouth, hon. This is going to taste so good to you." Gia gazed down at me—feigning kindness—but I didn't trust her for a second. I jerked my head to the side, and she immediately looked offended. "You don't like the treat? I made it especially for you. Thought it'd help you with the dehydration. Get some of your strength back up."

Is that what she'd told Noelle they were doing? Did Noelle even know Gia was in here with me right now? Where was she? My eyes frantically scanned behind her, but the door was still closed, and there was no sign of Noelle.

Gia grabbed my face with her other hand and tried to shove the Popsicle into my mouth, but I refused to budge. Rage filled her features. Unlike Noelle, she'd transformed throughout this experience. Her face grown hard and brittle like that of an old woman who'd been through three husbands and a couple of bad bouts of cancer. She squeezed the back of my jaw, painfully forcing it open, and smashed the ice inside my mouth. She clamped my mouth shut before I could spit it out. I struggled back and forth, refusing to swallow, but it didn't matter. The Popsicle melted in my mouth. The juice slid down my throat despite my best efforts. Cold. Thick. Syrupy.

I recognized the sweet feeling of opiates almost immediately. The feeling in the back of my throat. Candy-coated dreams. And then sweet nothingness.

It was just like before.

I couldn't open my eyes.

But I didn't need to. I could smell it. Feel it in my bones. I was home. Oriental Noir. The lavender bubbles around me. Noelle's melodic voice surrounding me, and in the next moment, I remembered she wasn't so sweet. Or nice. I tried to pull away, but I couldn't. All I could do was fall back to sleep, just like before.

Awake again.

They were still washing my body. The two of them. We were back home at our house. The big white soaking tub. Just like the night I'd come home from Crystal Meadows and told Noelle about Maddie's accident.

"Make sure you really scrub underneath her fingernails"—that's what Gia kept saying to Noelle. Her voice frantic and hurried.

If she was scrubbing my fingernails, I couldn't tell. I couldn't feel a single part of my body. I'd never been so high. I wanted to stay awake, but the lure to sleep was too great, and it pulled me back inside its vortex.

Only to wake to the sound of Noelle's crying. Followed by Gia's voice. "We'll do it together. At the same time. Just like we talked about, sweetie. Just like we practiced. That way it's just done, okay? It's over quick. Remember how I told you to cut?" I opened my eyes and watched as Gia raised up my arm. One hand circled around my wrist. A shiny razor blade glimmering in her other hand. "You go down. Just like this." She demonstrated with the razor on my wrist without actually touching my skin.

No! I screamed in my head. But I was trapped inside myself. Unable to move. Whatever they'd done to me, it'd worked. I couldn't speak or move.

"Oh my God. Oh my God." Noelle cried, sounding like she was going to hyperventilate. "I can't do that. I can't do that to her."

"It's going to be okay, baby. Really, it is. You'll see. Come on. Let's do this. Ready? Just don't think about it. Don't think about what you're doing. Remember what we talked about?" Gia's voice urged her on.

"I can't do it." Noelle sobbed.

"Yes, you can. You're so much stronger than you think, baby. You are. We're doing this together, remember? It's for Paris." Gia's voice was strong. Urgent. Forceful. "Equal responsibility? Come on, we can't stop now."

Yes, you can! Yes, you can, Noelle!

But all that came out of my mouth was a weird moan.

"Now she's waking up! What are we going to do if she wakes up?" Noelle shrieked. The anxious energy radiated off her. "Gia, please . . . Can't we think of something else? There has to be another way. I can't do this."

"She's only going to feel more awake the longer you wait. Right now she can't feel anything. That's why we have to do it now. While she's still totally numb. We can't wait. Come on. You've got this, baby. I'm right here. Right here with you. Ready?" Gia locked eyes with Noelle.

I was already outside myself and looking down at my body in the bathtub. Our huge white soaking tub. It was so pretty. The molding around it really was a good design choice, even though I'd fought Noelle on that one too. I watched as she gulped and stared back at Gia just as intensely. They were in their own world.

"Three. Two. One. Go!" Gia called out like it was the beginning of a race.

Noelle's eyes widened, and her mouth formed a perfect circle as she cut into my right wrist like she was horrified by her own actions but unable to stop them. Gia did the same on my left. Slicing just as deep and revealing the pink flesh inside. Noelle dropped her razor blade as the blood spurted and let out an anguished cry as she backed away. Gia leaned over the tub and smiled down at me.

HER
(THEN)

The world can change in an instant. That's all it takes to flip upside down.

One minute she was leaving the courthouse, deciding to make dinner to celebrate her decision. And in the next, she lay on the couch, staring at the tiles in the ceiling, paralyzed from drugs. She could still hear them arguing in the bathroom. Whatever they'd given her had knocked her out but still allowed her to hear. Or maybe it was that she'd left her body and was watching. Part of her thought she might already be dead.

But no.

She couldn't be yet. Her hand was still moving. She'd just seen it twitch. Her ring finger on her left hand. There it went again.

There was Aaron. Pacing next to the sink. The bathroom door still open.

They'd taken her by surprise. It'd all happened so quickly. She slid her key into the front door lock just as he slid up behind her. In one swift movement, he'd barreled his way inside the apartment with two of his buddies. They must've been watching her from the elevator. Her arms were full of groceries, so she could barely see. She'd dropped all of them as soon as she'd felt him pressing the gun into her side.

He was so mad. Practically fuming. Angry white boys—especially the entitled ones—were the scariest mammals.

"You're ruining my life. Why are you ruining my life?" he hissed in her ear as he wrestled her into the bathroom. She screamed and pounded against his chest. He pressed his hand over her mouth and slammed her against the wall. "You really thought you were going to get away with this?"

She'd screamed again, but his friends were in the living room, and they'd turned up the stereo as loud as it would go. Everyone would just think they were having a party. That's when Aaron stuck her with the needle. She didn't know what it was, other than strong. She'd turned to mush almost immediately. Couldn't even walk. They'd carried her to the couch and laid her down like she was about to take a nap.

She was plastered to the couch. Couldn't move, no matter how hard she willed her body to do something. Anything. People tried to do this to themselves on purpose. No thank you. She liked being able to feel her face.

Aaron paced circles in the bathroom. If she could open her mouth, she'd do her best to convince him not to hurt her. But it was never going to work. If she went away, so did her case against him. They couldn't charge him with something she wasn't there to testify for. She just hated that her past had made it so easy for him. Her goodbye letter to her family was still on the coffee table.

He was nervous, though. She could tell. The way he walked such tight circles. Muttering to himself. Running his hands through his hair over and over again. He was covered in sweat like he'd been working out. His friends weren't any help. They did nothing to try to talk him out of what he was doing to her. Or had done to her. They were probably the same guys that had come into the back room that night.

"Did you call Haley?" he yelled at them. It sounded like he was yelling at the end of a tunnel. "Call Haley. She knows what to do. Somebody has to text Paris. We can't because all our numbers are blocked. It has to be someone who's never texted her before, or it'll never get through. It has to get through."

"Bro, chill. We already did. She'll call us back. Give her a second."

"Okay, okay . . . good," he stammered. "Then let's move her, right? Put her arms on her chest or something. This shit is making me nervous." Was that Aaron or somebody else? Their voices were starting to blur together.

"You wanna call 911? They can probably Narcan her or something. Shoot, they probably have some here. Wanna look in the cupboards?" His voice wavered and wobbled. She thought he sounded like the one wearing the Hozier T-shirt.

Time dragged. Then sped up.

Another voice. Still male. "Okay, Haley said some girl, Laurel, is going to text her."

Laurel? Who's Laurel? She didn't know anyone named Laurel. Her head fell to the side when they lifted her arms. Slip sliding away.

"Jesus Christ. Oh my God, Aaron, she just looked at me. She opened her eyes and looked at me. She's going to know it's me. She can identify me. What do I do?"

"Relax," he said like he wasn't nervous anymore. "She's not going to be identifying you to anyone. Only thing she's going to be identifying is the dirt. What it looks like six feet under the earth."

And then they laughed. They'd always laughed.

She was floating. Or flying. She couldn't tell which.

"Okay, she did it. Haley said she did it. That girl Laurel texted her what you told her to say. Now just put her phone in her hand. We'll wipe everything down and get out of here."

Those were their last words.

Just as my phone buzzed on my chest with whatever message Laurel had sent me.

CHAPTER TWENTY-TWO

I watched the blood drain from my wrists. Just slide right through the pearly white folds like it was nothing. The water in the tub was red within seconds. There was just so much. I didn't know that much blood would come out of a person so quickly.

I sank in slow motion. It felt like I was melting. Holding my left wrist with my bleeding right wrist, trying to stop it. Nothing worked. All my muscles were jelly. Rolling along with the water.

Noelle.

She was my sweet angel princess. Even now the sunlight streaming through the window created a halo around her head. As she took slow steps back against the door and away from me.

"Noelle. Help me." The begging was gone. Just matter of fact. "Please."

The words didn't sound right coming out of my mouth. Maybe they didn't even come out. Did I talk? Gia came up behind her. Slid her arm around Noelle's waist. Noelle sank into her body in the same way she used to relax into me, and a small cry escaped my throat. She buried her face in Gia's chest.

"Do you know how long they think Paris was there before someone found her?" Gia looked down at me as I sank farther and farther into the water.

"I'm sorry, Gia, I'm so sorry," I said for what felt like the thousandth time. But I didn't think those words came out of my mouth either. I'd been apologizing for days. And I was sorry. The truth was, I deserved to die. Even as I felt the blood leaving my body and the primal part of me wanted to stay alive, the other part of me felt the sweetest resignation to my karma.

I've always wondered if people know they're dying while it's happening. The ones who pull the plug. Or who are trapped inside a car. At what point do you realize you're dying, and when you do, what does it feel like? Like, do you know you're dying?

We've all had those thoughts. Those terrifying thoughts. Keep-you-up-all-night thoughts.

Turns out, you do know.

I could feel the life draining out of me along with the blood. Probably in the same way Maddie had. I felt this strange connection to her. Felt her all around me. Had she never left? Was she the one guiding me through this investigation the entire time?

Death felt warm. Totally safe.

There was nothing scary about it. We spend all our time being so terrified of death. Paralyzed with fear about the afterlife. Lying awake at night. And once you hit thirty and those four-a.m. wake-up calls start coming? Drenching you in sweat and making you question every decision you've ever made? Rewatching the videos of your life. All the painful moments. The embarrassing ones.

It didn't hurt. I wanted to send a message to all the mamas in the universe who'd ever lost one of their babies: "It doesn't hurt!" It was like taking off a tight dress that you'd been wearing all night. Like someone unzipped the back, and you finally got to step out of it. You could breathe. You could just be.

And that was how I felt right now.

I was.

Was somebody else there? Here? With me? Coming to walk me home? Over the rainbow bridge? All the dogs. It didn't matter because I felt surrounded. Surrounded in the most glorious love. The most magnificent light. But not light like on this earth. Light of another kind. That was when I knew for sure that I was leaving.

And then, suddenly, there he was. Walking toward me. From somewhere and everywhere all at once. I'd recognize that smile anywhere.

"Daddy?" I cried out.

The glimmer of a cotton candy sky out of the corner of my eye. He'd taught me to enjoy the sunrise. It was like he heard me coming and he'd come running. He was carrying a cup of 7-Eleven coffee in his hand. A glazed doughnut in the other.

This indeed was it.

I ran to meet him.

It was true what they said—in the end, all that mattered was love. And I immediately wanted a do-over, because I hadn't done the best job at love. I looked up, but there was no longer an up. In the same way that there was no down. I was surrounded. And it was okay.

I'd done the best I could.

"You did a good job." My grandma's voice came from out of nowhere, and so close, as if she were standing beside me too. Whispering in my ear as she held my dad's other arm. Both next to me. And I did do a good job.

The universe was enveloping me. I could feel it. All encompassing. I was returning. It really was like a going home. Like they said. Returning to your center. And the other part of me, the one that chose to come here in the first place, knew I'd be back. As many times as I wanted to.

There was nothing left to do but let go.

I loved Noelle, and I forgave her. I looked at her one last time. She was the last face I wanted to see before I left this world. It didn't matter that she was holding a razor blade. Or that she'd been the one to plunge it into my wrist and cut straight through the vein. The love we had would always be real. Nothing else existed. Just like Marianne Williamson said in all her books. The ones we read together on Sunday mornings.

Except Noelle was gone now. She'd left me here. To die. That was what was happening. I knew it in the same way I'd known I was being born, even though I forgot from the moment I entered this life. Which is usually what happens. The forgetting and then the remembering.

Her love filled my heart. I wasn't angry or mad. I wasn't even sad. I wanted to weep the way you cry when babies are born—which makes no sense, because at this point, I was pretty sure I was no longer breathing. My heart might have even stopped beating.

Did it feel like this for everyone? Or just those of us who'd tried to take our own lives? Brought ourselves to this moment? The sweet release we'd been looking for our entire lives. The high we were always chasing. Because it was always about being okay. That desperate search was finally over.

I was okay. As okay as I'd ever been, even though I always was. The forgetting and then the remembering. At least they gave me drugs. That was nice of them. They didn't have to go that extra mile. I was comfortable. It didn't hurt. All the pain in my guts, from whatever poison they were feeding me, gone.

I wish everyone who'd lost a loved one knew this. It's not scary, I promise.

EPILOGUE
NOELLE

It's been three days, and I've done all the things on our list, exactly and precisely according to our plan. The only thing left to do is meet Gia here. But where is she? The evening sun is peeking through the hills. We were supposed to be on the trails already. I hope nothing happened to her. I can't wait to see her. I barely slept last night. Counting down the minutes.

Leave the house and go stay at the Four Seasons in West Hills for the weekend. That's all I had to do. She'd take care of the rest. She must've said it a thousand times to reassure me, but I've never stopped being nervous. I couldn't stay in the house with Laurel after I found out about her affair with Maddie. That's the story.

I was at the Four Seasons the night Laurel took her own life, I repeat to myself like I've been doing all morning. It's only a matter of time before I talk to the detectives. I can't keep putting them off much longer.

I haven't seen Gia since that night either. We haven't even spoken. Not even a text. This is the longest we've ever gone without communicating, from the moment we met four years ago.

I followed the plan perfectly. Obviously, so did she, but where is she? What's taking so long?

I pull my hat down. I'm wearing a baseball cap and shades. That part wasn't included in the original plan. It's an extra touch that I threw in when I packed my bags. We were just meeting for a hike to debrief. At least that's what the next part of our story would be. But not being recognized seemed like a good thing too. Nobody's talking, but I don't want anyone to start.

They haven't connected the two of us. Hopefully, they never will. Boone and Wallace are so busy digging into Laurel's past, they aren't even looking at us. Neither has anyone else. But I also haven't been out of the house other than to go to the hospital.

My hands shake. They haven't stopped shaking since I gave the report to the insurance company this morning. The one that said I got into a car accident. That I fell asleep at the wheel. That's what we're going to tell them. That's where we would be when the police asked us for our whereabouts during the time of Laurel's death and if they had any concerns about what I looked like. We even crashed the car. Drove it into a dumpster like Thelma and Louise drove off a cliff.

I haven't been out in public yet. I'm not going to for a while. There's a huge egg on my forehead. My two front teeth are practically gone. Chipped all the way to the top. They're so sensitive the air hurts when I breathe in. Gia's face isn't as bad, and she can cover up her eye and the scratches with makeup, so she's been able to be out in public. I look like I got my head bashed into the dashboard, so a car accident is definitely a believable story.

Moving Laurel back home was a bad idea. I said that from the beginning, but Gia insisted. Said there's no way that she'd take her own life at Gia's house. That it would look too suspicious. We had to say that I'd gone away because obviously I couldn't be there when something like that happened. It would've created too many questions. Leaving made better sense.

"Just stick to the story, okay?" Gia gripped my shoulders so tightly and peered into my eyes after Laurel finally stopped breathing in the bathtub. I was crying hysterically. "Remember? We practiced all this. You know exactly what to do. You've got this, honey. It's going to be okay."

I'm a terrible liar. Always have been. I stumble and stutter my way through it, and I can never keep the story straight. It's like everything leaves my head in that moment.

But that's not why I was crying.

Laurel was dead.

I killed my wife.

I still can't believe I hurt Laurel. The plan was to punish her. She deserved that, but she was never supposed to die. Never. All this just spiraled, from the moment things went wrong with Maddie. That's what I've been thinking about every night since it happened, while I lie in bed. It's not like I can sleep. I can't talk to anyone else, either, so it's all been driving me a bit mad. Gia changed her mind about everything after I hit Laurel in the head with the bat. Just took it upon herself to bring Laurel to her guesthouse and lock her up. She got so mad at me when I asked her about it, though. Said we wouldn't have had to do any of it if I hadn't hit Laurel. Except Gia was the one that said to stop her. To do whatever I needed to do to keep her from leaving.

"How will we explain her forehead?" I asked.

"Don't worry about it. Nobody's going to be worried about it," Gia said. "It'll just look like she fell in the tub. We'll set it up that way."

That answer wasn't good enough, but we didn't have time for anything else. But I am worried about her forehead. How will we explain that? Has Gia talked to the detectives yet?

I didn't want Gia to leave Laurel there in the tub, bleeding, but I didn't know what else to do. We could've taken her out of the tub. We could've called the police. Even the paramedics. We probably could've thrown her into the back of our car and driven her to the hospital in time. But we didn't.

We just stood there. Watching as the blood poured out of her body. She slowly crumpled to the bottom of the tub as it did. She never took her eyes off us. After a while, I couldn't look, but Gia watched it all the way to the end.

I turned around and squeezed my eyes shut. I kept telling myself she deserved it. Thinking about all the ways she'd made Paris suffer. How she'd been the one to push her over the edge. Bullied her into death. I meant what I said to Laurel that day. You couldn't say something like that and not have evil in you.

That's how I'll move past this. Every time the guilt threatens to overwhelm me.

Gia made me leave the house as soon as it was over. Said she would take care of everything, just like she told me to hit her with the baseball bat that night. I panicked when Laurel texted me from Crystal Meadows. I knew Laurel had figured it out and didn't know what to do. But Gia knows exactly what to do in any crisis situation.

What's taking her so long? She's never late.

What if the police arrested her? What if they're coming to arrest me? Fear creeps up the back of my throat. Would it always be this way? Living a life forever looking over my shoulder? I hope not.

I wish she'd hurry.

Come on, Gia.

I pull out my phone. It's 7:34. She's over an hour late. She's never been late before.

I quickly tap out a text to her on my other phone. The burner phones we've been using since last year. The ones nobody knows we have. The text comes back green, like I was blocked or she didn't have service.

I dial instead. The phone rings once, followed by "The customer is unavailable."

She disconnected the phone we used to talk to each other. That's okay. It makes sense that she disconnected the phone. But she's sixty-four minutes late, and Gia's always early.

I sit on the bench. Every single minute that she doesn't come drags. I try the phone again. Still out of service. Still green.

I've managed to dodge Boone and Wallace up until now, but I'm not going to be able to put them off much longer. Not for our official sit-down interview. The one where they ask me all the tough questions about Laurel. I need to know what to tell them. I need to know what we're going to say next. What Gia said when they talked to her. Our stories have to match up.

A small voice of doubt rises within me.

What if she's not coming?

I quickly throw off the thought. That's what happens when you find out your wife is a terrible person. How are you ever supposed to trust anyone else again?

Another hour passes.

Still nothing.

Panic grips my chest. I hurry back to the car. I can't wait at the base of the mountain once it gets dark. There are too many sketchy homeless people that come out of those bushes, along with the coyotes traveling in packs.

I slide into my car, hugging myself and rocking back and forth. I can't help it. My body will explode and shatter into a thousand pieces if I don't. My cells are already dividing. Coming apart at the cellular level.

She isn't coming.

I shake my head, refusing to believe it could possibly be true. Absolutely no way. She loves me. I give her life meaning. That's what she said.

Something happened. She just got held up. That's what I tell myself as I grab my regular phone and try the burner phone number again, just to see if it goes through on a different phone. I'm being so paranoid. How am I ever going to live this way? But I just need to talk to her. Hear her voice. Then everything will be okay. She'll know what to do.

"I'll walk you through all the steps." That's what she said in the beginning. When she showed me the pictures from Paris's funeral. Read me the letter Paris left their family behind. I've never cried so hard as I did when I read that letter. Gut wrenching is an understatement.

I thought that was the worst part of the story, but it was only the beginning. Gia's mother was never able to deal with Paris's suicide, and followed her into death three weeks later. Gia lost her mother and her sister within the same month. Her mom didn't leave a note, but she didn't need to. Gia never talked about her mom, though. Only her sister. That wound was too deep—that Gia wasn't reason enough for her mom to stay. Laurel's one act wiped out Gia's entire family.

I didn't know you could stop loving someone in an instant, but you could. I did. Right then. Every ounce of love I had for Laurel was gone, just like that, as if it'd never existed in the first place. I've been pretending since then. I meant every word I said to her about having the evil inside. I'm still not sure about the dying-for-her-sins part, though. That part doesn't feel real. I can't believe I killed her. Maddie was an accident, but I cut into my wife's flesh. The tremor moves through me. I've developed these weird uncontrollable shakes.

No.

Force myself to focus.

The phone gives me the same message when called from my cell phone. I laugh nervously at myself. As if she'd only block *one* of my numbers.

Where is she?

I can't push the button to turn on the car. I just rock. If you were to walk past the car, you'd think there was music. But there's nothing but silence. Deafening silence. The sound of being perfectly present while your world is shattering into a million pieces. Moving in slow motion. I pull up Gia's real number from my contacts and hit call. We've only ever spoken on our actual phones twice.

This time, the call goes right through. It rings three times before she picks up.

"Oh my God, I was getting so worried!" I gush. She's probably going to be furious that I called her cell phone, but I couldn't wait a second longer. I'm not cut out for this. I've never even had a speeding ticket.

"Hello?" a male's voice says, throwing me completely off guard.

"Um . . . hi, hello . . . this is Noelle . . ."

"Hi, Noelle, this is Andrew, one of Gia's assistants. I'm not sure we've met, but she's in the air right now, so she's having all her calls forwarded to me," he explains.

"She's in the air?" I think out loud, trying to process what's happening. Why is she in the air? She's supposed to be meeting me at Las Virgenes Canyon.

"Yes," he says, sounding slightly miffed. "Is there something I can help you with?"

"When will she be back?"

"Who did you say you were?" he asks.

I think fast. "I'm one of the producers on *Comeback Kids*. Gia left me a message to call her, and I was just getting back to her. I went offline for a few days after everything happened on set. I needed some time to process."

"So, then you know. Yes, it's just absolutely awful what happened. That's the reason Gia left. She was in the same space you were, it sounds like. She just needed some time to process, too, and really just wanted to be with her husband. That's all you want when something terrible like this happens, you know? Just to be with the ones you love."

"Totally. I get it. I did the same thing." I gulp, trying to keep the panic out of my voice. Gia never said one thing about a husband. Ever. He wasn't anywhere on her social media. Her LinkedIn. IMDb page. She didn't wear a ring. My brain quickly flashed through all the things. "I just have never heard her mention a husband. I'm so glad she has someone to be with right now."

"Nobody really does. They're both *very* private about their personal lives. Always have been. He's in Germany. Some super-eccentric photographer who's practically a recluse. Has zero social media? Can you imagine?" He laughs.

"Germany? She's headed out of the country?"

"Oh, sorry, did I not say that? Yes, she has dual citizenship. That's where she's originally from too. Most of her family is still over there. I imagine she'll be gone awhile. That's what she does whenever she needs a break from the stress of all this, the whole industry. And I mean, I'd go, too, if my husband looked like that. Baby, sign me up for the next plane." He laughs. "Anyways, I'll just be glad when this whole thing is over. It sounds like it's getting close, though. Between you and me, I heard they're pretty sure that therapist lady, Lauren or Laurie, something like that—whatever her name is—that she's the one who killed that poor girl. Personally, I never really got into the whole show. But anyways, that's who they think did it. They've just been trying to find her."

"They can't find her?" A hole opens inside my guts.

"They've been asking for anyone with information about her whereabouts to come forward on the news, so I'm guessing not."

It's been three days. Why are the police looking for Laurel? Gia was supposed to call them after I left for the Four Seasons. That was the plan. She would call them and say she'd gone there to talk to Laurel after she'd grown concerned when Laurel didn't respond to her calls or her knocks at the door. She was supposed to ask the police to do a wellness check on Laurel so they'd find the body.

That was the plan. That was the plan. No other thoughts would go through my head.

"Thank you. Thank you so much," I say to him quickly, because I'm seconds away from losing it. I end the call before he responds and whip my car out of the parking lot.

I head straight to my house—our house. The one I was never supposed to have to step foot in again. That house. The one that was supposed to be a police crime scene, just like the one at Crystal Meadows. That was the plan. That's what Gia said.

My heart races. Head pounds. There isn't enough air in the car. I roll down the windows, but that doesn't help either. This can't be happening.

No.

I hop on the 101 and speed all the way home. Pushing my Tesla faster than she's ever gone. Please don't let it be true.

That's all I can say. All I can think as I see the Coldwater Canyon exit and quickly hop back off. Within seconds, I'm home and pulling in to the driveway. The entire house is dark. None of the security lights activate when I get out of the car.

I walk to the house in slow motion, but I know what I'll find when I open the door. I punch in the code and step inside. Assaulted with the foul smell of a body that's been rotting there for days.

I sink to my knees and howl.

Acknowledgments

This one was promised to all my Booktok besties. Every male character in this book was named by one of you, so thank you. Specifically, Preston was called out over twenty times so he was a for sure thing. Thanks to Zoe Tosca for Spencer Yates and to @hellodavidson for tagging on the third. @HolliHalfcane is responsible for Tripp Kingston. ☺ Thanks for always being so supportive. Y'all are the best.

About the Author

USA Today bestselling author Lucinda Berry is a former psychologist and leading researcher in childhood trauma. She's written multiple bestsellers reaching millions of readers worldwide. Some of her bestselling works include *The Perfect Child, Saving Noah, When She Returned, The Best of Friends,* and *Keep Your Friends Close.* Her books have been optioned for film and translated into several languages.

If Berry isn't chasing after her son, you can find her running through Los Angeles, prepping for her next marathon. To hear about her upcoming releases and other author news, visit her on social media (@lucindaberryauthor) or sign up for her newsletter at https://lucindaberry.com.